THE AEGIS CONSPIRACY

A NOVEL BY
GALEN WINTER

CCB Publishing
British Columbia, Canada

The Aegis Conspiracy: A Novel

Copyright ©2010 by Galen Winter
ISBN-13 978-1-926585-72-7
Second Edition

Library and Archives Canada Cataloguing in Publication

Winter, Galen, 1926-
The aegis conspiracy : a novel / written by Galen Winter – 2nd ed.
ISBN 978-1-926585-72-7
I. Title.
PS3573.I565A74 2010   813'.54   C2010-900227-X

Publisher: CCB Publishing
              British Columbia, Canada
              www.ccbpublishing.com

In Memoriam

Douglas Robert Winter

Chapter 1

The man sat alone at a table in a restaurant in the Arturo Merino Benitez airport in Santiago. It was cold outside in the Chilean winter night, but comfortably warm in the section of the airport reserved for international travelers. For ten minutes, the man had been engrossed in reading the La Prensa articles describing the discovery of the body of Humberto del Valle. Without looking up, he reached for the small cup of coffee that rested on the table in front of him. He brought it to his lips. The coffee was cold. He glanced at the waiter and nodded slightly.

The waiter came to the table and the man said: "Otro cafecito, por favor."

The waiter answered "Si. Senor," and walked to the restaurant counter for another cup of the strong, black coffee the traveler seemed to prefer.

Though the government of General Augusto Pinochet Ugarte had been out of power for some time, the recollections of his administration's jailing and murder of left-wingers, opposition politicians and student dissidents had not faded. The report of the death of Humberto del Valle, the man who organized the vicious abuses, was front-page news.

His body was found in a cottage near Puerto Montt, a city only five hundred and fifty miles to the south of Santiago. One of the editorial writers wondered if friends within the current Chilean government might have provided del Valle with the sanctuary he enjoyed until only a few days ago.

Humberto del Valle disappeared when the Pinochet government fell from power. For years he had eluded his pursuers and avoided facing the consequences of his crimes. At various times he was reported to be hiding in Paraguay, in Spain and in Argentina. Protected by friends and fascist elements in those countries, he was consistently a step ahead of those who looked for him. Now he was dead. Someone had found him.

Two bodyguards protected del Valle. The body of one of them was found in a wooded area near the entrance to the Puerto Montt cottage. His neck was broken. The other bodyguard lay inside the building on the kitchen floor, a single bullet hole in the center of his chest.

Humberto del Valle carried a similar wound. He lay crumpled against the wall of his bedroom. A 9 mm Tokarev pistol was on the floor at his side. Empty cartridges found near his body and holes in the wall near the bedroom door confirmed it had been fired twice.

The man seated in the airport restaurant again read La Prensa's reports and editorial comment about del Valle's violent death. He studied each word and phrase to uncover any subtle suggestions they might contain. The newspaper articles and the government news release gave no indication there would be a serious attempt to find the man or men who killed del Valle.

The editorial writer of La Prensa was the exception. He wanted them found, honored and given lifetime government pensions. Like most Chileans, the writer was pleased to learn of del Valle's death. The man responsible for so much torture and killing was gone forever. It was the common presumption someone avenging the murder of a friend or a family member had performed the long overdue act. No one would shed tears for him.

The waiter returned with more coffee. Showing no reaction to the story, the man put the newspaper on the table, picked up the cup and drank from it. He looked around at his fellow passengers. It was easy to recognize the North American tourists and businessmen who wandered in and out of the tax-free stores lining the walls of the international flight waiting area. They congregated in separate groups, drawing attention by their dress and their conduct. They talked and laughed just a bit louder than Latinos. There was just a touch of flamboyant self-assurance in their gestures and in the way they walked.

Den Clark was indistinguishable from the Chilean nationals who were bound for the United States. Although he was a North American, his clothing and his demeanor were as theirs. He was reserved and drew no attention to himself. His spoken Spanish carried no hint of a gringo accent.

In his youth and early teens, Den Clark lived in Bogotá where his father managed the Colombian distribution office of an American business machine manufacturer. It was there he learned to speak the Spanish language as it is spoken in Colombia. It was there he developed both knowledge of and appreciation for Latin American culture.

When his flight was called and after the first class passengers received their preferential treatment, Den boarded the Chilean Linea Aerea Nacional jet together with the remaining travelers. He found his assigned row and eased himself into the aisle bulkhead seat. Den Clark was two inches over six feet tall and weighed a muscular 200 pounds. He needed the extra room provided by bulkhead seating.

Flights between Santiago and the United States leave Chile in the evening. On the following afternoon, they arrive in Washington D. C. It's a long trip - over eighteen hours. Spending that amount of time strapped in a seat, apparently designed to fit the body of a five-and-a-half-foot tall anorectic, was not a pleasant prospect for a man of his size, but Den always traveled in the tourist class section of the airplane.

A stewardess might remember a first class passenger. Few would remember a quiet traveler shoehorned into the crowded back section of the plane. Den Clark preferred the anonymity of tourist class passage. He was an agent in the Clandestine Services of the Central Intelligence Agency. He was returning to Washington after completing his mission in Chile. It had been his first assassination.

As a SEAL, Den had killed men. Killing the enemy was part of the Navy's Sea/Air/Land training and purpose. SEAL missions were team operations. Each man supported and was supported by his teammates. Den's Puerto Montt assignment was different.

The assassination of Humberto del Valle was a solo effort - one man entirely on his own. It was especially designed to be hidden behind the screen of secrecy. It was disclosed to no one except the men who conceived and organized it and the one man who carried it out. It was an operation carrying the faint odor of something that might be unacceptable if exposed to the light of day.

When the LAN flight was in the air, Den tried to relax. La Prensa's speculations about the death of Humberto del Valle were reassuring. Everyone assumed he had been killed by Chileans. There wasn't a suspicion the murder might have been planned and carried out by the CIA. Still, Den Clark was not at ease. When the flight attendant pushed the beverage cart down the aisle, a Scotch and water helped him unbend. It helped quiet the tiny whispering voice of disapproval.

Den knew the del Valle killing was a test. It was a necessary test. Those who planned it had to know if he was able to skillfully carry out an assassination. Den knew he had performed well. He proved he was resourceful and efficient. He passed their test. He told himself his future missions would have a stronger national purpose. It was a thought that made him feel better.

After dinner, eaten tourist class fashion with his arms pressed tightly against his sides, Den took the pillow offered by the flight attendant. He removed his shoes and tried to find a comfortable position. Two hours later there were few overhead lights shining in the cabin. It was quiet. Only the people who were unable to sleep on airplanes were still awake. Den was one of them.

He shifted his weight and crammed the tiny pillow behind his head, trying unsuccessfully to make it do the work of two. He couldn't tilt his seat backwards without disturbing the lady and the baby who sat behind him. At least the infant was not squalling. Stretching his legs seemed like a good idea. He decided he wouldn't walk to the flight attendant's station. The modest exercise and the coffee he would probably drink would keep him awake.

Den reshaped the tiny pillow and put it behind his neck. It didn't help. Sleep continued to elude him. He shut his eyes and tried to clear his mind. He thought about Gigi Grant. He wondered where she was. He wondered what she was doing. He told himself she would approve of what he did in the isolated cottage in the forest near Puerto Montt. He told himself she would have understood. It was a comforting thought.

* * * * *

For a few years before she came to Washington, G. G. Grant was one of the newer associates in a prestigious Phoenix law firm. The firm was large and her work was routine. Gigi was smarter and worked harder than most of the younger attorneys, but she was assigned mundane duties. Her male counterparts got the more interesting work. They were also the first to be advanced. Later, Gigi would refer to that part of her life as "my factory worker phase". She left the firm when her application for Central Intelligence Agency service was accepted.

Den Clark met Gigi Grant during their CIA indoctrination training. She was a pretty woman and the competition for her favors was active. Gigi was not displeased by the attentions she received from the new agents, but she was well aware of the usually narrow focus of their intentions.

One of the agents she met in the cafeteria, however, treated her as if she were a human being and not merely an example of the female of the species. Gigi selected Den and that was that. Any further male attempts to attract her interest were unmistakably and immediately frozen into cold immobility.

Den and Gigi's affair was intense, but short-lived. Neither had any serious interests in the commitments and the compromises that lead to permanent engagements. They enjoyed the laughter, the companionship and the fun of each other. However, they knew their chosen work denied the possibilities of a long-term relationship. The lives they planned for themselves wouldn't allow it.

When the time came to end the affair, they parted as good friends. They told themselves it was over. It was time to turn the page. Now, only a few years later, in their reveries, each would often revisit the time they spent together and each would smile.

Den remembered waking in the early morning and feeling the warmth of Gigi's body. They had slept, pressed against each other like two spoons. He remembered when he softly moved his arm that held her to him and left the bed, careful not to disturb her. Minutes later, he returned with her coffee mug - the one that carried the legend: QUIET!! DON'T TALK UNTIL I'VE FINISHED THIS. He remembered her bright surprise when he kissed her awake.

Those were happy days filled with smiles and fulfilled expectations. Now they were memories - good ones with only a touch of the bittersweet. Gigi was in the Near East. She had been sent to the Damascus Station. After a boring period of basic analyst's labors, Den found his home in the Central Intelligence Agency's Directorate of Operations. In the Agency's descriptive shorthand, it was called "Clandestine Services". They both thought they would probably never meet again, but they had great memories.

Recalling Gigi's smile and the sounds of her voice and laughter and in spite of the cramped LAN tourist class accommodation, Den Clark finally went to sleep.

Chapter 2

Denver Clark was named after a paternal grandparent who was born in the railroad station on the evening the infant's homesteading parents' arrival in Denver. Two generations later, someone had to carry on grandfather's name and the new-born baby, unable to defend himself, was elected. Though he wasn't pleased with that decision, the child was glad his grandfather had been born in Denver rather than in Bismarck, North Dakota or, even worse, in Florence, Wisconsin.

Denver Clark seldom acknowledged his first name and preferred to be called "Den". By the time the Clark family moved from Bogotá to a Minneapolis suburb, no one knew him as "Denver". In Minnesota, Den Clark became an avid hunter and fisherman, a fact that explained why his face and hands were well tanned.

He also developed the attractive characteristics of self-assurance and self-reliance. Perhaps it was a result of the experiences derived from life in different cultures or perhaps it was that same undefined genetic quirk that caused his great grandfather to migrate to Colorado and his father to take a position in South America.

In any event, when he reached university age, Den was afflicted with both a strong sense of independence and an irresistible curiosity. He had "sand in his shoes". His idea of hell would be an eternity of routine. He could not - would not - reduce his life to an endless series of boring tomorrows, each one a carbon copy of its pointless predecessor. It was his temperament and his curiosity that caused him to disappoint his parents by dropping out of Cornell and joining the Navy. Den Clark became a SEAL and acquired the scars that now marked his body.

During the first weeks of the Second Gulf War, Den and his SEAL team were inside the military portion of the Saddam International

Airport some ten miles to the west of Baghdad. They had already found and radioed the positions of the airfield's defensive installations. Beginning on the morning of April third, his team began their attacks on the reinforced aircraft shelters where Republican Guards were awaiting the arrival of the advancing American armies.

Only two of Den's team survived the ensuing firefights. Only one would have survived except for the courage of a big Chicago Irishman. When Den was shot while crossing an open landing strip, Mick McCarthy left the comparative safety of a hanger and, under fire, ran to where Den lay bleeding in the middle of the tarmac runway. He grabbed Den and dragged him back to the hanger, receiving two small arms gun fire wounds in the process.

Later that day, when 3rd Army infantrymen arrived and drove most of the Iraqis from the field, they searched the airfield for pockets of resistance and found Mick McCarthy weakly calling out to them. He insisted an unconscious Den Clark was still alive. The two men received medical attention from the corpsmen and were helicoptered to a hospital ship in the Gulf.

Mick recovered quickly and returned to active duty in SEALS. Den's wounds required more time to heal. He was still in the hospital when he was interviewed by the Central Intelligence Agency. SEAL training and native-like fluency in Spanish were special qualifications. Den guessed the Agency was looking for a man to perform covert operations in Latin America. What more could a man want.

As soon as Den was recruited into the Agency, he called Mick McCarthy and told him what had happened. Mick didn't show the unhappiness he felt when he heard of Den's decision. He and Den had become close friends during their years in the SEALS. He knew the life of a CIA foreign intelligence officer would certainly appeal to Den. It would be a great job for him. Mick also knew he would miss Den and he suspected Den would miss him.

He encouraged Den and then thought: "*What the hell. Why not?*" He asked Den to tell him how to apply for a job with the CIA and then asked him to recommend him for the same work Den was going to do. Or, at least, the sort of work Den thought he was going to do.

After completing his training at the CIA's Sherman Kent Center,

Den received a disappointment. He did not become a covert agent in some CIA Latin America station. He was assigned to the CIA's complex in Langley. He became an analyst specializing in reviewing facts and events developing in Spanish speaking countries. The work of an Agency analyst inside the Belt Line held little appeal for him. Perhaps it was only a temporary warehousing and his abilities would soon be put to their proper use.

Den invested one full year behind a desk heaped with reports and Spanish language newspapers. He spent hours studying them. Looking for needles in the haystacks of trivia that were piled on his desk became unbearably boring. His expectation to become one of the Agency's field officers went unfulfilled.

Reluctantly he concluded he had been permanently sentenced to an analyst's chair. He would have preferred a prison term. There were other alternatives. Den planned to quit the Agency and look for them. Before he could execute his plan, he was called to a meeting with Teddy Smith.

Den didn't have a clue about the reason for the meeting. After making inquiry, he learned Smith was in the Projects Branch of the CIA's Foreign Intelligence Service. The Projects Branch screened proposed operations to be undertaken by field operatives. A CIA organizational chart would show both the Projects Branch and the Foreign Intelligence Service were a part of the Directorate of Operations. Also called the Clandestine Service, it was the part of the CIA involved in overseas espionage.

Den suspected he would be interviewed for some sort of planning position in the Projects Branch. It would be another desk job, probably one like preparing logistic support for an off-shore covert plan to break into someone's office and steal the plans for the enemy's super-secret portable outhouses. Den was sure it would be a position in which he would slowly sink and drown in the swamps of the Washingtonian bureaucracy.

He wasn't in a good humor when he arrived at a part of the building he had never before visited in Langley's complex of 1,400,000 square feet of CIA office space. After being properly identified, a Marine corporal took him through a maze of corridors and, finally, to a door identified only by a number. The corporal led him into a suite of offices, turned and left.

Three people were already seated in the anteroom. They were mildly surprised and somewhat irritated when the receptionist told Den he was expected and immediately ushered him into one of the inner offices.

A bald man got up from behind an uncluttered desk and, smiling, walked toward him. When men with desk jobs pass beyond the fifty year mark, they tend to go to pot. The man who arose to greet him had avoided that tendency. His stomach was flat. He was tanned and well muscled. He watched his diet, exercised regularly and jogged every morning,

"Good morning, Denver," the man said. "I'm Teddy Smith and I've looked forward to this meeting. I've heard good reports about you." He extended his right hand and used his left to hold Den's elbow. It was one of Smith's studied maneuvers, meant to show warmth and friendship.

Den winced. *"He called me 'Denver'. I haven't used that name in years,"* he thought. *"How in hell did this guy find it out?"*

He was happier when Smith said: "If you get the idea I'm an informal cuss, you're right. I want you to call me 'Teddy'. Everyone else does."

Den was happier because he now had the chance to say: "And I hope you will always call me 'Den'. No one ever calls me anything else."

Den immediately realized Teddy Smith must have ordered a careful investigation of his background. Obviously, those inquiries were more than a simple review of the files. Den had taken pains to conceal his actual given name. All Navy and CIA written records and even his passport carried it as Den Clark. Teddy Smith had dug deep enough to learn his birth name.

"I'd offer you a dram of The Macallan," Smith said, "but I don't have any. The guys here in Washington are a cautious and timid lot. They're afraid of the press. If a reporter got even the slightest rumor of there being Scotch whisky in a CIA office, we'd all be painted as a bunch of drunks. I sometimes think the country's most dangerous enemies aren't Middle Eastern terrorists. They're our own gentlemen of the press."

Smith liked to engage his visitors in friendly conversation. It gave him an opportunity to observe their reactions. It also created a proper atmosphere. A man spoke more freely and, possibly, more honestly if he were comfortable and satisfied that he was talking to a friendly sort of guy.

Den was capable of playing small talk games, but, today, he had no time for them. In his mood, small talk was an irritant. He wanted to know why he had been called to Teddy Smith's office. He expected to be offered a job he didn't want and had already decided to refuse. He would resign. He would look for a job with some international personnel security outfit. With his Spanish language ability and background, he would be a natural to act as a bodyguard for an American businessman working in some troubled part of Latin America.

"You may be right about the press, Teddy," was Den's non-committal observation. Then, in order to end the interview as quickly as possible, he abruptly changed the subject. "There are three people in your waiting room. I'm sure they have important matters to talk about, but your secretary let me in first. You've uncovered the name on my birth certificate and you know my preference for single malt - right down to the brand. Why all the attention, Teddy? Why am I here?"

* * * * *

Teddy Smith was tired of watching Senators and Representatives impose restraints on the Central Intelligence Agency. At one time, if diplomatic maneuvers proved unsuccessful, the CIA could be expected to be used as an instrument for executing foreign policy. The men who, only a few decades ago engineered the overthrow of Mossadiq in Iran and Arbenz in Guatemala would no longer recognize the Agency.

Unequivocally, but quietly, Teddy objected to "Sense of Congress" resolutions, Presidential mandates and Agency policies that shackled the hands and sometimes threatened to punish the men who planned and carried out covert operations. He watched as the Agency's purpose was slowly changing into one which, he was sure, would ultimately be limited to the collection of information. Satellites, foreign newspaper articles, reports from friends in foreign countries and gossip from embassy parties might, he feared, become the sole arena of CIA activity.

The Agency's constant development into an ever larger and more complex bureaucracy also discouraged him. Bureaucracy and timely action were seldom close companions. Teddy came to believe an organization's effectiveness was inversely proportional to its size. His opinion was shared by many of the Agency's old timers.

As the Central Intelligence Agency grew and changed, Teddy became more restive. When he was a field agent, certain amounts of discretion were allowed. An agent was expected to use his imagination. A rule might be bent a bit or even fractured if the result advanced the mission. Now it seemed as if procedure was far more important that substance.

You might be able to lie or cheat or blackmail to get information, but you couldn't torture. Everybody knew that. But nobody really knew exactly what constituted torture. Apparently, the definition of torture was subject was to change, depending upon the gravity of the situation.

The old adage of the wild West: "Shoot first and ask questions later" was, Teddy believed, changed into: "Ask a lot of questions first, analyze the hell out of the answers, have some Congressional Committee meet in closed session a few times, leak the deliberations to the press and then think about if you should shoot and what sort of weapon you should use and what you should shoot at." Teddy became convinced it was time for someone to reverse the trend. Many of the CIA's old timers were likewise convinced.

And now Denver Clark sat before him, asking why he was here.

Chapter 3

On paper, Den Clark was the kind of man Teddy sought. He was a SEAL, trained to handle himself in difficult situations. He was tough and resourceful. He was battle tested. He had courage, a fact that was amply proven by his record. During this short interview, Clark had already shown he was perceptive as well as smart.

Teddy's problem involved uncovering Den's core beliefs? How do you find if a man is trustworthy? Teddy would have to make decisions based on the way Den reacted when he got an answer to his question: "Why am I here?"

Teddy took a Dominican Republic cigar from a humidor atop his desk. "Care for one?" he asked. Den shook his head. Teddy lighted the cigar. He studied its glowing end and, satisfied, blew a smoke ring. "Of course you want to know why you're here and, of course, I'm going to tell you."

Teddy began by disapproving politicians' interference in CIA affairs. "It hamstrings the Agency's ability to effectively perform its functions. For decades they cut our budgets," he complained. "They nearly destroyed our on-the-ground sources of information," he continued. "We used to get solid reports from felons, perverts, prostitutes, drug dealers, disreputable types of all sorts. They weren't nice people so the politicians told us we couldn't use them.

"As a result, we had no accurate information about the Ayatollah Khomeini when our politicians managed to get us thrown out of Iran. We didn't even know the man our politicians put in power after that Haitian mess. He was an admirer of Castro. Look at the problems we've had in Iraq trying to get local informants.

"We used the Mafia to keep the docks operating in World War II. The OSS used them in Italy, too. That's all changed. Now our people on the ground have to be squeaky clean. Remember when some fools believed we could get all the information we needed through satellite surveillances?

"These same idiots are busy burying us under layer upon layer of bureaucracy. Defense, State, the military, the Agency - we all had intelligence operations. Now we are magically interrelated. It's a classic example of the strange and clearly insane belief that 'change' means 'progress.'

"You don't keep secrets by telling them to ten governmental agencies and five congressional committees. Hell, Den, those guys would tell a reporter everything they knew if they could get even the slightest personal advantage from it.

"And that's not all. Lines of communication are confused. The connections between authority and responsibility are vague. Who reports to who?" Teddy asked without expecting an answer. "Who decides what projects are to be pursued? The Defense Department? Those wimps at State? Damned politicians."

Den had heard it all before. It was a common subject in CIA casual conversation. There may have been some truth to the complaints. On the other hand, they may have been based on nothing more than the Belt Line bureaucrat's nightmarish fear of losing turf.

"And that stupid Executive Order 12333," Teddy said as he blew another smoke ring and carefully watched for Den's reaction. "Isn't that one for the books?" Then he was silent. Den knew Executive Order 12333 forbade CIA involvement in assassinations and he also knew Teddy was waiting for a response.

Again, Den's comment was non-committal. "Twelve-three-three-three is one of the rules of the game and I suppose we have to live with it," he said. But he thought: *I wish Smith would get to the point.*

"Do you really think so?" Teddy asked. "Let me ask you a question, Den. Suppose someone high up in the Agency - I mean very high up in the Agency - asked you to develop a plan calculated to cause the death of a person not only antagonistic to our national interests, but, to use that hard-to-define phrase, 'a clear and present danger.' Suppose you were told you would he officially disowned and castigated if your plan ever came to light. You could expect no help or support from anyone. What would you do?"

Teddy immediately held up his hand, silencing any answer Den might make, and added, "Let me make my proposition more concrete. If it was 1938 and Executive Order 12333 was in effect, would you create and execute an unofficial and unauthorized plan designed to kill, say, Adolf Hitler?"

"Now there's a loaded question if I ever heard one," Den thought. *"Well, Teddy expects an answer and I'll give him one."* Aloud he said: "Only the silliest academic would answer that one in the negative. A tougher question is: If it were 1928, when Hitler was nothing more than the leader of a small super-nationalistic German socialist political party, would I plan and carry out his assassination?"

The friendly, pleasant face Teddy Smith presented to the world seemed to erode. His expression appeared to harden and his eyes, without any movement, were fixed on Den's face. "If not in 1928," he asked, "How about in 1930? How about in 1932? '34? '36?"

"Is assassination appropriate only after an enemy has attacked us? Admiral Isoroku Yamamoto planned Pearl Harbor. We killed him in April of 1943. We discovered his flight plans and we sent a group of fighters to shoot him out of the sky. Do you know we had to go to the President of the United States to get the go-ahead to shoot him down? We were at war, Den, a war for our survival - and this was long before the 12333 Order.

"We had no CIA and we had no OSS when World War II began. Today we have a much more extensive intelligence community. We are capable of uncovering the very early development of growing and serious threats to our country. It's a rapidly changing world. Can it be said we have not only the right, but the duty to perform pre-emptive strikes?" Teddy paused for only a few seconds before adding: "You served in the Second Gulf War, didn't you?"

Den didn't answer. Of course, he knew Gulf War II was a pre-emptive strike. He saw the logic of Teddy's argument. How many millions of people were killed because of Hitler and Mussolini and Tojo? More recently, how many Southeast Asians were slaughtered in the killing fields of Pol Pot? Still more recently, would an assassination have avoided 3000 deaths on September 11th?

Teddy's question, Den began to suspect, was not a part of a mere casual conversation. Teddy had hinted at the presence of people inside the CIA structure who were dissatisfied with Agency policies limiting their abilities to act. Slowly, the light began to dawn. *"This guy is in the Projects Branch. He plans clandestine operations. He is suggesting the possibility of assassinations planned secretly within the Central Intelligence Agency. He is asking me to join the group."*

Part of Den's brain told him to refuse Teddy's overture. Den entered the CIA for covert field work. Sitting behind a desk in the Projects Branch and planning the logistics or even the mechanism for killing some foreign politician or head man in some terrorist organization held little appeal. His immediate reaction to Teddy Smith's unspoken invitation was negative.

By refusing the offer, Den would be rejecting an invitation from the people Teddy described as "high up in the Agency". Rejection would limit his future in the CIA, but such a probability was not a factor in his considerations. He had already planned to resign.

Another part of Den's brain told him to consider Teddy's as yet undisclosed proposition. If the nation's intelligence services uncovered a serious threat requiring drastic and direct action, should 'policy' require inaction? In a world of terrorists willing to commit suicide by flying airplanes into buildings, atomic explosives that can be carried in suitcases and deadly disease that can be poured into water systems, should 'policy' tell us we must wait for disaster before striking?

Den decided to postpone any immediate decision. He would wait to see if he had accurately analyzed the reason for Teddy's interview. That meant he had to give the answer Teddy wanted. Den returned Teddy's unwavering gaze. "If we were sure one of our enemies represented a real danger to the country, I wouldn't hesitate for a moment. I'd work out a plan to kill the son-of-a-bitch."

That was what Teddy wanted to hear. He quietly speculated for a few moments and then made his decision. "I know your record," he began. "You've undertaken some dangerous missions for your country. You've been shot at and you've been wounded. You are a patriot. Now, I'm going to tell you things. You're not going to remember any of them. This conversation never took place."

Teddy waited, looking down at his desk. He wanted to give Den a good opportunity to object before proceeding. When he looked up, he saw Den ever so slightly nod his head. Confirming Den's guess, Teddy explained the reason for the interview.

Over the years, some men inside the Central Intelligence Agency had become increasingly alarmed by policies and regulation imposed by college professors and politicians who had no true understanding of the dangers of international threats. A group of CIA officials considered the changes in Agency authorities and objectives to border on the suicidal.

A few of them, Teddy confided, decided to disregard policies that had little application to the kinds of dangers faced in today's world. Teddy described those men as a closely-knit group of patriots, some of them occupying the highest of positions in the Central Intelligence Agency. Some of them were part of the Directorate of Operations - the Clandestine Service. Others were inside other Agency Directorates and in their Branches and subsections. Teddy admitted he could only guess who they might be.

These men, Teddy explained, believed there were circumstances demanding the assassination of people who represented growing threats to the country. They did not look for any kind of authorizations for their programs calling for the killing of our enemies. Teddy emphasized how very careful they were in determining when an assassination became necessary.

"These men consider themselves to be the shield of the Republic," Teddy said. "They call themselves 'Aegis'. Clandestine Services does not know they exist'. No one outside of Aegis has even a suspicion of its existence."

Aegis projects left no records of their activities. They were carefully concealed within other authorized missions given to officers under the jurisdiction of the Directorate of Operations - the Section of the CIA involved in overseas espionage. Teddy finished his comments by stating an imperative. No one outside the circle should ever learn of the existence of Aegis. Even the most remote danger of the discovery of their invisible organization could not be tolerated. It would have to be avoided at all cost.

Teddy's last words were; "The men who carry out Aegis plans, must be more than merely capable of carrying out assignments. They must be particularly dedicated and completely trustworthy." Then he leaned back in his chair and waited for Den's reaction.

Den's reaction was immediate. *"This is not desk work,"* he thought. *"Teddy wants me to carry out assignments. He wants me do the killing."* Den looked for confirmation. "I suppose you are running a risk right now because I've been checked out and someone wonders if I might be willing to undertake," Den paused for a second before saying, "a special project." Teddy nodded.

"I suppose this is all you're going to tell me about Aegis?"

Teddy shifted his eyes and studied the ceiling of his office, "If you were in the top level of the Agency and you knew the public exposure of an assassination plot could destroy the CIA as well as, perhaps, the President and his Administration, you wouldn't want anyone to be able to identify your associates, would you? And if you, yourself, were involved in executing such a plan, wouldn't it be better if you didn't have any such dangerous information?"

Den nodded. "Give me a few days."

Teddy got his answer the next morning.

A week later, Den was sent to the CIA station in Santiago, Chile. Officially, he was expected to perform the jobs usually given to agents on their first overseas posting. His station associates didn't know he had been given another unannounced assignment. Aegis provided him with the reported location of a political murderer who had successfully hidden from the justice that, long ago, should have been meted out.

The few attempts to capture Humberto del Valle had been frustrated. Carefully developed information of his whereabouts was consistently accurate and consistently stale. Den's assignment was to determine if Humberto del Valle was in Puerto Montt. If he found him, he was told to kill him.

Chapter 4

A few days after Den left for Chile, Henry Putnam was ushered into Teddy Smith's office. Henry Putnam still had some hair. He combed it around on this pate to try to make it look like there was more of it. He wore rimless glasses and, unlike Teddy, he had developed a paunch. Henry was a bit optimistic when he considered himself to be middle aged. Psychologically, at least, he had moved far beyond that classification.

Henry Putnam had been in the Agency since the 1970s. As the years went by, he recognized how Congresses and various Administrations clamped down on the Agency's clandestine operations. Like Teddy Smith, he watched the CIA become what he considered to be a bureaucratic monstrosity. Henry's morale went into a steeper decline in each succeeding year.

Now he was the Chief of Station in Damascus and, unlike Teddy Smith, he had no professional interest in anything, except marking time until he could retire and enjoy the condo he owned in Hawaii. Henry Putnam's professional life was governed by three rules: (a) Follow orders, (b) Cover your ass, and (c) Don't screw up.

Teddy Smith and Henry Putnam were casual acquaintances. Over the years they had met and talked a few times. On rare occasions, they may have had a drink or two together. However, a stranger listening to Teddy's jovial greeting would think they were the closest of old friends.

When Henry entered his office, Teddy, smiling his broadest of smiles, got to his feet. "Henry, great to see you. You look good. Syria must agree with you." He shook Putnam's hand and, as usual, held his visitor's elbow with his left hand.

Teddy exuded friendly interest. "Great history in Syria. I was surprised to learn Damascus is the oldest continuously inhabited city on the planet. Must be a very interesting place. Sometimes I wish I were there with you instead of being chair bound here in Langley. Come. Sit. Not there. Here on the couch. The chairs are for strangers. The couch is for friends."

Teddy's few minutes of practiced inconsequential chatter followed before he asked: "What brings you here, Henry? What can I do for you?"

Henry took off his glasses and slowly wiped them. It was an affectation he often used for the purpose of getting a few seconds to think about what he was going to say and how he was going to begin.

Henry faced a problem. Covering his ass and keeping his head down had run into a serious conflict with the requirements of Agency policy. There was a slight chance that his worrisome problem might not exist. To learn if, in fact, he had a problem, he had to bring Teddy into his confidence. That, too, was dangerous, but he was reassured by Teddy's friendly welcome

"Well," Henry began, "I've got a little problem, Teddy."

Teddy quickly interrupted. "If I can help, of course, I will. After all, what are good friends for?"

"We've got a younger guy in Damascus and he seems to be some kind of a maverick. He took it upon himself to do a free lance operation," Then Henry quickly added: "I didn't know about it and I didn't have anything to do with it. It was purely his idea. I don't want anybody up here to think I was in on this guy's scheme."

Teddy nodded. "I'll do everything I can to make sure nothing rubs off on you. Now tell me what happened. Tell me everything. I'll need to know it all."

"This guy - his name is Jacobson - decided to bribe a terrorist in order to get a list of local and traveling Palestinians who were engaged in killing Israelis, kidnapping westerners, blowing up airplanes and the like." Putnam paused, audibly exhaled and slowly shook his head. "Without any authorization of any kind, Jacobson took money from an Agency account to fund his bribery. I didn't have a thing to do with it, Teddy."

Teddy nodded sympathetically. "How much did you lose?"

"We didn't lose a cent, the bribe was never delivered."

"Then you don't have much of a problem. What nobody knows won't hurt you."

"There's a complication," Putnam said in an uneasy tone. "When Jacobson tried to pull it off, one of our guys got killed. I'm pretty sure he wasn't in on it. He hadn't been in Damascus for more than a couple of days. I think Jacobson talked him into being a delivery boy. Because of Jacobson's unauthorized bribery, one of our men is dead." Putnam emphasized the word "unauthorized".

"Of course, I called for an investigation. I assigned it to another of our newer people, Agent G. G. Grant. She did a good job - possibly too good a job. She dug up the whole story. I've got her report with me. Here it is." He handed a folder to Teddy, saying: "Take a look at it. I'm afraid Jacobson might lie to save his skin and try to implicate me."

Teddy quickly skimmed the report. "Have you filed this thing, yet?"

"No, I haven't." The purpose of Henry Putnam's visit then became apparent. "I hoped, maybe, you might have given Jacobson some special Projects Branch work?" Putnam's rising inflection changed the statement into a question. "I know you don't have to tell me anything, but I have to ask you: Was Jacobson operating under some kind of Clandestine Operations authorization? If he was, I can file my report and be in the clear."

Obviously, Henry Putnam was a very worried man.

Teddy saw the potential of an advantage coming out of Putnam's dilemma. He wouldn't let Henry think it was as easy as Teddy knew it to be. When Teddy solved his problem, Henry Putnam would be obligated to him. Bread upon the waters. At some future date, Teddy might need help from him. Teddy picked up the report and told Putnam he needed time to think about it. "Can you come back tomorrow?" he asked. "I do my very best to find a way to get you out of this mess."

That evening, propped up by pillows, Teddy leaned against the headboard of his bed. Agent G. G. Grant's report of Jacobson's theft and insubordination and the extent of his involvement in the death of

Agent Mick McCarthy lay beside him. Teddy smiled when he remembered how he had operated without Chief of Station authorization. He was on a drug assignment in Colombia. A fellow agent had been detained by the Baranquilla police and was being held in the city's colonial-age prison.

The plan to liberate the man consisted of packing a car with explosives, parking it next to the prison's central exercise area and blowing a hole in the wall. Teddy objected to the scheme as dangerous and unnecessarily complicated. The Chief of Station overruled him.

At three o'clock, when the prisoners were allowed a half-hour of recreation outside of their cells, a Jeep was parked adjacent to the prison courtyard. The driver left the vehicle and, when a safe distance away, pressed a button setting off the charges hidden inside the car. The blast made no more than a dent in the prison's five-foot wide eighteenth century wall.

The explosion had two immediate effects. It blew the hell out of the Jeep and it scared a burro. Wild eyed, the animal, carrying a bundle of fire wood, galloped down a narrow street, its owner trying his best to keep up with it. The explosion also set the stage for potential disaster.

At the very least, the as yet unidentified prisoner would be found to be an American. It would be a miracle if some of the editors of the anti-gringo press didn't claim he was a CIA agent. In any event, the incident was sure to result in new rounds of gringo bashing.

Without authorization, Teddy withdrew funds from a hidden agency account and walked to the prison. Within the hour, the agent was free. The two guards who escorted him from the old fortress were each ten thousand pesos richer. The newspapers printed the rumor that the escaped prisoner was a Canadian drug dealer, busted out of confinement by local drug lords. Teddy received a commendation.

That was thirty years ago. If he tried it today, like Jacobson, Teddy would run the risk of being cashiered.

Now, as the head of a Section of the Projects Branch, Teddy was not known as a maverick. He had the reputation of being an administrator who was more than merely competent. He was dedicated to the work of the Central Intelligence Agency in general and specifically to the undertakings of the Clandestine Service.

Teddy enjoyed the respect of his superiors. He was reliable. His ability to successfully manage covert operations was impressive. The Deputy Director of the Foreign Intelligence Service, Cullen Brewster, had nearly absolute confidence in him.

Teddy Smith was regarded as an intelligent, good humored and pleasant man. Beneath that façade, less obvious qualities were hidden. Teddy Smith was a consummate pragmatist. He was as cold, as calculating, and as ruthless as he was ambitious. If his family had a coat of arms, its motto would be: The ends justify the means.

Teddy's personal life was carefully regulated. He never married. Except for an occasional professional, he had no time for women. Teddy's associates incorrectly assumed he enjoyed social functions. Others had also been misled. Teddy attended Washington parties only as a matter of office politics. Whenever he saw someone who had or might some day have a position of authority, Teddy found a way to meet him. He smiled and was charming. Silently wondered how that someone might some day be useful.

* * * * *

Henry Putnam may have thought he had a problem. Teddy didn't think so. If it ever became necessary to "adjust" a Station's financial records, the work would have to be done very carefully. In Langley, accountants were meticulous in their review of foreign station money management. They were responsible for catching more than one man with his hand in the till.

But no money had been lost from Damascus accounts. It was not necessary to adjust the Station's financial records. Poor old Henry Putnam didn't have to face that most difficult problem of hiding a completed embezzlement. With no bogus financial records for some zealous Agency Finance Officer to question, the balance of Henry's problems would be easy to manage.

A clean record of the agent's death and a transfer of Jacobson was all that was needed. Some judicious amendments of Agent Grant's investigation report and the re-assignment of Jacobson to some place where he could do no harm would clear up everything.

Teddy was ready with a workable suggestion. He glanced at Gigi Grant's report and considered the necessary changes. If, instead of delivering a bribe, Jacobson and McCarthy were going to meet a man who promised to give them information and if that terrorist had set a trap to kidnap them, Henry would be able to sleep secure in the knowledge that there was nothing in the investigation report that could embarrass him.

Jacobson would certainly keep his mouth shut. Henry would have to make sure Grant didn't spill the beans. He'd probably tell her it was "orders from above". Teddy would make sure that only a barren abstract of Agent G. G. Grant's report of the death of McCarthy would find its way into the Agency's records.

Teddy put Gigi's report on the bedside table and re-arranged the pillows. Before he went to sleep, he reviewed Jacobson's scheme. It was an imaginative plan requiring contact with the terrorist, stealing the Agency funds and, finally, using an innocent to be blamed in the event the plan misfired.

Teddy recognized Jacobson's mistake. A common bond unites the Palestinian people and those who support them. They all hate the Israelis with an almost unimaginably deep and pervasive hatred. That animosity joins them into a brotherhood with mutual loyalties able to withstand great pressure. An offer of five thousand dollar might get a man's attention, but it wouldn't break the kind of bond between people who share deep-seated hatreds.

The amount of the bribe being offered wasn't nearly enough to insure reliability. Ten thousand up front and another ten when the work was done together with the promise of much more for continued cooperation might have been enough.

Before he went to sleep, Teddy thought: "*This man, Jacobson, is not overawed by Agency rules and procedures. I think he might be useful.*"

Chapter 5

Den's return from his Chilean assignment was uneventful. He disembarked from the Linea Aerea Nacional plane in Washington, picked up his luggage and took a cab to his Arlington apartment. He was tired, but knew he had to postpone the few extra hours of bed time his body demanded. There was other work to do. Without taking the time to unpack, he showered, shaved and changed from the clothing he had worn when he left Santiago's wintry season. Then he taxied to Langley and went directly to the Project Branch. In the anteroom, Den waited to be called into Teddy's office.

Receptionists and secretaries form an information network of surprising efficiency. Bits and pieces of Agency gossip pass among them with computer-like speed. Teddy's receptionist knew Den had just returned from South America. She knew he had recommended Sean McCarthy for foreign service work and she also knew McCarthy had been killed in Damascus. She wondered if Den knew his friend had lost his life. Den's reaction told her he did not.

"Killed? When? Where?"

This was not the first time Den experienced the loss of a SEAL friend. It was to be expected in their line of work, but it was always painful. The men of SEALS are bonded in an exceptional manner.

Den had little time to digest the news of the death of the man who dragged him from danger on the open tarmac of the Saddam International airport - the man who insisted on his timely treatment by the navy corpsman.

Deputy Director Cullen Brewster left Teddy's office, acknowledged Den's existence by way of an undersized nod and left the anteroom. After only seconds, the intercom buzzed and Den was ushered into Teddy's office.

"Den, Den," Teddy said, faking sincere enthusiasm as he arose from behind his desk and reached out to shake Den's hand. "You look good, Den. Chile must agree with you. Pretty place. Magnificent scenery. Excellent wine country. I wish I could have been there with you instead of being chair bound here in Langley. Come. Sit. Not there. Here on the couch. The chairs are for strangers. The couch is for friends."

Teddy spent a few minutes engaged in pleasantries. Den was now accustomed to the ploy. He played the little game. Finally, Teddy got down to business. "Don't hold me in suspense any longer, Den. I know you pulled it off. I want to know how you did it. I want to know what went right and what went wrong. Give me everything. All of the details."

There would be no written record of Den's report of the assassination of Humberto del Valle. There would be no written report of any Aegis associated activity. It was, therefore, important that verbal reports were complete. There was no room for a subsequent "Oh, I forgot to tell you" or a later "Now I remember something else." During Den's report, Teddy Smith seldom had to interrupt him for additional information or explanation.

Den confirmed the presence of Humberto del Valle in a cottage a few miles from Puerto Montt on the Gulf of Ancud in Southern Chile. The land and climate there were similar to that of the Pacific Northwest. It can be clouded and wet and cold - that penetrating kind of cold that often accompanies foggy places. Den's first two trips to Puerto Montt were made for information. The purpose of the third was execution.

Two bodyguards attended del Valle. One of them stayed close to him inside the cottage. The other was usually outside the building. He kept watch in the wooded area surrounding the house and paid special attention to the gate and the lane that led up to it. Del Valle used the same system employed by the residents of Mexico City's Lomas de Chapultepec district. It is an upper middle class neighborhood where robberies are not uncommon. If a thief kills the outside dog by tossing a poisoned chunk of meat over the wall surrounding a targeted home, the owner's inside dog will still be able to raise a warning.

The outside bodyguard had placed a chair in the woods. It was near the trail that ran from the roadway through the iron gated entrance and on to the cottage del Valle occupied. Den spent a cold, damp and uncomfortable night, wrapped in a wool blanket, shivering as he leaned against the base of a tree not far from the empty chair.

The sun was not fully above the horizon when the outside bodyguard, carrying a thermos bottle, came from the cottage. It was his practice in the early morning to sit and watch the gate while warming himself with hot coffee. When he was seated, Den silently came up behind him. The man was unable to make a sound before he dropped to the ground. The outside dog was silenced.

Unseen, Den approached the house. He ducked low and, on his hands and knees, he began crawling past the cottage windows as he made his way to the building's kitchen entrance. He passed under the windows and was approaching the door when it opened. The second bodyguard came out to relieve himself. Den and the man saw each other at the same instant. The bodyguard raced back into the kitchen for his Uzi. Den stood and ran after him.

By the time Den reached the open kitchen door, the bodyguard had picked up his weapon and was swinging its muzzle toward him. Den stepped back putting the kitchen wall between them and dropped to the ground as slugs from the Uzi slammed through the wall only inches above his head. When the burst stopped, Den rolled and, on his stomach at the bottom of the open door, he fired a single shot. As the second bodyguard fell backwards, the man's fingers tightened and an un-aimed burst of gunfire exploded from the Uzi.

Den ran through the kitchen and into the living room. It was empty. The front door of the cottage was open. One of the bedroom doors was also open. Den looked at the front door and then at the bedroom. Someone standing inside it would have a clear view of anyone leaving the cottage. Instead of running to the front door, Den looked inside the bedroom. He quickly pulled his head back.

As he suspected, Humberto del Valle was standing in the shadows at the side of the bed. He was pointing a Tokarev automatic at the open front door. Screaming "hijo de puta" he fired twice at Den's disappearing head. Den again appeared and fired back.

The bullet hit del Valle in the chest and knocked him back against the wall. The Tokarev fell from his hand. Del Valle's blood stained the wall as he slid to the floor.

There were no nearby houses and there were many pine trees in the surrounding forest to muffle the sounds of the gunfire. Though the chances of someone finding him at the scene were small, Den quickly left the area. A difficult two mile cross country hike brought him to a rural road where he had hidden his rented automobile.

The sun had set when he arrived in Santiago. Twenty four hours later, he was in the Arturo Merino Benitez Airport, awaiting his flight back to the United States. Den had operated quickly and silently.

Teddy listened to Den's report with few interruptions. When it was finished, he showed no interest in the man whose murder he had planned. He asked only one question. "How did you explain your absences to the guys at the station?"

"I told them I was going fishing or sightseeing" Den answered. "There were a lot of good excuses for two and three day excursions. I even went fishing a few times - in the line of duty of course." Both Den and Teddy smiled. "To establish my bona fides, I gave a mess of trout to the people in the car rental Agency."

"Good enough," Teddy said. "Did they buy it? Do you think anyone at the Station has an inkling of what you were up to?"

"I don't think so. As far as they were concerned, I was clipping newspaper stories, attending embassy parties, meeting the important and nearly important locals and sending reports, observations and gossip to Langley once every week - all standard work. On my own time I was fishing and sightseeing. I didn't see or hear a thing to suggest anyone may have suspected the other mission."

"I know it was a tough assignment, Den. You came through it with flying colors. One of the truly unfortunate aspects of our job is the fact that successes aren't acknowledged. A few of us know the important work you have performed. You didn't fail us. I wish I could do more for you."

Teddy left the couch and returned to his desk. He opened the middle drawer and removed a thick envelope. "Here's some walking around money and a ticket to Bozeman." He smiled when he added:

"It's first class and it's an aisle seat. There'll be a car waiting for you at Hertz and I've booked a week at one of the best fishing lodges on the Madison River. This isn't a lot, but it will give you a hint about how much we all appreciate your work."

Dealing with the news of Mick McCarthy's death had to be postponed during Den's report to Teddy Smith. Now it forced its way to center stage. Surely Teddy could answer his question. "I hope you appreciate me enough to give me some information." He didn't wait for any response. He asked: "How did Mick McCarthy die?"

Teddy Smith's face remained expressionless. It didn't betray his immediate reaction to Den's questions. *"Why does he ask? What does he know?"* With equal speed, Teddy divined the answers to his questions. *"It was Den who recommended we get McCarthy into the Agency. They had to be friends from back in their SEAL days. Den Clark doesn't suspect a thing. How could he? This is nothing more than natural curiosity."*

"There's not much to tell. It was Agent McCarthy's first assignment. I think he was in the wrong place at the wrong time. He hadn't been in Damascus for more than a few days. He and another agent got ambushed. I'd guess one of those crazy Palestinian groups may have discovered the other agent's identity and tried to engineer a kidnapping. Hold him for ransom and get publicity - their usual procedure. Our guys fought them off, but McCarthy was wounded and died before he could get help."

Teddy leaned back and watched for any sign that would tell him Den might suspect what had really happened. He saw none, but, after Den left his office, he experienced an uneasy feeling. Teddy decided to warn Jake Jacobson. *"I think Jake should get a heads-up on this one,"* he thought

* * * * *

Jake Jacobson was in grade school in Massachusetts when he earned the nickname "Weasel". He was a small kid with glasses and braces and big ears. Jake was never able to develop any close friendships. He was always the last one picked when the boys chose

29

sides for sandlot baseball. With the cruelty common in children, the boys in his neighborhood picked on him and laughed at him. He was the butt of their jokes.

Young Jake reacted by becoming introspective. He satisfied his ego by dreaming of revenges that were never acted out. As he matured, he found he could build his self-image by detracting from others. He took delight in ridicule and sarcasm.

Later, at the university, he enjoyed publicly criticizing fellow students, corrosively exposing any weakness he could uncover. His sarcasm goaded a few of them into hitting him. When confronted, Jake's immediate and unvarying response was to run. He was widely disliked.

Jake's had an excellent academic record, but his post-college employments always ended abruptly. He alienated his immediate superiors as well as those who worked with him. The personnel manager who fired him from his third job suggested he might try government work where, he believed, discharge because of personality defects was rare. Jake was hired by the Central Intelligence Agency.

During indoctrination and initial preparatory assignments, Jake succeeded in keeping his assessments of his associates to himself. He had learned that open antagonism to others produced an equal and opposite antagonism toward him - a condition which not uncommonly resulted in being fired. While in Washington, Jake Jacobson developed the reputation of being a loner, smart enough, but not at all friendly.

His first off-shore post was Damascus, where he quickly concluded the station chief was an imbecile and his associates uniformly moronic. He began looking for some scheme that would show his obvious superiority and result in promotion from the field and back to Langley.

When he was called back to Washington after his failed attempt at bribery caused the death of Agent Mick McCarthy, Jake knew he would again be fired. He intended to defend his actions. He'd fight back, but he knew he wouldn't get a fair hearing. The old timers would hang together, although, certainly, they must have long ago recognized the incompetence of that old fool, Henry Putman.

If it hadn't been for Gigi Grant, the nosey little bitch, he could have blamed everything on that big, dumb ox, Mick McCarthy. But she had seen through him. McCarthy hadn't been in Syria when Jake took the money from the Agency's concealed account.

Jake tried to reason with Grant. After all he was just trying to do some good work for the Station and the Agency. The Agency got the money back. Who would be hurt if his "misstep" wasn't mentioned in her report? But, no, she wouldn't listen to common sense. There was nothing he could do about it right now. He had to satisfy himself by promising to get back at her someday.

To Jake's surprise, he wasn't called on the carpet. He didn't have to defend his actions. No one mentioned his Syrian "misstep". He was re-assigned to the CIA's Directorate of Operations. At first Jake could not believe his good fortune. He believed it had to be a trick. The scenarios he developed to explain the reason for the pleasant treatment he received at Langley reflected his innate paranoia.

Perhaps the CIA didn't want to fire him immediately for fear of some newsman uncovering his failed bribery and learn the facts surrounding the death of Mick McCarthy. Perhaps they would keep him in the Agency until the Damascus matter was obscured by the mists of time. Then, in a year of so, they would sack him.

Jake produced an even deadlier scenario. Perhaps the CIA couldn't run any risk of his Damascus debacle becoming known. Perhaps they intended to insure against any such possibility by waiting for a year or so and then killing him. That is what he would propose if he were in their shoes.

* * * * *

Teddy Smith dispelled Jake's fears when he invited him into the Aegis group. Jake was a willing recruit. He was more than comfortable in his conspiratorial assignments. He reveled in it. What Jake thought would be the end of his CIA career turned out to be his ticket to a position of higher responsibility.

He was promoted and given a post in the sensitive area of planning covert operations. Jake had a position in the Project Branch of the Clandestine Service. His boss was Teddy Smith. For the first time in his career, Jake Jacobson had a boss who protected him.

Most of the other people in the Project Branch had an idea of what Jake did. He designed programs to further the development of foreign intelligence. No one knew he served additional undisclosed functions. Jake was the man Teddy Smith called upon whenever he faced a special problem requiring an extra degree of duplicity and deception. He also called on him when he needed to surreptitiously insinuate an Aegis assassination into some project already approved by the Directorate of Operations.

Teddy knew Jake had an IQ substantially above the national average. He suspected Jake would enjoy the intrigue involved in fulfilling the requirements of Teddy's special Aegis assignments. It didn't take Teddy long to confirm his suspicion.

Of course, Teddy also knew Jake was woefully deficient in the personality department. Jake's many detractors in the Projects Branch couldn't bring themselves to admit how bright he was. They preferred to characterize his intelligence as a kind of well-developed, animal cunning.

Jake soon established a reputation as a ruthless office politician. If Jacobson didn't like an associate, that man could expect trouble. Jake Jacobson was both hated and feared by the people who worked with him. Being hated didn't bother Jake. Being feared pleased him.

The more he was feared, the more he could intimidate others and the higher his self-esteem. Jake's ego blossomed. He had power and he enjoyed the protection of Teddy Smith. He thought no one would dare to challenge him.

Chapter 6

Den sat in his apartment, the ice cubes slowly melting in his untouched drink. He was preoccupied. Teddy's description of McCarthy's death didn't come close to satisfying him. There had to be more information available.

Den decided he would ask for a file search. He'd find and read the Damascus report of the killing. He was sure it would give a more complete picture of what had happened. When he asked for the file, he was told it was not available. He asked "Why?" It was a simple question. The answer was equally simple. "The file is not available to you because it is classified."

It took three dinners with a rather plain girl who had access to the Agency's Classified Information records. Without authorization, she let Den read the file he sought. The report of the circumstances surrounding McCarthy's death was brief and overly concise. It contained no reference to any investigation into the death. It reported only that Agent McCarthy was killed in Damascus by a group of terrorists. Date, time, and location were reported - only basic information, the facts that might satisfy a statistician, but nothing more.

It was as sterile and barren as Teddy's description. Den was more than merely dissatisfied. He was angry. He wanted to know the specifics of the death of his SEAL comrade - the man who once saved his life. Why couldn't he find out exactly what had happened to him?

Den's instincts told him there was more to the story of the death of Mick McCarthy. The small voice living deep within him was again whispering. That same voice had warned him when he crossed the tarmac at the Saddam Hussein airfield in Baghdad. It told him something was astir during his first meeting with Teddy Smith. Den had disregarded the little voice when it told him to quit the Agency and forget Teddy's offer. Now it was again telling him something was wrong.

Why was the report so lacking in corroborating fact? What was so secret about it? Why had it been classified? Was someone trying to hide what happened to Mick McCarthy? Was someone trying to avoid any record that might cause someone else to become curious and ask questions? Who was the agent with Mick when the shooting started? Why doesn't the report identify him?

Den decided he would look for that man. He would find him and talk with him. He'd find out what happened to Mick. But how could he identify the agent who stood with Mick McCarthy in Damascus? Where would he begin his search? Den found a way to answer those questions when he remembered Ferdie Robbins. *"Ferdie might be able to help,"* he thought.

* * * * *

Ferdie Robbins looked like a cartoonist's idea of an accountant. He was narrow framed and weighed, maybe, a hundred and fifty pounds. His face seemed too small for the large tortoise shell rimmed glasses he wore. He was a quiet man - an introvert, just a bit uncomfortable in the presence of anyone. It had been facetiously rumored that he was part mouse. Certainly, he wasn't flamboyant and, certainly, he wasn't courageous.

Secretly, Ferdie dreamed about being an undercover agent. He fantasized about meeting and overcoming the kinds of desperate peril found in Hollywood's lurid spy movies. In real life, however, Ferdie avoided any kind of potential danger with the same indefatigable attentions he would employ to avoid the Black Plague. Though he spent much of his time badgered by varying degrees of fright, he performed his work at Langley with efficiency and intelligence.

Ferdie worked in the Agency's Clandestine Service. He arranged transportation for CIA field agents. He also provided another special service. If an agent traveled for some covert purpose, it was Ferdie who prepared the cover, the passport and other documents that would prove he was anyone from a Chicago plumbing contractor to a Belgian investment banker.

It was Ferdie who arranged Den's transportation to Santiago as well as the alternate identity he might assume in the event of any unforeseen problem with Chilean authorities. Because of Ferdie's job responsibilities, he was collaterally involved in many of the Agency's covert operations. Den knew Ferdie probably managed the transportation of every person who had been sent to Syria.

Ferdie would know who was in Damascus when Mick was killed. He would probably be able to name every officer who might have been with Mick the night he died. If Mick was involved in some secret operation, Ferdie would know about it. He would have provided the necessary cover. Den's problem was getting Ferdie to tell what he knew. Ferdie was tight lipped. He made a clam look like a Hollywood gossip columnist.

In the spying business, a covert agent's fear of exposure is constant. That kind of fear can migrate to other people in the intelligence services who are not involved in covert operations. Suspicion is pernicious. If a man is suspected of treachery, his friends and associates also become suspect.

When the suspicions of the presence of a Soviet penetration of the CIA's Langley offices were high, many in the Agency, from secretaries on up, wondered who could they trust. Perhaps the man at the next desk was a Soviet mole. To be able to work in an atmosphere of such widespread mutual suspicion is difficult.

When Soviet moles were uncovered and the leaks were plugged, much of the fear subsided. Ferdie Robbins, however, remained alarmed by the possibility of being accused of disloyalty. True to his cautious and timid nature, Ferdie became inordinately fearful of the consequences of being seen outside the office with anyone associated with the CIA. It could start rumors. It could cause trouble. In fact, Ferdie was convinced, soon or late, it would cause trouble.

Like many others in the Agency, Ferdie disliked Jake Jacobson. Ferdie made the arrangements to move Jacobson from Damascus back to the United States. After he had been promoted into the Projects Branch, Jacobson called Ferdie and complained about the quality of his temporary motel facilities. He insisted on better accommodation in any future hotel/motel stay and warned Ferdie of dire consequences if he ever overlooked those demands.

Jake's imperious attitude led Ferdie to make careful inquiries. Who was this man? Was he as important as his manner indicated? Ferdie's acquaintances in the Project Branch were unanimous in reporting their dislike of Jacobson. One went so far as to call Jake "a sneaky, egocentric asshole," and a secretary from the Damascus Station, being transferred to New Delhi, said she believed Jacobson might have caused the death of a fellow agent.

It was easy for Ferdie to identify the fellow agent who had been killed. During the time Jacobson was in Syria, only one man, Sean "Mick" McCarthy, had been killed in Damascus.

When Jacobson learned Ferdie had questioned his Projects Branch associates, he charged into Ferdie's office. In a voice loud enough to be heard in surrounding offices, he gave him a tongue-lashing. It was Ferdie's dislike of Jacobson that induced him to talk to Den Clark.

* * * * *

"I'm going to trust you," Ferdie almost whispered. It was early in the evening. He and Den shared a back booth in an Arlington cocktail lounge. A few customers were at the bar, but the booths adjacent to Den and Ferdie were empty. Ferdie wanted it that way. He had screwed up his courage to meet with Den and, temporarily at least, he overcame some of his usually timidity. He wanted to cause trouble - trouble for Jake Jacobson.

"I'm going to trust you," he repeated and immediately added the disclaimer: "It's only a rumor, nothing more." He drank from his Coca Cola before he spoke again. "I'm going to trust you to forget about where you heard this." Den nodded and Ferdie continued. "Jake Jacobson might have had something to do with Mick McCarthy's death. Whatever that 'something' was, it might have been covered up."

Den asked no questions. He knew Ferdie Robbins would tell only what he wanted to tell and not another single syllable. Ferdie appreciated the silence. He didn't want cross-examination. Any cross examination could become very dangerous. The mere fact that someone had asked questions of him was dangerous. It could ruin his future in the Agency. If he answered any of those questions, he might, inadvertently, give away some terribly important Agency secret.

After a moment, Ferdie looked up from the soft drink he had been nervously studying. "He's sucked up to Teddy Smith something fierce," he said. "He even took an apartment close to him so he could jog with him. Teddy relies on him. Jake is as powerful as he is pompous. He can get you transferred to the backwoods of Ecuador. He can get you fired. Behind his back he's called 'that asshole', and for good reason. The man is dangerous."

Ferdie again looked down at his Coca Cola and tried to find a way to tell Den what he suspected had really happened to Mick McCarthy.

"You've read the file, I suppose?"

Den nodded his head. "It doesn't say much. Mick and I were friends - good friends. I want to know what happened and there's nothing in the file that will help me."

This time it was Ferdie who nodded in agreement. He waited a few seconds and then said: "Well, I'd like to help you, but that's all I know." He looked around to be sure no one was eavesdropping and slid out from behind the booth table. "Thanks for the drink. I've got to go now." As he put on his overcoat, he tried to casually change the subject.

"I suppose you don't know any of the people in the Damascus Station? They're a nice bunch. I just finished moving one of them back to the States. She's being re-assigned. Her name is G. G. Grant. She's at the Four Points Sheraton right now." Ferdie scrunched his head down into the protection of his upturned coat collar and walked toward the lounge's door. Without looking back at Den, he added: "Room 310."

"*Gigi!*" Den thought. "*She's here! She's back in Washington.*" Den's looks and actions did not betray the feelings he had unsuccessfully tried to deny since he and Gigi went their separate ways. Those feelings were filed away in his memory, but never far from the surface where they could make fleeting re-appearances. They often came to him during those early morning seconds when the mind hovers briefly between consciousness and sleep.

Den's memories of Gigi again emerged from their partial exile. Again they commanded his attention. *"Gigi!"* he repeated. *"She's here."*

Den left his unfinished Scotch and water, dropped a ten on the table and walked to the lounge's bank of telephones. He called the Four Points Sheraton and asked for a connection with room 310. He hoped Gigi hadn't left for dinner and was relieved when he heard her voice.

"Hello, hon, this is Den."

"Den! For God's sakes, where are you?"

"I'm here in Washington and I want to see you."

Gigi paused before answering. She was not in one of her better moods. Being brought back to Langley for re-assignment often signaled an opportunity for advancement, but she knew her recall meant the end of her Central Intelligence Agency career. She knew she had incurred the displeasure of the "powers that be" in Langley. Her investigation of the death of Agent McCarthy had stepped on someone's toes.

"I'd love to see you again," she told him, "but I'll warn you, I don't think I'll be very good company."

"What's wrong, hon? Can I help?"

"No. Nobody can help. Thanks, anyway. Don't worry. It isn't the end of the world."

Den knew Gigi was worried. It wasn't only the words she had spoken. Her voice was flat, even a bit sad.

"You'll survive, hon," he said, attempting reassurance. "We're both survivors. We can handle anything. I'll be over in twenty minutes. Have you eaten?"

"Yes."

"Then we'll talk."

"I'd like that."

Den hung the phone. Gigi might be able to tell him what happened to Mick, but she sounded like she had her own problems, problems causing her to speak in short sentences, volunteering little and devoid of her usual, almost lilting effervescence. He didn't know the reason for her uncharacteristic depression. Whatever it was, Gigi's tone made it sound serious and Den knew it was no time for her to be alone.

He also knew it was no time for him to question her about Mick. Den would defer his interest in what happened to his friend. Gigi needed cheering up and he would give her the sympathetic support she needed. Den left the lounge, hailed a taxi and made his way the Four Points Sheraton.

Since receiving notice of recall to Langley, Gigi had to face the reality of closing what turned out to be an unpleasant chapter of her life. She had expected so much from her career in the CIA. Now, her disillusion dismayed her. Alone in her room at the Sheraton, again and again she went over the sanitizing of her investigation of Jake Jacobson and the punishment she was suffering because she told the truth. She had lost two years of her life. Damn Jake Jacobson, Damn Henry Putnam. Damn the CIA.

Two emotions fought for ascendancy within her. She felt the frustration of being victimized by office politics, the frustration of being penalized because she had been right. She also felt the helplessness of being unable to defend herself. Her thoughts swung back and forth between the anger born of her frustration and the depression that came from the realization of her inability to do anything about it. She couldn't fight the bureaucracy.

Den's call lifted her spirits. If there ever was a time when a lady needed a friend, this was it. She knew Den Clark was, indeed, a friend. He had been much more than a friend. She was transported back to their days together in the Sherman Kent School for Intelligence Analysis. It was more than fun. They had shared their lives, honestly and completely.

When Gigi heard the knock on her door, the lingering feeling of isolation - of being alone - left her. The sense of relief she felt when she answered the phone and recognized Den's voice returned to her. She hoped Den hadn't changed. She hoped he was still the man she knew so well at the Kent School. She needed more than just a friend. She needed someone to hold her.

When Gigi opened the door, Den saw the pretty woman who had attracted him in that cafeteria two years earlier, but her smile seemed to be a bit tentative. Den thought she showed signs of stress. He wondered if she had changed. He wondered if she had moved on with her life. He wondered if she was the same woman who shared his life at the Kent School. He hoped so.

At first, they spoke in short impersonal sentences. Den said she looked great. She said he did, too. Could he come in? Yes, of course. Sit. Make yourself at home. Good to see you again. You too. Then, after a few moments of uncomfortable silence, Den removed any reason for further embarrassment. He wasted no time. "What's wrong, hon. I'm someone who loves you. Remember me? I'm on your side. You can talk to me."

Gigi was reassured. This was the Den she knew. He could always read her moods. His sympathy was never false. He was more than a once-upon-a-time lover. He was her most intimate friend. She knew she could trust him.

Gigi wanted someone to know how Jacobson stole money from a CIA account and tried to use it to bribe a terrorist. She wanted someone to know how Jacobson feared a double cross and used an unsuspicious Mick McCarthy to deliver the bribe. She wanted someone to know how Jacobson had driven from the scene at the first sign of trouble, leaving McCarthy alone to face terrorist gunfire. She wanted someone to know the Agency had engaged in a cover-up. Her story might never become a part of the official record, but she wanted someone to know it.

Gigi told Den everything she had uncovered during her investigation of McCarthy's death. When she had finished, she leaned back in the chair. "Jacobson tried to get me to whitewash him. Of course, I wouldn't do it. I gave my report to Henry Putnam. He's the Station Chief. He took it to Langley. When he came back, he showed me a doctored document. Jacobson wasn't even mentioned.

"He said he was told to change it by top echelon people. The reason wasn't explained: 'Need to know' basis only and I, of course, didn't need to know. I was told to destroy my report and keep my mouth shut. Henry filed the doctored report and Jacobson was given a position in the Projects Branch."

The cover up was obvious and it was extensive. Even Gigi's,

watered down investigation report was not made a part of the record. Something, indeed, had been wrong in Damascus. Ferdie Robbins told him Jake Jacobson was involved in Mick's death. Gigi showed him Jake was more than merely involved.

Den showed no outward reaction to her revelations, but, inside, his anger increased. It was an anger   caused by his empathy with the pain Gigi had to endure and, equally, by his own reaction to the CIA protection of the man who embezzled funds - the man who caused the death of Mick McCarthy.

Before Den could say anything, Gigi made an additional statement. "I've been recalled for reassignment. It won't be a promotion. Tomorrow, I'll be offered a transfer. I suspect it will be to a file clerk's position in the lowest level basement of the Langley complex. Jake Jacobson and whoever is protecting him are behind it. They want me out of the Agency. I know too much about Jacobson."

Den asked her: "What are you going to do about it?"

"I'm not going to do anything about it. McCarthy's case is closed and nobody is going to re-open it. I can't fight the Agency. I'm going to quit. I'll going to put all this behind me. I'm going to Tucson and I'm going to hang out my shingle. From tomorrow on, I'll be 'G. G. Grant - Attorney and Counselor at Law'. If you ever need a divorce, care to start a corporation or want me to probate your estate, look me up."

Then, for the first time, she smiled. "I feel much better now," she said.

"You've had a tough time, hon," Den said. He expressed his own feelings as well as hers when he said: "Jacobson is a bastard - and so are his friends in the Agency. You've made the right choice. Get out of here and start again in Arizona. You don't want Jacobson or his friends in your life." He put his hands on her shoulders and, face-to-face, told her he would make Jacobson pay.

Gigi almost melted when Den put his arms around her and held her to him. They talked about how they had met, the good times they had shared. The talk of happier times helped to restore her. Perhaps life wasn't so bad after all. She asked him if he remembered their first kiss. He did. He also remembered the first time they slept together. So did

Gigi. She looked up at him and, ever so slightly, raised her chin.

"I'd like to kiss you," Den said.

"That would be nice." She answered, "very, very nice."

The sun had risen when they awoke. They showered together and breakfasted in Gigi's room. When it came time to leave, they kissed again and Den promised he would be there for her, should she ever need anything.

Chapter 7

After he left the Four Points Sheraton Den's thoughts moved from Gigi to Damascus to Mick McCarthy and then to Jake Jacobson. Now he knew what happened to Mick. Jake Jacobson put him in a dangerous situation and when the fight started, he deserted him. That was the act of a coward, an act completely foreign to Den's character. A man who would leave a comrade in danger was detestable.

Den wondered why the son of a bitch was not exposed. Why wasn't he kicked out of the Agency? Jake showed his true colors in Damascus, but he was still in Clandestine Operations. As he drove to his apartment, Den remembered Ferdie's warnings: Teddy Smith relies on him. Jake Jacobson is powerful. The man is dangerous.

Jake was now assigned to Teddy's Projects Branch. No one was assigned to that Branch without the most careful of background checks. Teddy was aware of Den's birth name, his favorite brand of single malt Scotch and even his preference for bulkhead aisle seats in airplanes. Surely, he must have known what Jacobson did in Damascus. Was it a case of someone telling Teddy to bring Jake into the Projects Branch?

Or could Teddy be Jake's benefactor? Teddy said Mick was killed while working with another agent. Why didn't Teddy tell him that agent was Jake Jacobson?

There was no point in trying to make Jacobson pay for what he did by going through official channels. When the Syria Station chief came to Langley, he must have talked with somebody who had enough clout to be able to scrub the record clean and move Jake into the Projects Branch. Someone up there liked the little bastard. Den had no doubts. Jacobson's friends would continue to protect him.

Den promised himself Jake Jacobson was not going to get away with abandoning Mick. He wasn't going to get away with forcing Gigi out of the Agency.

Later that morning, Gigi Grant was notified of reassignment to a station of such modest significance that those who went there were considered by their fellow agents to have received early retirement. As Jacobson had presumed, Gigi Grant immediately resigned from the Central Intelligence Agency. She went to Tucson and reactivated her membership in the Arizona Bar Association.

* * * * *

Jake Jacobson learned important lessons from his disastrous bribery attempt in Damascus. He had long known it was all right to denigrate people below him in the chain of command. It was also entirely proper to quietly attack the competence and credibility of those who shared his same level in the organization chart. Since they were his competition for positions up the corporate ladder, Jake believed their reputations had to be destroyed.

Prior to Damascus, Jake had been almost completely insensitive to the concept of deferring to the people above him in the chain of command. They were the men he wanted to replace, so he had adopted the practice of attacking them. It was his way to show what he truly believed was his own intellectual superiority. He would look for real or imagined defects in his immediate superiors. He would bring them to light, often. He made no effort to disguise his signs of disrespect. The signs were not missed by the targets of his attacks.

After Damascus, Jake learned the value of a friend with clout. He learned it was a terrible mistake to treat superiors with anything but sycophantic respect. The boss's ability to think may be on a par with that of a garden slug, but keep your mouth shut. Praise him. In times of adversity, he can help you. Putnam could have helped Jake, but he didn't. Why should he? Why should Putnam or anyone else help a man who so obviously held him in contempt?

Jake knew he had been unreasonably lucky in Syria. Henry Putnam was a spineless idiot. If he had any guts at all, Jake would have been peremptorily fired. It took Teddy Smith, a perfect stranger, to convince

Putnam to protect him. Putnam could have prepared his own report. He could have provided him with cover, but he didn't. Teddy was the one who saved his ass. The lesson was clear. It was essential for a man to have friends "up the line".

In Langley, Jake carefully cultivated Teddy. He agreed with whatever Teddy said. He complimented him whenever he could find an opportunity. He studied the ways Teddy acceded to Cullen Brewster, the Deputy Director. He tried, unsuccessfully, to be as adept and subtle as Teddy in dealing with his superiors.

Of course, Teddy recognized Jake's false subservience. It didn't bother him. He had an accurate assessment of Jake Jacobson. Teddy knew Jake would turn on him if it ever became advantageous for him to do so. Given the same motivation, Teddy would turn on Jake just as quickly. The word "loyalty" could not be found in either Jake or Teddy's dictionary. As long as Jake bent every effort to please him, Teddy would be happy, but he was careful not to trust him.

Jake's CIA associates of equal rank didn't like him. They knew him as a sarcastic and arrogant back-stabber. Whenever one of them used the phrase "that little prick" or "that asshole" everyone knew he was referring to Jake Jacobson. As long as Jake had the support of Teddy, if made no difference what his fellow planners in the Projects Branch called him. He didn't give a damn what they thought of him.

* * * * *

At four o'clock in the afternoon, Jake left his office in the CIA complex at Langley. The office regularly closed at five o'clock. Jake often left early. It was an action that did not go unnoticed by his associates. He enjoyed his little game of "conspicuous early exit".

Leaving at four gave him the advantage of missing some of the late afternoon traffic, but Jake did it for another reason. It was a quiet and pointed reminder to everyone in the Section that he was a man of special privilege. He could violate the rules without fear of reprimand.

A half hour after leaving Langley, Jake arrived at The Bellavista, an apartment building in nearby McLean. The Bellavista's management catered to career government employees in the upper quadrants

45

of pay grades. Jake hadn't yet reached that income level, but The Bellavista address was a status symbol and Jake Jacobson was abundantly sensitive to status symbols.

There was another reason for Jake's selection of The Bellavista. It was less than a quarter mile from the apartment of Teddy Smith. The selection of The Bellavista was part of Jake's plan to develop a friendly and personal relationship with Teddy. Living close to him helped create that relationship. Jake would sometimes jog with Teddy and afterwards, on weekends, they would occasionally breakfast together.

Arriving at The Bellavista, Jake pressed the button on his garage door opener and the security gate to the building's underground parking area slid open. He parked his Audi in the place assigned to him and took the elevator to the third floor. As he walked down the corridor, his sense of satisfaction was complete. He was protected by Teddy Smith, feared by his associates and envied by his inferiors. Vain and arrogant, Jake Jacobson was pleased with his life.

He pulled a ring of keys from his pocket and inserted one of them into the lock of his apartment door. As soon as the door swung open, someone came from behind him and struck him between the shoulder blades with such force that Jake's dark glasses flew from his face and he was propelled inside the room and onto the floor.

As Jacobson got to his knees, he was kicked in the ribs. He fell against the hallway table, sending the vase and flower arrangement crashing to the parquet floor. In pain and gulping air, Jake struggled to his feet. He was grabbed by his coat lapel and jerked upright. A fist was driven into his stomach and, as he doubled forward, he was hit on the side of his face. His jaw was broken.

More punches brought blood from his mouth and nose. A downward blow broke his collarbone and, barely conscious, Jacobson collapsed, falling to the floor where he assumed a protective fetal position. He was kicked again. Finally, he lay unconscious.

Den turned to leave the apartment and spoke for the first time. "There, you miserable son of a bitch. You're lucky I didn't kill you."

* * * * *

Den left Jake Jacobson's apartment. He took the elevator to the underground parking floor and retrieved his suitcase from where it rested behind one of the cement pillars. Then he stood in the shadows next to the security gate. Within minutes a resident opened the gate as he drove his automobile into the parking area. Before it closed, Clark walked out of the building and continued up the ramp to the street. He waited on the sidewalk until he could hail a passing taxi.

At Reagan National Airport, Den boarded a commercial jet and left Washington. When he arrived at Miami International, he showed a false passport to the clerk at the Aerolineas Argentina counter. She took it from him, looked at the picture and then glanced up at him. The passport picture looked as much like Den as most passport picture look like their owners.

The clerk returned his passport, checked his bag and handed him his flight documents. Then she smiled the same rehearsed smile that automatically appeared whenever she handed a boarding pass to a traveler. Like every well trained Aerolineas Argentina ticket counter clerk, she added the required comment: "I hope you will enjoy your visit to Argentina, Mr. Peabody."

Den took the ticket, returned an equally meaningless smile and thought: "*At least she didn't say 'Have a nice day'.*" Den didn't have time for the rote and phony cordialities so common in the English language. When someone asks: "How are you?" he really doesn't give a tinker's dam how you are. Den admired the people who answer such empty inquiries with words like "terrible".

As he waited to board his flight to Buenos Aires, Den reviewed his beating of Jake Jacobson. It had not been a cold and calculated deliberate punishment. It was an expression of anger at the way Jake destroyed Gigi's career and at the way he put Mick in danger and ran when the shooting began.

What Jake did could not be changed. At least he had let Jake know he knew of his cowardice and his betrayal. At least he had vented his anger and given Jake some sort of repayment for his actions.

* * * * *

Jacobson awoke in a hospital. His jaw was wired shut. His arm and shoulder were in a cast. His ribs were taped. He ached, but it wasn't only the stabbing torment of his injuries that caused his agonies. Jacobson knew the man who had beaten him was Den Clark.

"*Teddy warned me Clark was asking questions*," Jake said to himself. "*He must have found out what happened in Damascus. If he doesn't know, he must have guessed.*" Jake tried to forget his pain and analyze his problem. "*Yes*," he concluded, "*Clark knows and he wants me to know he knows. That's why he made no attempt to hide his face.*"

Jacobson turned his head toward the window and, catching his breath because of the sharp pain the movement caused, he continued his thoughts. "*If Clark had firm proof,*" he reasoned, "*I think he'd try to have me tossed out of the Agency. No, Clark either guessed or else someone told him what happened, but I don't think he can prove a thing. Otherwise, he would have tried to get me fired. Well, he made the mistake of his lifetime. I'll get back at him. He'll pay for this.*"

Jacobson lay in the hospital bed and planned the shape of his revenge. "*I could whisper in Teddy's ear,*" he thought. Jake knew he could count on Teddy. "*Teddy could easily arrange to send the son of a bitch to a permanent posting in the Sahara or to Nome. He could get him reduced to the status of a supply clerk or, better yet, kicked out of the CIA.*"

Jacobson quickly rejected those alternatives. He knew Clark wouldn't go quietly. "*If he got canned, he would certainly tell everyone why he beat me up.*" Jacobson didn't want that reason to become public knowledge. Moreover, getting Clark thrown out of the Agency wasn't nearly enough. Jacobson wanted more, much more. There was only one way he could satisfy himself.

"I will kill him," he said aloud through his wired jaw and clenched teeth. He nodded his head and slowly repeated, "I will kill you, Den Clark. I'll get my chance and then I will kill you."

Chapter 8

Every year, huge quantities of illegal narcotics are smuggled into the United States. They come from Southeast Asia, from the Middle East and from Latin America. It's a profitable business for the suppliers. There are human costs associated with the business. Violence is its constant companion.

Warfare between cartels and the murder of competing suppliers are only the tip of the iceberg. The robberies and prostitutions committed by those who have no other ways to support their addictions destroy an even larger number of lives. The bill society pays for the illegal drug business is enormous.

The arrests and incarcerations of dealers and drug lords are complemented with programs for the education and treatment of victims. The effect of these activities can be debated. Certainly, the drug associated violent deaths do not seem to diminish. Neither does the volume of illegal drugs imported into the country.

The identification and destruction of drug production and distribution, wherever they are located, is an objective of our government. The phrase "wherever they are located" includes many of the Republics in Latin America. In those Republics, as in other countries of the world, destruction of the drug production is difficult.

Newspaper editors who have the courage to speak out and judges who sentence offenders are threatened and often murdered. Those who remain silent are rewarded. Army officers and policemen and Senators and judges and Mayors and corrupt government officials all become wealthy by looking the other way while cocaine is produced and shipped from and through their countries. As long as there are people who will offer bribes, there will be politicians who will take them.

Any attempt to stop coca leaf production and harvest is nearly impossible. It is an important cash crop for the peons and small farmers who plant it. Funding the programs of Latin American governments to replace the peon producers' income by cash payment fails when confronted by reality. Government intermediaries steal most of the monies and the small amount that goes to the farmers is welcomed as an addition to the coca leaf income - not a substitute for it.

Rather than try to pay peon farmers to plant other cash crops, it had been argued, a more effective approach would be to terminate such funding and direct more assets to demolishing local production factories and destroying sophisticated international distribution networks. The pervasive corruption of local officials too often stymies those efforts. Cooperation from local army, police and drug enforcement personnel is far from adequate.

Some men believe there is a better way to fight the narcotics wars. They point to the drug lords' nearly universal practice of murdering their competition. When the surviving drug lords have established their monopolies, these men argue, the deaths of the men who then direct the drug production and distribution networks will be the more effective way to fight the drug war.

* * * * *

Joselito Montoya came from humble origins. He was now a Bolivian millionaire often described as the continent's most elusive drug lord. His cocaine empire rivaled that of Colombia's Cali and Medellin cartels. United States Drug Enforcement Agency personnel, working in Bolivia with their local counterparts, were unable to damage his operations.

Urban and rural locations were often raided and buildings were searched. They were always too late. Traps were laid, but no one came close to capturing their quarry. Joselito Montoya had provided himself with the most effective of early warning systems. The Bolivian hounds made a great show of chasing the drug lord fox, but the fox controlled the hounds. Joselito Montoya, through massive bribery, knew the plans of the Drug Enforcement Units as soon as they came off the drawing board.

In Argentina's northwest Province of Jujuy, a few days after deplaning in Buenos Aires, Den Clark entered the Republic of Bolivia. His false passport would carry no Bolivian "entrada" stamp. There would be no record of his entry into the country. Late at night, alone and unburdened by any sort of official approval, he hiked into the country, avoiding Bolivian Custom and Immigration checkpoints. The USA's local DEA people, their Bolivian counterparts and Joselito Montoya never knew Den Clark was there.

Den was sent to Bolivia to quietly and secretly locate the places where coca leaves were harvested and processed. His assignment also included the identification of Bolivian politicos, police and army officials who accepted drug lord bribes in exchange for protecting Montoya.

Den had another unofficial assignment. It had been planned in Langley by men in the Aegis organization. They were the only few who were aware of it. Den Clark's undisclosed mission was the assassination of Joselito Montoya.

For months, Den studied Montoya and his organization. From the cities of Trinidad in the Province of El Beni, to San Ignacio in the Province of Santa Cruz and into the country's more populated cities, Den Clark watched and learned. The outlines of Montoya's operations were not difficult to discover. They were well-known.

In towns and villages, a handful of Bolivianos spent in a cantina identified places and names, including the names of local officials growing wealthy by cultivating impaired vision. More detailed information required more substantial amounts of Bolivianos. Care and caution had to be exercised because the man who would sell him information about Montoya would also sell Montoya information about Den Clark.

* * * * *

Joselito Montoya was bothered. Not frightened. Not worried. Just bothered. For months he had heard reports of someone asking questions about him. He had been unable to identify the man who was asking the questions and that bothered him.

It wasn't a gringo. The questioner spoke Spanish without an accent. I wasn't anyone in the local Bolivian or American drug control units. Montoya knew them all and many of them were on his payroll. If some new program was to be undertaken, Montoya would know its details before it began.

Montoya believed the unknown questioner may have been in the employ of someone who wanted to replace him as head of his cartel. Montoya killed two of his own men who were acting suspiciously, but the reports of the presence of the stranger continued after their death. The stranger had an educated accent. Someone with an educated accent was trying to take over. Could it be someone from Cali or Medellin?

The police in the various Provinces and Montoya's own men were on the lookout for the man. Montoya was sure they would find him. They would deliver him to Montoya. The usual vigorous method of questioning would be sure to give Joselito the information he most desired: Who sent the man to Bolivia? Then he would be killed.

In the meantime, Joselito added two automatic weapons to the arsenal he carried in his especially armored automobile. He carefully avoided any routine of movement that might endanger him. The only exceptions were his visits to his mistress. His chauffeur and one bodyguard were sufficient protection for those trysts.

Joselito Montoya left an apartment building in an exclusive Sucre neighborhood. It was the place where he kept his mistress. His bodyguard, a well-armed man who seldom left his side, was waiting for him in the hallway. The bodyguard was a large and powerful man. He shielded Montoya as he left the apartment and told him he had neither heard nor seen anything to disturb him while he kept watch at the hallway door.

Together the men took the elevator to the ground floor of the building. They unlocked and walked through the ornate wrought-iron gate that protected the interior of the building from thieves. According to the report of the Sucre police, the man presumed to be Montoya's chauffeur, his face obscured by a black felt hat, hurried around the automobile and opened the door to the back seat.

When Montoya and his bodyguard approached to enter the car, the chauffeur pulled a weapon from beneath his jacket and killed both of them. Then he calmly walked into the gathering crowd and disappeared. Montoya's real chauffeur lay dead on the floor of the front seat. No one was able to give a description of the man who killed them.

Shortly after the death of the Montoya, Nathaniel Peabody stepped from the Aerolineas Argentina flight and entered that part of the Miami International Airport where United States Customs officials check passports and occasionally review the contents of luggage being brought into the country. Minutes later, Den Clark, his baggage transferred to the Delta flight to Washington, emerged from Customs.

A few days later, a courier from Washington delivered a thick envelope to the American DEA Office at La Paz. The envelope contained a comprehensive report. It described the operation of the Bolivian drug trade from the collection of coca leaves grown in Northern provinces, through laboratory processing and on to warehousing and shipment out of the country. The report identified national and local politicians as well as Bolivian army Drug Enforcement officials who were in Montoya's pay.

Nothing happened to any of the politicos. Some of the officers in the Bolivian army's Special Drug Unit were reassigned or allowed to retire. Other officers were replaced. An American DEA official left a note announcing his resignation and disappeared from the La Paz office.

A few successful drug raids followed. Then the officers who replaced their corrupt predecessors began to show signs of newly acquired wealth and the Bolivian drug trade returned to business as usual.

* * * * *

When Den returned to Langley, Teddy Smith acknowledged the success of his endeavors in Bolivia. The Agency had provided the DEA with a comprehensive picture of the Bolivian drug trade. Both the CIA and the DEA were convinced a rival or an overly ambitious lieutenant in Montoya's own organization had engineered the man's murder. They had no suspicion of what really happened.

Den was somewhat surprised when Teddy said he had another assignment and told him he would have to handle it immediately. Teddy told him an across-the-border invasion from Canada was underway. Den would be expected to disrupt it. Then Teddy told him the invasion consisted of migrating Woodcock.

"Take two weeks," a smiling Teddy said. "I'm sure you will need some special ordnance. I'll take care of that problem for you." When Den returned to his apartment building, the doorman handed him a parcel. It contained an engraved Spanish AyA double barrel 28-gauge shotgun. Den left Langley for a hunting vacation in Maine. He hoped Teddy would send him on more and more of these kinds of assignments.

* * * * *

During Den's work in Bolivia, the Republic of Guatemala began to experience growing political turmoil. A military Junta had been in power for over two years. For decades, there had been what Latinos call "anti-social" elements operating in rural parts of the country. We would call them gangsters and drug traffickers.

The Junta used their presence as an excuse to refuse to hold the elections promised after their successful coup. The Junta's attempts to control the press and its heavy handed treatment of dissidents fueled a growing popular demand for change. Students protested against the military junta. The church spoke out against it. Support for the movement to overthrow the Junta grew. The Junta reacted as oppressive dictatorships usually react.

They attempted to wipe out the opposition. A reporter was killed. So was an activist priest. Rumors of "death squads" directed by the Junta were circulated. Of course, the Junta's opposition grew. It was possible that the military Junta would be removed from power. It was also possible that it would be replaced by a government unfriendly to the United States.

In Washington, the military attaché to the Guatemalan Embassy contacted the Department of State. He didn't bother to fully inform his own Ambassador of the reason for the contact. The Attaché's disregard of his own country's Ambassador might be explained by his lack of experience. There was a more accurate explanation of his actions.

Major Ernesto Rodriguez was only recently given an army commission and sent to the Guatemalan Embassy in Washington. He was the nephew of Colonel Máximo Rodriguez, a member of the Guatemalan ruling Junta. The Major was following his uncle's orders.

Colonel Máximo Rodriguez directed the Junta's Internal Security Forces. It was his responsibility to protect the government by keeping its opposition under control. To perform his function, the Colonel needed help. He sent his nephew to Washington to explain the problem and request assistance.

The State Department quickly denied the Colonel's request. The United States could not support a repressive military Junta by involving itself in the killing of an opposition leader. The effects of such a killing on relations between the United States and all Latin American Republics far outweighed any temporary (and highly questionable) advantage in Guatemala.

Both the CIA and Director of Clandestine Services had no problem with the State Department's position. Certainly, such an improper involvement in the internal affairs of another government was unacceptable. It was Teddy Smith who pointed out the dilemma to Deputy Director Cullen Brewster.

Teddy said the Guatemalan drug traffickers would happily fund revolution. If a revolution was successful, the drug lords' influence in the new government would be enormous. There were plenty of examples of Latin governments' active cooperation with local drug cartels. In Panama it had required the intervention by United States troops.

Teddy also pointed to another danger. Venezuela's anti-US postures and its agreements supporting Iran were disquieting. The establishment of another Castro or Chavez kind of anti-US Latin government in Central America was unthinkable, particularly if an alliance with drug traffickers was a potential.

After presenting those problems, Teddy Smith made a suggestion. While giving Colonel Rodriguez the assistance he requested was out of the question, steps might be taken to destroy the cocaine based funding of the Junta's opposition. A successful program to weaken the drug lords would weaken anti-American Guatemalan revolutionists by removing both organizational and financial support.

Teddy proposed a man be sent to Guatemala to study the illicit drug organization and prepare a plan to do substantial damage to it. He pointed to Den Clark's investigations in Bolivia. Teddy admitted his suggestion could result in keeping the Junta in power, but he recalled the Eisenhower administration's comment concerning a friendly Latin dictator. "Yes. He's a son-of-a-bitch, but he's our son-of-a-bitch."

Both Departments of State and Defense thought the scheme had merit and the proposal was adopted. Clandestine Services directed the Projects Branch to create the plan of operation. As they had done in the Bolivian matter, Teddy Smith and Jake Jacobson created the plan that would send Den Clark to Guatemala to undertake an assessment of the country's drug trade.

The review of the Guatemalan project ordered by the Directorate of Operations was perfunctory. Jake did his usual creditable job and it received the approval of the Directorate.

At the same time, Jake developed related plans. The Directorate of Operations would never have the opportunity to see, review or give their stamp of approval for this concealed mission. The hidden mission quietly attached to the authorized Guatemalan Drug Control Project was designed to carry out the proposal of Colonel Máximo Rodriguez. It was the same proposal the State Department and the CIA had flatly denied.

In addition, the Aegis plan was intended to carry out Jake's own personal agenda. It provided for the death of Den Clark.

Chapter 9

Jake sat in the chair facing Teddy's desk. He had never been invited to sit on the office sofa. Privately, he and Teddy were discussing the unauthorized actions hidden within the Directorate's officially approved Guatemalan project. Teddy was satisfied with every element of Jake's plan - with one exception. He wanted to know why it had to include the killing of Den Clark.

Jake was prepared for Teddy's objection. There was a good reason to require the death of Clark and Jake was ready to explain it. Perhaps the word "eager" would be more descriptive. He began his argument by recalling the Aegis assignments Den had successfully carried out.

Den went to Chile for mundane first posting jobs and del Valle was killed. He went to Bolivia to carry out the Directorates plan for an independent investigation of the drug trade and Montoya was killed. Den performed well in Chile and in Bolivia. That performance, Jake insisted, now marked him as a danger to Aegis.

Teddy showed polite interest, but hoped Jake would get on with it. He was sure it was Den who gave Jake the beating at The Bellavista. Jake's story about surprising a burglar and being attacked in his apartment didn't hold water. The Bellavista building was secure. No one could just walk in, get to the third floor and then enter Jake's apartment.

Besides, nothing was stolen. What kind of a burglar would attack a man, pound the hell out of him, leave him unconscious and then neglect to take his wallet? Teddy knew Jake hated Den. He expected Jake to come up with some imaginative reason to justify killing him. Teddy had no intention of accepting it.

Jake continued to argue his case. Sooner or later, he said, someone in the Directorate of Operations would make a discovery. Every time

Den Clark was sent on an offshore assignment, somebody living in the country he visited was killed. The discovery of those "coincidences" was sure to be noticed by someone. Teddy began to pay closer attention to Jake's argument.

Jake asked if it would be logical for someone to wonder if these coincidences might be more than simply a case of a Clandestine Service agent taking it upon himself to violate Executive Order 12333. Would it not be logical, he asked, for that someone to wonder if there might be a group of men, hidden within the CIA, who were planning and carrying out the assassinations?

Would it not be logical, he asked, for that someone to initiate an investigation of Den Clark's associates including his boss in the Projects Branch? Now he had Teddy's full attention. That potential chain of events had not occurred to him.

Jake didn't have to point out Teddy's personal danger of exposure. They both knew it wouldn't be difficult for an investigator to find it was Smith and Jacobson who planned the CIA's Bolivian drug cartel project. It wouldn't be difficult for him to find it was Smith and Jacobson who planned the CIA's Guatemalan drug cartel project.

Nor would it be difficult to find Smith and Jacobson's hand in the planning of any future assassination assignments involving Den Clark. Would it be difficult, Jake asked, to discover the two people who had the best opportunity to meld unauthorized assassinations into Directorate approved missions?

As Jake was counting down the threats of the exposure of Aegis, Teddy realized he could not dismiss the danger Jake had identified. The need to keep the existence of Aegis hidden from view could not be compromised. If a Guatemalan killing took place while Den was there, and if the Chilean and Bolivian operations were carefully scrutinized, it would be hard to claim "coincidence".

Jake watched Teddy Smith's reactions. At first he listened politely, but his face and body language reflected disinterest. As Jake's argument unfolded, Teddy's expressions changed. First, Teddy showed interest, then he showed serious consideration and, finally, he began to nod acceptance.

Jake leaned back in his chair, satisfied that he had shown the danger of exposure faced by Teddy and by Aegis. He had led Teddy directly to the conclusion he so desperately wanted. From the way Teddy listened to him and voiced no objections to his arguments, Jake was sure Teddy would agree to the elimination of Clark. "*At last,*" he thought, "*At last. I get my revenge. That son of a bitch will die.*"

Three assassinations occurring during Den's first three off-shore assignments, Teddy agreed, were almost guaranteed to attract the kind of attention that could be ruinous. Aegis could not run the risk of exposure, but Teddy saw no need to eliminate Den. He was one of Aegis' most valuable assets. Teddy didn't want to lose him.

"I think you're right in your assessment of the threat," he told Jake. "If we can't use Den, I suppose there's only one thing to do. We'll have to scrap our part of the Guatemalan venture. We'll have to lie low for a time and give Den regular assignments that don't include any hidden agendas. That will break the pattern."

This was not the result Jake wanted. "*Damnit,*" he thought. "*Why can't this idiot think straight?*" Jake wasn't willing to give up. He'd try again.

Jake said it didn't make any difference if the Aegis portion of the Guatemalan Project was scrapped or carried out. It didn't matter if Den were ever used in another operation or removed from all future Aegis projects. Sooner or later, the existing pattern of his assignments and local assassinations would emerge. The death of Den Clark, before that pattern came to light, was the only way to remove the danger.

The situation in Guatemala was not the problem, Jake contended. Den Clark was the problem. The questionable connection between Den Clark and the Latin American murders, Jake insisted, would be broken only if Clark died. The Guatemala project gave them an opportunity to resolve the problem once and for all.

Clark's death would give Rodriguez additional cover and, at the same time, protect Aegis. As far as the Directorate of Operations and the rest of the world would know, Den was killed while in Guatemala on a mission to uncover and identify illegal drug activity. Latin American drug lords have killed more than one CIA agent. Den wouldn't be the first one and he wouldn't be the last one.

If, at some later date, a hint of that pattern was suggested by anyone, Den Clark wouldn't be around to confirm or deny or, more importantly, to be questioned. Any suggestion of the existence of a conspiracy to assassinate could be passed off as some insane, anti-CIA conspiracy foolishness. There was nothing more for Jake to say. He did not like the look of Teddy's furrowed brow. He did not like Teddy's hesitation.

Jake didn't know it, but he had succeeded. The need to protect Aegis from exposure was absolute. Teddy's furrowed brow and the hesitation weren't caused by any reluctance to agree to the death of Den Clark. It was quite something else. Den had proven his ability to handle Aegis assignments. Teddy trusted him.

"If Den is killed in Guatemala," Teddy asked, "who will take his place? Where will we find another man capable of replacing Den Clark?"

Now Jake's need to avenge the beating Den Clark had administered depended upon finding another man who could carry out the special assignments Aegis might order. If he could produce that man, Den Clark would soon be dead. Come hell or high water, Jake told himself, he would convince Teddy he could find another man to replace Den Clark.

Jake developed a convincing answer to Teddy's question. He made it up as he went along, passing off guess and hope and wish as fact. Using another CIA agent to carry out Aegis assassinations after Den was gone, Jake told Teddy, was subject to the same objections making Den's removal necessary. The more projects the man successfully completed, the more likely the emergence of a pattern. An outside man was needed.

Any direct connection between that man and the Agency, Jake claimed, had to be avoided. In fact, the potential for trouble would be reduced if the man had no connection to the United States. Teddy began to slowly nod his head. If any accusation of the existence of assassination programs were ever made, Jake continued, charges would be more difficult to prove and official denials would be more credible if the alleged assassin were a foreign national living outside the country.

"Think of the possible defenses, if such a man turned us in," Jake said and he counted them on his fingers. "The man's a foreigner. He's a killer who would say anything to save his neck. He hates the United States and the CIA. This is nothing more than speculation by people who want to destroy the Agency. It's a foreign plot to weaken this country's eyes and ears in the dangerous world of international politics."

Jake stopped when he saw Teddy slowly nodding in agreement, supported by just a hint of a smile. When Jake suggested Den could be replaced by an experienced terrorist, a Jordanian, Teddy's cautious smile disappeared. His eyes widened and showed his surprise. Before he could voice his objection, Jake hurriedly listed the advantages of using a Near East killer.

With such an outside man, Jake argued, Aegis would not have to disguise their projects within other CIA missions. Aegis could operate independent of legitimate Agency projects. There would be no coincidences hidden within Directorate projects to draw attention and cause an internal Agency investigation.

Teddy heard enough. "Get real, Jake," he said, interrupting him. "The theory is great, but don't you see just a few problems in translating it into reality?

"An Israeli might be a possibility, but how do you convince an Arab to work for the United States. Jordanian terrorists are not too enthusiastic about our policy of supporting the people they've sworn to exterminate. They don't trust us and I could never trust one of them. And just how would you suggest we look for such a man? Put an ad on Al Jezeera television or in some Gaza strip newspaper?"

Jake ignored the sarcasm. "I have someone in mind," he answered. "He is a very experienced and a very capable assassin. He's the man who killed Mick McCarthy."

Teddy couldn't believe his ears. Had Jacobson forgotten the results of his first attempt to bribe him? The man had double-crossed him and tried to kill him. Teddy didn't doubt the Jordanian was probably an effective assassin, but how could Jacobson suggest he work with a terrorist who had already killed one of the CIA's own Agents?

It wasn't hard for Jake to guess the thoughts that crowded into

Teddy's mind. He answered Teddy's questions before they had been asked. His arguments echoed Teddy's own innate, cynical sentiments. Jake began to speak Teddy's own language.

Both men believed everyone looked out for Number One, first, last and always. Neither of them believed there was any such thing as unconditional reliability. Anyone could be bought if the subject matter of the offer or the amount of the offer was right.

"Everyone has a For Sale sign on his forehead," Jake said. "The only thing that differs among men is the price tag. I made a mistake in Damascus. I didn't offer enough money."

Teddy remembered the Damascus investigation report Henry Putnam had given him. When he first looked at it, he told himself Jake's bribery offer was too small. Now, despite his initial reaction to Jake's proposal, Teddy began to think Jake's scheme might deserve some consideration. "I'm listening," he said.

Jake pressed his argument. Things weren't going too well for the terrorist profession in the Near East. The haven and support from Libya and Iraq were things of the past. The leaders in various support groups had been targeted and killed in Afghanistan, in Pakistan and Yemen.

If an American Afghan surge or a Pakistani anti-Taliban campaign was successful, the terrorist havens would be further diminished. If Iran was surrounded by pro-Western governments, support from the mullahs could diminish. Jake admitted Palestinian hatred of the Israelis and the West was a potent factor, but he emphasized his belief that the man he tried to bribe in Damascus was ready to work for the CIA.

"I've met with him many times," Jake lied. "In spite of my history with him, I know him to be a realist. I think he'll abandon any cause if the price is right. I believe I can convince him."

Teddy reviewed Jake's track record. The plans he created in the Projects Branch were somewhat ornate, but well designed to conceal sources and mislead the enemy. The man had natural abilities for the espionage business. His proposals deserved a hearing. Teddy was well aware of the fact of double agents. They were nothing new in the world of international espionage. Nevertheless, he harbored serious reservations about Jake's proposition.

Teddy didn't trust Jake. Jacobson, quite possibly, was dissembling. He doubted Jake knew enough about the Jordanian to be able to forecast his reaction to an offer to change sides. On the other hand, it was possible that Jake was telling the truth.

Teddy thought the possibility was substantially less than fifty percent, but if Jake could pull it off, the rewards would be great. If Jake couldn't convince the Jordanian, the down-side loss would be minimal. Teddy decided he was willing to take the gamble. There was a way to find out if Jake's assessment of the terrorist was right.

Den was hunting in Maine when Jake flew to Damascus to meet with the man who tried to kill him.

* * * * *

The man Jake Jacobson knew in Damascus as "Abdul" was born in a Palestinian refugee camp in Jordan. He grew up in poverty and on a steady diet of hatred for the Israelis. He despised them and anyone who helped them. Hezbollah recruited him when he was a young man. They took him to Lebanon where he proved his loyalty to the Palestinian cause by killing Israeli soldiers. He organized attacks on outposts and set up urban ambushes.

Later, various national and international political initiatives to end the violence began to develop support among those Palestinians and other Arabs who were tired of the chaos and bloodshed. To discourage any negotiated settlement, Abdul progressed from the killing of enemy soldiers to the murder of fellow Moslems who were willing to make peace with the Israelis. He kidnapped them. He planned bombings to kill them and their families. He shot officials who would compromise with the Israelis.

After the Osama bin Laden inspired attack on the United States and the start of the Second Gulf War, the links between national and international terrorism were under attack. Terrorist bombings of Arab civilians in Jordan and Iraq made some of the more enlightened Moslems begin to substitute a hatred of the various terrorist organizations for part of their hatred of Israel and the United States.

Support of those the West called "terrorists" softened. Saudi funding began to dry up. Philippine, Algerian and Indonesian cells came under attack from their own governments.

The man Jake knew as "Abdul" would never lose his fanatic hatred of the Israelis and anyone who offered them aid or comfort, but in recent years self-interest began to intrude in his thoughts. He had killed Israelis, sympathizing Arabs and Americans without any significant material advantage for himself.

Once before, the CIA had offered to pay him for information. Abdul wondered if the man he killed in Damascus might have been carrying the money he had been promised. Perhaps, Abdul thought, he should have met with that man, given a false list of names and taken the money before killing him.

These thoughts had more than once run through Abdul's mind before he learned Jake Jacobson was in Damascus and was again trying to contact him.

Chapter 10

Jake Jacobson did not like the idea of returning to Syria. He did not want to be seen by anyone in the Damascus Station. Undoubtedly, some of them knew what had been written in Gigi Grant's original report of the investigation into the death of Mick McCarthy. Some of them knew Jake had sent a new man into the tavern in the souks - the old part of Damascus - where Abdul and his friends waited. Some of the people in the Damascus Station knew he had quickly driven away at the beginning of the firefight that killed Agent McCarthy. Jake didn't want to refresh their memories and set their tongues wagging.

Jake was even more afraid of a meeting with Abdul. Jake had two face-to-face talks with him when the bribery scheme was originally proposed. He remembered Abdul as sullen and suspicious. The man's expressions never gave an indication of what he might have been thinking. Jake remembered his eyes. They were dark eyes set further back in a swarthy face. They were intense eyes that seemed to look inside him and divine his thoughts.

Jake's flight from Rome was not one of his happier experiences. The closer the plane got to Damascus International Airport, the more Jake reflected on the alarming fact that Abdul had once set a trap, intending to murder him. Jake was sure the trap would have caused his death if he hadn't smelled a rat and sent McCarthy in his stead. If he managed to contact Abdul, he wondered where he could find a place to meet with him - a place where he ran no risk of being killed. Was there any such a place in Damascus?

Jake had no alternative. If he had not promised Teddy he could get Abdul to work with him, the part of the Guatemalan venture that would end in Clark's death would have been jettisoned. Jake would do anything to keep Clark from escaping his planned revenge. Now he had to pay the price for his distortions. He was committed to contacting a man he didn't trust, a man who tried to kill him and who might try again. He had to convince that man to work with him.

With a feeling of resignation, Jake filled out the Customs forms the stewardess handed to him. Jake had to look at the documents Ferdie Robbins had provided when he filled out the parts of the Entry Declaration that called for name and passport number. Jake was now identified as Albert S. Simpson, a travel agent from St. Louis. He never recognized the tiny bit of Ferdie Robbins' revenge represented by the initials of the name in his false passport nor did he see the sardonic humor of his answer to the question: Purpose of Trip. He had written: "pleasure".

The spaces for the listing of potentially dangerous or taxable items brought into the country were quickly check marked "none". Of course, he brought no weapon with him. He couldn't get a side arm from the Station without announcing his presence and there was good reason for keeping his visit to Abdul as quiet as possible. He could never disclose the reason for his visit to Damascus. If he met with Abdul, he would be unarmed. It was not a pleasant thought.

Jake would stay at the Le Meridien. At least that nebbish fool, Ferdie Robbins, had made reservations at a Five Star hotel. As soon as he was in his room, Jake phoned the number he had used when he contacted Abdul two years earlier. As he expected, he heard Arabic words completely unintelligible to him.

Jake answered in English speaking slowly and enunciating clearly. "I am Jacobson. I want to speak to Abdul. He will be interested in what I have to say. I am at the Le Meridien Hotel. I am registered under the name Albert S. Simpson. I will be here for 24 hours." After a few seconds of silence, the connection was broken.

Perhaps Abdul was dead. He may have been killed. He may have been moved into the Gaza strip or sent to Pakistan. If Abdul didn't return his call, Jake wouldn't consider entering the murky Damascus world of car bombers and murderers to find someone else to replace Den Clark. It was far too dangerous an undertaking. He would return to Langley. He would tell Teddy Abdul had been killed. His plan to kill Den Clark in Guatemala would have to be dropped.

In spite of the peril represented by a meeting with Abdul, Jake hoped his pipeline to the Jordanian had not been broken. He hoped Abdul was still in Damascus. He hoped he would return the call. He smiled when he remembered the line from The Godfather movie. This time he would make an offer that could not be refused.

As Jake waited for the phone to ring, the dangers of a meeting with Abdul began to displace his thoughts of revenge. He remembered his feeling of panic when he heard the shooting from inside the souks tavern. He remembered seeing Mick McCarthy, standing in the narrow alley and firing at the men who pursued him.

Jake could have been the man who fell into Abdul's trap. Another meeting with Abdul could be another trap. This time Jake would not be seated in an automobile, able to leave the scene if shots were fired. Jake's hopes to contact Abdul began to wane as his fear of the dangers of a meeting grew.

* * * * *

Abdul was surprised when told Jacobson was in Damascus and wanted to talk to him. What was the man's ulterior motive? Was this an elaborate scheme to avenge the death of the CIA agent he had killed? That hardly seemed probable. With the help of the Israelis, the CIA could have found an easier way to kill him in Syria. No, he concluded, the meeting with Jacobson was probably not part of that plan.

Jacobson tried to bribe him once. Was it possible he would again try to buy him? Well, there was little danger in answering Jacobson's call.

Jake was staring out at the Damascus cityscape when the phone rang. He hesitated before he picked it up. Jake thanked Abdul for calling. Abdul said nothing. Jake told him he had an attractive proposition for him to consider. It would make him wealthy.

After a few seconds of silence, Abdul decided he could not repeat the mistake he made in Damascus. He killed the man before actually receiving the bribe. This time it would be different. He would talk with Jacobson. If Jacobson offered money, He would take it. Then he would kill him.

Abdul spoke one word: "Talk".

Jake talked.

"Would you like to come to the Western Hemisphere and take assignments from the Central Intelligence Agency? If you listen to what I have to say, I will give you ten thousand dollars. Just to listen, Abdul, nothing more. Just listen to my offer. You can accept it or you can reject it but I'll need your decision before I leave tomorrow afternoon."

Abdul was cautious. Of course, he expected duplicity from the Americans. As far as he was concerned, anyone who believed anything a CIA agent told him had completely lost touch with reality. Abdul had no intention of working for the CIA, but he would not overlook the potential of a ten thousand dollars payoff.

Jake waited for thirty seconds before Abdul again spoke. "Where shall we meet?"

"I'm at Le Meridien."

"Why don't you invite me into the basement of your Damascus Station?" was Abdul's sarcastic response. "I have a better suggestion. Remember where we met in the bazaar in old town? In souks? In Straight Street? We can have coffee in the back room."

Now it was Jake's turn to be sarcastic. "I remember it well, Abdul. That's where you waited to kill me. The old town is your territory. I'd suggest something more open where the risk to either of us will be limited. You don't like the Le Meridien? How about another Five Star? How about the Sheraton?

"No."

"All right, you name the hotel."

This time the pause was only a few seconds. "The Metropolitan," Abdul said. "Top floor. The Oasis barroom. Ten minutes." Then he hung up.

Abdul named the barroom at the Metropolitan as their meeting place because two trustworthy friends worked there. The bartender and the young man who ran errands, carried cigarettes, liquors and other supplies from the storage room to the bar and seemed to constantly sweep the carpets, empty ash trays and clean the table surfaces. Jake

Jacobson also knew the Metropolitan and the Oasis Bar. It was popular with Americans.

When Abdul abruptly hung up, he left Jake with no alternative. It was the Oasis or nothing. Jake hesitated and vacillated. Abdul could send a suicide bomber. Top floors of hotels were not the best places for a bomber to plant a bomb and set off an explosion. The Oasis Bar was as safe as any place in Damascus.

No place in Damascus was entirely safe. A meeting with Abdul anywhere in Damascus was dangerous. Still, a meeting with Abdul was Jake's only opportunity to insure the death of Den Clark. In the end, Jake reluctantly decided to meet with Abdul. He went to the Oasis Bar.

Jake left his taxi, walked into the Metropolitan Hotel and took the elevator to the top floor. The Oasis was empty except for two TV newsmen at the bar and Abdul who was seated at a table where he could quickly exit through the service door. The younger of Abdul's two friends was waiting behind that door, ready to help him make his escape.

Jake wore slacks and a shirt, showing he had no place to hide a weapon. Abdul carried a knife sharp enough to use as a razor. It rested in a sheath beneath his jacket. Jake approached him and, before sitting, handed him an envelope containing ten thousand dollars.

Abdul opened the envelope. He counted one hundred bills. Each carried the picture of Benjamin Franklin and each one looked legitimate. He slipped the envelope into his inside jacket pocket. He would listen to what the American had to say. Then he would slit his throat and, with the help of his friends, quickly leave the Metropolitan.

Jake didn't mention the existence of Aegis. He said he expected Abdul to be skeptical about the suggestion that he work with the CIA. He made his arguments as brief and as powerful as possible. Abdul was in the business of killing people. The CIA had use for his services. The CIA would pay much better than anyone else. Abdul was curious and wanted to hear more - so he showed false signs of interest and Jake became more explicit.

Abdul was to remain in Syria until notified. Then he would disappear from the Near East scene and quietly re-appear in Mexico.

When Abdul arrived in Mexico he would receive another ten thousand dollars. He would be expected to establish his residence there. From time to time he would receive an assignment from Jake.

The amount of the payment for his services would depend on the degree of difficulty involved in the assassination. Half payment would be delivered when Abdul accepted the assignment. The balance would be paid upon the successful completion of the job. The Jordanian presumed the CIA's objective was to use him to kill fellow Moslems. He knew the language and the culture and could move about Moslem communities without attracting attention.

Abdul had fought for the Palestinian cause for many years and was an accomplished killer. The CIA could certainly use a man with his special qualifications. Abdul, however, would never kill a fellow jihadist Moslem. Nevertheless, he told Jake he would consider working as a CIA assassin. His words were lies, calculated to mislead. He had no intention of working for the "CIA dogs that did their Israeli master's bidding."

The Jordanian decided to defer his plan to cut the throat of the man who sat across the booth from him in the Oasis barroom. The delivery of the ten thousand dollars and the promise of liberal payment for his services saved Jake's life. Abdul amended his plan. He agreed to wait in Damascus until Jake contacted him. Then he would go to Mexico. He would collect the additional ten thousand dollars, kill whoever delivered it, and then return to Syria.

* * * * *

Jake returned to Langley and assured Teddy he had secured a competent replacement for Den. He told him the Jordanian terrorist had agreed to undertake projects from the CIA. Jake recommended they give him the same code name assigned to him when, as a young man, he had been recruited by Hezbollah to kill Israelis.

Jake hoped Abdul hadn't lied to him and would come to Mexico for the additional ten thousand dollar payment. Privately, he didn't put much faith in Abdul's promises. Whether or not the terrorist actually became an Aegis assassin was not important. Jake's enthusiastic and confident assurances were made for the purpose of getting Teddy's agreement to kill Den Clark in Guatemala.

Teddy gave his approval to all aspects of Jake's Guatemalan project. Jake was happy. Clark would die.

That evening before he went to sleep, Teddy reviewed Jake's Plan. He thought briefly of Den and recalled the succinct advice of 18th century buccaneers. Dead men tell no tales.

Chapter 11

It was a Sunday afternoon when Den returned from the Maine Woodcock hunt. He was refreshed. A few weeks in the autumn woods can, temporarily at least, erase the cares and troubles that beset a man during his usual urban occupations. Den unpacked and, alone in his apartment, felt relaxed and comfortable. He opened his apartment's kitchen cabinet and removed the bottle of The Macallan. Minutes later, he was seated in an easy chair - Scotch and water in hand.

It didn't take him long to realize he was again inside the Belt Line. The solitude he had enjoyed in Maine quickly slipped away. As he took his first sip of The Macallan, he noticed the red light blinking on his telephone. He listened to the message Teddy had left. "Den. Hope you enjoyed Maine, you lucky dog. Come, tell me about it when you get a chance." Den knew what it meant. Translated into English, Teddy told him to get to the office as soon as possible.

Den suspected Teddy's message also meant a special operation had been planned by Aegis. He expected he would be asked to execute it. When a new operation was in the offing, Den became impatient. He wanted to know about it ASAP. He did not enjoy watching a minute hand struggle around the face of a wall clock while he waited to be told just what he would be asked to do, but it was too late in the afternoon to travel to Langley. It would serve no purpose. Teddy wouldn't be there. Den limited himself to a few "damnits" and resigned himself to waiting until the morning.

Den turned on the TV and clicked through the channels, looking for something - anything interesting enough to attract his attention. Some guy was fooling around with an alligator. He tried to make it look like he was in danger. His cameraman associate evidently felt safe. The man continued to film the episode, taking a number of shots of the alligator's head and teeth without as much as a camera-shaking tremor.

By the repeated use of the clicker, Den escaped the plague of soaps and quasi-soaps that threatened him. Finally, after deciding he had no interest in buying ersatz gemstone jewelry and still less in watching automobiles speeding around a circular track, juvenile cartoons or replays of the Senate chambers during a Quorum Call, he said "damnit" again and pressed the Off button.

He swiveled his chair so he could look out the king sized window in his apartment. He was reduced to watching the air traffic at the Reagan National Airport. He was no longer at ease. He was restless and he couldn't do anything about it. He had to wait until meeting with Teddy on the following morning. In the meantime, he glowered, sipped The Macallan and watched another airplane land at Reagan.

That night he had dreams, many of them, only short scenes and brief episodes, all immediately forgotten and not one of them told any kind of pleasant story or left him with even a momentary impulse to smile. He awoke in the morning, not rested by the evening's sleep. He breakfasted automatically, without tasting what he ate, got into his car and drove to Langley. In only a few hours, Den had been re-adjusted from life in the woods to life in Washington D.C.

* * * * *

"Den. Great to see you," was Teddy's greeting as he got up from behind his clean and shining desk and extended his large hand. "I haven't hunted Woodcock in years and years. I remember they were usually in such thick stuff that I had trouble raising my gun barrel." Den knew he was in for a few minutes of chatter before Teddy explained the reason for the meeting. He had to struggle not to say *"Cut the crap, Teddy. Get to the point."*

Finally, Teddy broached the subject. "There is a problem in Central America." He thought for a moment and re-phrased it, "I guess I could describe it better by saying our friends in Guatemala have a problem. The locals can't or don't want to handle it themselves. They've asked us for assistance and we should help them out."

Teddy continued with his explanation. "Here it is in a nutshell. A group of bad guys are starting to stir things up down there. The Guatemala security people are convinced a terrorist cell in being organized. It scares the hell out of them. They tell us it's not a big group right now, but they are worried. They say the Iranians are behind it and the local ringleader has a history as an effective rabble-rouser.

"We're told the guy is one of those charismatic types. You know - a kind of Fidel Castro. The Guatemalans are afraid he'll ally himself with the local drug merchants and bandits. If he does, he'll have money and he'll have the protection of the local politicos. It looks like most of them are getting pay-offs from the drug people.

"If, or when, the terrorists and the drug guys get together there will be the devil to pay. In short, the Colonel in charge of the Guatemala Security Police wants us to take out the leader of the cell before he becomes something very, very serious." Teddy stopped and waited for a reaction.

Before he learned of the Damascus whitewash and Jake Jacobson's transfer to the Projects Branch, Den had confidence in Teddy Smith. Now the worm of doubt was beginning to chew at him. Jake worked for Teddy. Den didn't know if Teddy was Jacobson's protector or if he was following orders from some unseen Aegis principal.

Den felt his best course was one of caution when dealing with Teddy and, for that matter, with anyone who might be in the Aegis network. As far as Den knew, that could mean anyone in the CIA. After a moment, he asked: "That doesn't seem to be such a difficult problem, Teddy. Why call us in? Why don't the Guatemalans take care of the matter themselves?" He didn't wait for an answer. His next question followed immediately. "Are you telling me the whole story?"

Teddy Smith lit a cigar and puffed a few times. He checked the lit end and was satisfied with it. He smiled when he answered. "Den, you old fox, there is a bit more to it. Somehow, I knew you'd ask." His smile was not returned. "Neither of us was born yesterday. Both of us are painfully aware of the antagonism we have to face from the media. It's not only a problem here in the States. It's just as bad for our friends in Central America.

"You've read the reports of the so-called 'death squad' assassi-nations down there. Of course, there's some truth in them. All local security guys in Central America are scared silly of death squad publicity. They are particularly sensitive because of the effects such reports have on some of our goddamned, panty-waist Congressmen.

"The Agency has labored long and hard to convince our Senators and Representatives of the necessity of military assistance packages for friendly Latin American governments. Death squad stories nullify our work and endanger those programs.

"The people who have confidence in you think all efforts..." Teddy paused for emphasis and then repeated ... "all efforts should be expended to avoid an organized terrorist sponsored presence in this hemisphere. We had enough trouble with Castro and the USSR fomenting revolutions in Africa and supporting red rebels in Nicaragua and Salvador. They almost got away with a big airfield in Grenada. Reagan understood the danger and we nipped that one.

"We can't afford to run the risk of an anti-US take-over in Central America. We've got to help our Guatemalan friends before it's too late. At the same time, the Guatemala Aid package is being debated in Congress and it can't be jeopardized." Teddy leaned back in his chair and added nothing more. It was Teddy's way of asking for questions. Den had a question.

"Just how would our operation result in insulating our Guatemalan friends from charges of death squad assassinations? Down there, if someone active in any Junta's opposition is found dead of causes natural or otherwise, all fingers can be expected to point at the government. It's automatic."

Teddy blew another smoke ring. "A good question and a good observation. Of course, we've thought about it. I'll start from the beginning. The Directorate has given us the responsibility of coming up with a plan to study illegal drug activities in Guatemala. We have more than a suspicion that the drug traffickers are ready to promise the terrorists all the money they need for a successful coup. Your official mission will be to analyze the drug lords' operations and find the way or ways to shut them down before drug funding becomes available to the bad guys."

Teddy again waited for Den's reaction. Again, there was none. "Your unofficial mission," Teddy continued, "will be to eliminate the coup ringleader. That will solve our problem as well as Rodriguez' problem. The Colonel can be trusted. He'll be an asset you can rely upon."

"Some of our guys have come up with a scenario to remove any death squad accusations." Teddy looked down at his desk and pursed his lips. He was thinking of Jake Jacobson. Without looking up he said: "Frankly, some of our guys are long on scenarios, but awfully short on field experience." Then he looked up. "That's a thought I hope you won't allow to escape from this room."

"What would happen if a gringo appeared in Guatemala City? What would happen if he got into some posh hotel, threw a lot of money around, and, in a fairly amateurish way, let it be known he was looking for a steady supply of large amounts of cocaine?"

"What would happen if, a week or so later, the bodies of a Guatemalan terrorist leader and some of his friends were found out in the hills with cocaine scattered around him? Would a drug gang shoot-out in Guatemala look like a death squad killing? Would a drug gang shoot-out in Guatemala endanger the Guatemala Military Aid Bill now before Congress?"

Den cautiously nodded. He asked: "If that chain of events came to pass, how might that gringo get out of those hills?"

Another smoke ring floated in the air. Another answer followed. "A Guatemalan army helicopter might appear at the scene and take the gringo to a friendly landing strip near Belize. An Agency jet will be waiting. When you're back in the States you can file your official report.

"Colonel Rodriguez is the head of the Security Police. He's been collecting information about the drug lords for years. He's ready to provide you with all the information you'll need about the local drug operations." Then, once more, Teddy waited for a response.

Den had another question. "What does Colonel Rodriguez know about Aegis?"

"Nothing," Teddy answered. "He doesn't know anything about us and he never will know anything about us. He asked the State

Department for help in getting rid of the terrorist and got a flat turn down. He thinks the CIA has agreed to secretly overrule State and that State doesn't know about it. Of course, State knows all about the Directorate's decision to investigate Guatemala drug trade and find ways to stop it."

"Rodriguez will keep his mouth shut. If he does spill the beans, he'll accuse the CIA, not Aegis. If push comes to shove, we'll be ready to prove you had nothing to do with it, that a Rodriguez death squad did it and that the Colonel is falsely accusing the CIA because he doesn't want his death squad killing to come out. Rodriguez can't hurt us. You'll be protected and Aegis won't be discovered."

Quickly, Den reviewed the project. A terrorist organization in Central America constituted a serious threat. If allied to the money, the organization and the political connections of the drug lords, that threat would be multiplied. The project was a worthwhile undertaking. Den looked at Teddy and gave a short, quick nod.

Teddy smiled. "Let's call our little program 'Ocelot' - Operation Ocelot."

Chapter 12

The firing lasted for no more than fifteen seconds. It was followed by silence. Nevertheless, Den waited, listening for any sounds that might signal unsuspected danger.

"Paco! Are you OK?" he asked.

"Si, senor Den, I am OK." The voice came from one of the two Guatemalan Security Guards who had driven them to this sandy road at midnight. They had hidden the Scout and the three crouched in the undergrowth at the side of the trail until well after the sun had risen. That was when the Volkswagen Thing approached them.

Den yelled to the other guard, "Ernesto? Estas bien?"

"Estoy bien," answered his other unseen companion.

Den, holding his Model 12 Beretta sub-machine gun in front of him so that it could be fired instantly, stood and surveyed the scene before him. When he was satisfied, he used the barrel of the weapon to motion to one of the Security Guards.

Slowly and carefully, Paco arose from where he lay concealed behind a larger clump of the broad leaved grass that grew at the borders of a road leading from the flat valley lands up to the forested foothills of the Alto Cuchumante Mountains. Ready to give supporting gunfire in the event it was needed, he came to the edge of the trail and kept his weapon pointed at the open top, corrugated looking Volkswagen Thing that now rested half on the other side of the road and half in the shallow ditch.

Den came from behind the tree that partially sheltered him during the firing. He, too, stepped to the edge of the roadway. His eyes rapidly moved over the two bloody bodies that lay on the dirt road. There were no sounds and no movements. With his Beretta raised and ready to fire, he crossed the dirt road and cautiously approached the automobile.

There had been four people in the open Volkswagen. The ambush worked flawlessly. All of the terrorists carried .45 caliber automatics, but not one of them had time to remove his weapon from its holster. Den had concentrated his initial fire on the passenger in the front seat. That man, he reasoned, would probably be the leader. The two in the back seat would be the bodyguards. They were only secondary, but necessary targets.

It was academic now. They were all dead. Two of them were in the center of the road. The driver was slumped over the wheel and the fourth man laid face down, in the shallow ditch. Carefully, Den moved to the far side of the vehicle. After a moment, he stood erect.

"It's OK," he confirmed. "They're all dead."

Den removed the partially spent 40 round magazine from his weapon and replaced it with a new one. Their sub-machine guns were manufactured in Brazil. Large numbers of them had been produced and chains of ownership were impossible to trace. That's why the Berettas had been provided to them. Den removed the scarf that partially covered the face of the man in the ditch - the one who had occupied the passenger side of the front seat.

"My God," he said in nearly a whisper. He rolled the body onto its stomach and took a wallet from the dead man's back pocket. "My God," he repeated, this time in a louder voice.

"What is it?" Paco asked.

Holding the man's wallet in his hand, Greg pointed the muzzle of his gun at the body. "This is our man." He paused before he said "man" and his voice betrayed the disgust he felt. Joselito Montoya needed killing and the world was better off with Humberto del Valle in his grave, but, he feared, Operation Ocelot had no such justification. Alvarez, the dead man lying at his feet, was too young to be a leader of terrorists. Was he twenty years old?

"Our man?" Den repeated in a questioning tone. "He's only a kid." He lifted the head of the one behind the wheel and looked at the bodies on the road. "They're all kids. Look at them. Not one of them is able to grow a beard. What in hell have we done?"

A voice came from the other Guatemalan Security Guard who still lay hidden in the undergrowth. "Todos son muertos?" it asked. "Alvarez es muerto?"

"Yes," Den answered, "every one of them is dead," His voice was flat. Then he remembered Ernesto didn't speak English. "Si," he amended, "Si. Son muertos. Alvarez y los otros. Todos. Son muertos."

Another sound came from the direction of the hidden voice. It was the sharp metallic click made by a shell as it leaves a clip and enters into the firing chamber of an automatic weapon. Paco dove back into the cover at the far side of the road and Den reacted immediately.

He dropped into the shallow ditch behind the Volkswagen while bullets from both Security Guards filled the air. They smashed into the Volkswagen and thudded into the body of the dead driver. One of them creased Den's side and another struck him in the shoulder.

The firing stopped. From the safety of the ditch, Den raised his head and cautiously looked toward the place where the two guards were hidden. He listened, but remained silent, disregarding his pain and slowly moving his Beretta into firing position. Den waited and watched. His field of vision was limited to what he could see, looking from his ground level vantage point and past the underside of the Volkswagen. He heard the men quietly talking.

"They're close together," he thought, *"close enough to whisper to one another. They're wondering if I'm dead - wondering what to do."*

Soon he heard them moving. Together the men left the cover of the roadside vegetation and stepped onto the open dirt road. Slowly, weapons raised and ready, they came toward the car. Den could see only the feet of the men as they approached the vehicle. When they got to the center of the road, he fired. His shots passed under the Volkswagen and, flying parallel to the ground, the bullets smashed into the men's feet and ankles. They screamed and fell. Den emptied his magazine into their bodies, not twenty feet from where he lay.

Den ripped the sleeve from his wounded left arm and made a tourniquet. Blood gradually oozed from his grazed ribs and he tried to stem the flow by pressing his upper arm against them. He went to the bodies of the men who tried to kill him. Paco still carried the cocaine that was supposed to be left at the scene.

Den took his wallet. It contained a card identifying him as a

Security Guard. The printing of his name and other personal information was superimposed over the design of a Seguridad Nacional badge. There was no picture. Den took the card. Then he hurried back to the Scout that brought them to the scene of the ambush. He drove away as fast as the two rutted road would allow.

Two men from the Guatemalan Security Guard had tried to kill him. That was not an action they would take without direct orders from above. That meant the orders came from Colonel Máximo Rodriguez, the man who had been his primary Guatemala contact. Den knew no army helicopter would appear to take him to Belize.

When Paco and Ernesto did not report back to the Colonel, someone would be sent to the ambush site. They'd find a lot of bodies, but they wouldn't find him. Colonel Rodriguez would know he was still alive and a search would be made for the gringo who was supposed to be lying dead beside the bodies of the four young men. Den had no illusions about what would happen to him if they found and captured him.

Den had planned an alternate overland escape route to Belize in the event the mission misfired or the Guatemalan army helicopter didn't appear. As he drove past the bodies lying on the road, he discarded that plan and elected an entirely different one.

Den hoped Rodriguez would think he would try to get to the Agency jet at the Belize airfield - the place the Guatemalan army helicopter was supposed to take him. Instead of going to the northeast and the Belize border, Den would travel in a westerly direction to the border with Mexico. It was much nearer, less than 200 miles away, but, first, he needed medical attention. The nearest town that might have a doctor was Ticopetenango.

* * * * *

Dr. Mario Hernandez was only beginning to enjoy his evening meal when his nurse tapped on the door of his apartment. He knew she would not disturb him unless a patient had come into his downstairs sanatorium. "*Another cold meal*," he thought. He crumpled his napkin and dropped it on the table. "Pase," he said and the nurse opened the door. She told him a man, bleeding from what appeared to be gunshot wounds, was in his waiting room.

Dr. Hernandez patched up the wounds and with the aid of the medication he provided, Den slept until wakened by morning sunlight shining through the open windows. He was in the four room, antiseptic smelling, private hospital attached to Dr. Mario Hernandez' Consultorio and living quarters. Bandages were taped over his injured ribs and his left arm resting in a sling. He had slept, nearly upright, leaning against a bunch of pillows in the hospital bed.

Now he heard the sounds of stores being opened for business and the murmurs of people talking in the streets as they began their daily routines. Den swung his legs over the side of the bed. The pains in his shoulder and ribs were not bad enough to seriously hamper movement. He left the bed and walked to the waiting room where Dr. Hernandez' night nurse slept, resting her head on folded arms cushioning her office desk top.

Den woke her and asked her to leave her post long enough to buy him another shirt. He gave her a generous tip when she returned from a nearby shop bringing a T-shirt decorated with the face of Mickey Mouse. She helped him remove the sling and put it on. When she left his room, Den waited until he was sure she was back at her station. Then he quietly opened the back door of the Sanatorio Hernandez and drove toward Quezaltenango and the Guatemala/Mexico border.

* * * * *

On the previous evening, Dr. Hernandez left his unfinished dinner and walked down to the first floor of his home where he maintained a small private hospital. As his nurse had guessed, the stranger had been shot, but his injuries, while requiring careful attention, did not appear to be life threatening. The man showed a bloody identification card and identified himself as a member of the National Security Forces. Given their ruthless reputation, Dr. Hernandez felt it would be imprudent to ask any questions.

Now, in the light of day, the doctor was uneasy. His patient seemed older than 25, the age shown on his Guardia identification card. The man spoke Spanish, but the doctor thought he might have detected a slight accent - like the Spanish spoken in Mexico City or, perhaps, in Colombia.

Another curious matter attracted the doctor's attention. The injured man's vocabulary was that of an educated man, not that of the kind of man one would expect to find in the Seguridad. Dr. Hernandez feared the man was involved in the drug trade.

The doctor finished his breakfast and phoned the Comandante of the Ticopetenango police. When the Comandante arrived at Sanatorio Hernandez, the doctor's patient was nowhere to be found. Upon being questioned, the nurse confessed to leaving her station and buying the Mickey Mouse T-shirt. She didn't mention the money Den had given her.

The Comandante and Dr. Hernandez shared unspoken relief. Each was pleased the wounded patient had disappeared. He was no longer a problem. They could both make believe he never existed. Back at his office, the policeman had second thoughts. The stranger claimed to be Paco Gomez, a member of the Security Forces. Though he had shown an identification card to Dr. Hernandez, in all probability, the wounded man was not Paco Gomez.

"*Perhaps,*" the Comandante thought, "*this man killed Gomez. I might be criticized for not reporting the presence of the wounded man to the Security Fuerzas.*" That thought caused him to telephone the offices of the Colonel Máximo Rodriguez in Guatemala City.

* * * * *

As Den drove on roads that surely must have seen better days, he winced whenever the Scout found an unexpected pothole and his ribs and shoulder were jolted. Before noon, he came to Quetzaltenago and the highway that ran north and entered into Mexico at Tapachula, a larger city with an international airport. Den turned onto the highway and drove a few kilometers. Then he left it in favor of a less traveled secondary road and continued his journey to the border - but not directly to Tapachula.

Den's use of Paco's identity card might pass muster at a small border town where customs officials were more casual in performing their duties. If they became too inquisitive, a handful of bills might solve possible problems and induce memory loss. Personnel at the larger, more popular ports of entry, like Tapachula, were more professional and the risk of encountering an unbribable official was greater.

Den decided to enter Mexico through Ciudad Tecun Uman, a smaller town some thirty kilometers southwest of Tapachula.

Driving in the countryside past the dormant volcanoes lining the Sierra Madre Mountains, Den wondered why Rodriguez wanted him dead. He pushed the question to the back of his mind, reminding himself to concentrate on the problem at hand - getting out of Guatemala and into Mexico.

When he arrived at La Union, he estimated he was only thirty-five kilometers from Ciudad Tecun Uman. With luck, he would be there in another half hour and Mexico was on the other side of the river. Den was half way to Tecun Uman when his luck changed. Following the roadway, the helicopter came from behind him. He didn't hear it until the pilot swooped low over him to confirm identification.

The pilot wasn't able to get a clear view of Mickey Mouse, but the white T-shirt was enough for him. He circled the Scout, intending to fly next to it, giving his companion soldier an easy broadside target. "Damn it," Den said, aloud. Rodriguez probably had alerted his men at every border town. Now that goddamned Colonel knew Den was planning to enter Mexico through Tecun Uman.

As the helicopter came alongside the Scout, Den stood on the brakes. The soldier fired only nanoseconds after the Scout came to an abrupt, squealing, swerving stop. His bullets dug into the road ahead of the vehicle. Den leaped from the car and ran into an adjacent wooded area while the helicopter swung in a wide circle and then returned and hovered over the Scout. The soldier fired again. Bullets from his automatic rifle hit the gas tank and the Scout exploded into flame.

After taking another turn, the helicopter landed in the middle of the road. From the safety of brushy undergrowth, Den watched as the soldier emerged and cautiously approached the burning Scout. Using his arm to shield his face from the heat, the man tried to get close enough to see if a body was inside the vehicle.

The heat was intense and the soldier backed away. He remembered the report of the six bodies on the trail near the Alto Cuchumantes. If the gringo wasn't in the Scout, he had to be somewhere nearby. The soldier didn't want to be ordered to search a forested area for a man who had already killed six people. That man was very dangerous and, probably, very well armed.

The soldier went back to the helicopter and reported the heat was too great to get close enough to be sure, but he thought the man was inside and, almost certainly, he was dead. The helicopter rose and disappeared over the horizon. Den left his hiding place and, avoiding the open roadway, he made his way toward Tecun Uman and the border.

The sun was down when he got to the town. Den walked toward the river. When he came close to the bridge, he saw a Customs station and a few Guatemalan soldiers guarding it. Their rifles leaned against the building and, seated on chairs, they smoked and talked and joked among themselves.

Den changed direction and walked a short distance down a side street. Out of sight of the soldiers and unchallenged, he made his way across the river and into Ciudad Hidalgo. He was in Mexico.

After buying a guayabara and tossing his Mickey Mouse T-shirt, Den started the next leg of his trip - the hike to the airport in Tapachula. As he walked down the Mexican road, illuminated only by the moon and the stars, a peculiar question occurred to him: If a gringo sneaks into Mexico by crossing a river, is he called a "wet front" or a "dry back"?

Chapter 13

At Tapachula, Den boarded an Aerovias Mexicana flight. At noon he was in Mexico City. After buying a ticket for the flight to Dallas, he called Langley. As soon as he identified himself, Teddy broke in.

"For God's sakes, what happened? They told me you were dead - got killed in a gunfight somewhere out in the hills. What in hell happened down there? Jesus Christ. Are you OK?"

"I'm all right. I'm carrying a couple of bandages, but I'm able to sit up and take nourishment. It's a long story and I'll tell you about it when I get back. I'm leaving in two hours. American Airlines. I'll be in Dallas at 4:15."

"OK. I'll have a plane and a doctor waiting for you."

Den was met as soon as he stepped out of the tunnel that led from the plane into the Dallas-Ft.Worth International terminal. He was immediately taken back to the tarmac where a waiting Jeep carried him to an Agency jet. A few hours later, an ambulance met him at the Andrews Air Force Base. He was taken to Walter Reed Hospital.

Apparently, Dr. Hernandez did a creditable job when he performed his patch-up in Ticopetenango. The army medicos reviewed his work. They did some cleansing, some re-bandaging and little more. They insisted Den spend the night resting in the hospital. The shoulder wound, they agreed, was not life threatening, but it would require time to heal. Physical therapy would help.

Early in the morning, a doctor stuck his head into Den's room and asked how he felt. Den said: "OK", the doctor said: "Fine" and his head disappeared back into the hallway. In some ways, the Walter Reed hospital was like any other hospital.

Later, with a breakfast inside him, Den took off the open backed nightshirt garb all hospitals use to embarrass, intimidate and humiliate their patients. He tested his wounds. His rib cage was still tender and his shoulder was sore, but the bandages showed only small traces of blood.

Den felt good enough to go to his apartment. Checking himself out of Walter Reed was, at best, an iffy proposition. Nevertheless, he would try it. Underpants, socks and pants were in place when the door opened and Teddy Smith entered the room.

Teddy saw Den, with bandaged side and shoulder, sitting on the edge of the hospital bed. This time there was no small talk. "How are you feeling, Den?" he asked. "Should you be sitting up?"

"I'm going to live," was Den's response. "I'll heal up in a week or so and I'll recover faster if I'm on the outside. Hospitals depress me. Can you threaten a few doctors and nurses and get me out of here?"

Teddy paid no attention to the question. "Rodriguez told me you were dead. He said you were killed before his men finished off Alvarez and three other terrorists. He sure jumped the gun," he said, smiling and gently putting his hand on Den's good shoulder, "I can't tell you how happy I am to see you. You feel up to telling me what the hell happened down there?"

Den told Teddy of the ambush set up by Colonel Rodriguez' Security Forces. He told him Alvarez and all of his three friends were too young to represent serious threats to anyone. "Those kids were no more terrorists than you or I."

Teddy's act was convincing. He showed indignation. Through clenched teeth he said: "That double crossing bastard, Rodriguez. It looks like he wanted to wipe out student protest. In Latin America, university students are almost always the children of wealthy families. The son of a bitch was afraid to kill the sons of important people. He got us to do it for him. He sold me on the idea of a terrorist organization being formed. Terrorists? A bunch of kids playing 'revolution'."

"I knew Rodriguez had a reputation for being a ruthlessly son of a bitch. There is nothing delicate about the way he stamps out any opposition to that Junta and there is no doubt about his connection with Guatemalan death squads. No one has ever been able to prove it. It looks to me like you might have had a brush with them."

Den nodded his head. The word "brush" didn't begin to describe his experience with the Rodriguez death squad. Den told Teddy about the second ambush - the one that came close to killing him. Teddy nearly exploded in a combination of surprise, and anger.

He let go a few expletives. There was no mystery about the reason for the Colonel's attempt to kill him. Packages of cocaine, the bodies of the students AND the body of a dead gringo, known to be looking for drug connections in Guatemala City, would have been found on that dirt road.

It was obvious. It was the Junta's plan to contend the students were buying cocaine from an American drug trafficker. A Guatemalan drug lord decided to eliminate the gringo competition. He would be accused of killing the student witnesses. Den's body would be all that was needed to pass the whole thing off as drug killings. Nothing would give the slightest hint of a death squad and Den wouldn't be alive to tell the truth.

"Sooner or later there'll be a change of government down there," Teddy said. "It won't be long before Rodriguez will be looking for asylum. I'll get my chance at him. Believe me, I'll make the son of a bitch pay for this."

Teddy squeezed Den's right arm. "Come on, Den. I'll help you put your shirt on. Let's get out of here."

* * * * *

The day after Den returned from Guatemala, Jake Jacobson was livid. "*How did he get out of Guatemala alive?*" he asked himself again and again and again. Now the fat was in the fire. Not only had Den survived Ocelot, but he was wounded at the same time students were killed during what the Guatemalan newspapers called a gun battle with drug traffickers.

Den's presence during assassinations in Chile and Bolivia was bad enough. His presence in Guatemala and his drug investigation mission made thing much worse. The smell test would certainly fail if it were applied to the "coincidence" of Den's wounds being received concurrent with the so-called Guatemalan drug trafficker's shoot-out.

Jake tried to convince Teddy it was essential to the safety of Aegis that Den Clark be unable to answer any investigator's questions. He recommended Den be killed as soon as possible. Teddy didn't want to see Den eliminated. Emotion or sense of loyalty had nothing to do with it. If Den were murdered inside the Belt Line, the Senate and the House would investigate and the media would be sure to make a fuss. The Washington Post would speculate the hell out of it.

More importantly, the Agency's attention would be drawn to Den's Guatemalan assignment. If the Agency did its own in-depth investigation, the "coincidence" deaths of Montoya and el Valle would be discovered. The existence of Aegis might be suspected. Teddy felt it would be much safer if Den died during his next off-shore assignment. It was best to let the matter rest for a while.

In the meantime, Teddy hired a nurse to visit Den at his Arlington apartment to change his bandages and provide physical therapy to rebuild his injured muscles. Teddy's motives had nothing to do with an interest in Den's well being. He had to be sure Den would cause no problem while he recuperated.

Teddy asked the nurse to get Den's confidence, encourage him to talk and then report the conversations back to Teddy. At first the nurse was disinclined to act as an informer and violate confidences, but Teddy made a convincing argument.

He told her he was worried about her patient's state of mind - even more than his physical recovery. He swore her to silence and confided that Den was being considered for an important position in the Agency. If there were any indications that the experience of being shot might affect his ability to make decisions that could put men in harm's way, the Agency had to be advised. The nurse agreed to act as Teddy's spy.

Teddy intended to create one more overseas assignment for Den. It would be the last one he would undertake. In the meantime the danger to Aegis could come not only from suspicions of assassination projects discovered by someone within the Agency. It could also come from the possibility of a planned or inadvertent disclosure by Den Clark.

If Den showed signs of wavering, Teddy would no longer be able to dismiss Jake's often-repeated proposal to kill him in Washington.

The nurse was Teddy's insurance policy. If she reported Den showing indications of second thoughts about continuing the work he had been doing, he would have to be eliminated as quickly as possible and regardless of collateral risk.

Teddy took what appeared to be a personal interest in Den's rehab program. He made sure Den's supply of aged single malt Scotch was a bit more than adequate. He often visited Den and, sharing a drink or two, he led conversations to Ocelot and Rodriguez, hoping to find if Den suspected the truth about the double ambush.

Den was unaware of Teddy's ulterior motive. He believed Teddy was sincerely interested in his recovery. He came very close to concluding Teddy must have hired Jake because he had been ordered to do so. Nevertheless, the voice of that tiny skeptic within him continued to urge caution. This time, Den listened to it.

As he recuperated, strengthening his left arm and exercising the muscle that had objected to the injuries around his ribs and upper arm, Den had time to think. Undoubtedly, justice was served by the death of del Valle, but there was no pressing national interest that called for his assassination. He was a test and Den could see how Aegis would consider the test necessary.

Montoya, on the other hand, presented a stronger case. The killing of such a drug lord was higher up on the scale of national interest - on a societal, if not on a military level. The Ocelot Operation, however, was nothing more than garden variety murder. Den tried, without success, to forget he was the one who probably killed Alvarez as the young man rode in the front seat of the Volkswagen.

On the surface, the Guatemalan Colonel appeared to be the villain, but Teddy Smith had withheld information on the death of Mick McCarthy and someone in Aegis had engineered a cover-up. Den's confidence in both Teddy and Aegis continued to erode.

Den began to realize he had entered a dark world where he was a pawn, a tool, manipulated by men like Colonel Rodriguez and the people who protected Jake Jacobson. He didn't like it. The thought that he should end his association with Aegis and the CIA crossed his mind with increasing frequency.

* * * * *

Den paced the living room of his apartment and squeezed a soft rubber ball in his left hand. His nurse had given it to him. She said he should use it. It was an exercise that would strengthen his arm muscles. She knew her nursing services would end when he was pronounced "recovered" and Den was nearly at that point.

When she asked if he would return to the work that caused his injuries and could easily have killed him, Den momentarily dropped his guard. He told her he wasn't sure. He told her it wasn't the danger that bothered him. It was something else. Now he wondered what might have motivated her questioning.

Squeezing the ball with his entire hand presented no challenge. When Den tried to use only his thumb and little finger, the ball slid from his grip. As he bent over to retrieve it, the king sized double paned window in his apartment shattered above his head. Den immediately dropped to the floor. He crawled to the wall and, carefully reaching up, turned off the lights.

Still on his hands and knees, he saw the red dot of a laser above him. It slowly moved back and forth along the back wall of the room. Den knew someone had shot at him from the building on the other side of North Hancock Street. Someone wanted to kill him.

As soon as Den's apartment lights were turned off, the man who tried to shoot him knew he had missed. The red dot of the laser told Den the man had access to some high-tech equipment. It also told him the man was waiting for another chance to kill him. It meant this wasn't a casual amateurish shot. The shooter didn't quickly disappear. He calmly waited to fire again. It smelled of professionalism.

Den watched the red dot as it swept the room and finally found the door that led from the apartment to the hallway. There it stopped. "*The son-of-a-bitch is going to wait until I try to leave,*" he thought. Keeping his eye on the red dot, Den crawled to the desk. He removed his .357 revolver from the middle drawer and then pulled the phone to the floor. He dialed 911.

"I just watched a man murder a woman on the fifth floor of the building at 1267 North Hancock," he said, giving the address of the

91

building across the street. Then he hung up.

Soon, sirens announced the arrival of the police. The red dot disappeared and Den left his apartment. He took the stairway to the basement, opened the service entrance door and entered the alley running parallel with North Hancock Street. Den left the alley when it met a side street. He turned away from the police cars' flashing lights and the noise and confusion in front of his apartment building. As he walked, Den's adrenalin flow ebbed and he began to organize his thoughts.

"He's a persistent bastard, whoever he is," Den thought. *"If a man misses his first shot, he usually gets the hell out of there in a hurry. That red dot didn't leave until the cops' sirens were close by. This guy, Red Dot, is serious about trying to get me. Who is he?"*

"Máximo Rodriguez?" he asked himself. It seemed improbable that his tentacles stretch as far as Washington. It was possible, but not probable. Rodriguez might not even know he was still alive.

The second name was Humberto del Valle. Did some far right wing Chileno ideologue friend of del Valle discover he was the one who killed him in that cottage at Puerto Montt? Certainly, that possibility was a stretch. Still, a right wing conspiracy nut blew up a Federal Building in Oklahoma and left wing nuts shot judges and robbed banks in California. Extremists are capable of almost anything.

Den's third scenario was a hit man hired by a drug trafficker who wanted to make a statement about the impropriety of assassinating Bolivian drug lords.

The chances of any of those three being behind the attempt to kill him, Den thought, were a hundred to one. On the other hand, the chances of being eaten alive by a polar bear in Arlington are a million to one - but once is enough. Den had to consider all alternatives. There was another candidate and Den believed he was the more viable possibility. That man was Jake Jacobson.

Of course, Jake knew it was Den who broke his jaw, cracked his ribs and sent him to the hospital. That might be motive enough for a borderline psychotic like Jake. Den suspected Jake was the most probable man behind the attempt on his life. He had no proof. It could have been someone else, but . . . Den stopped in mid-thought. A fifth alternative occurred to him.

Aegis! What if it wasn't Colonel Rodriguez who quietly planned his death in Guatemala? It could have been Aegis. Aegis planned Ocelot. Den could have been no more than an expendable element of that plan. Aegis might have been willing to let him die in order to protect Rodriguez and his death squads. If Den survived, he might suspect that truth and he would have both the information and motive to destroy Aegis.

Aegis could not run that risk. It would have to permanently close his mouth. Now Den's lists of probable suspects had grown to five: a Chilean fascist, a drug lord, Colonel Rodriguez, Jake Jacobson, or an Aegis assassin.

"I got lucky tonight," Den thought. *"I got a warning. If they get another chance, I may not get lucky again. Jacobson or some Aegis agent or whoever fired that shot will try again. I'll have to change my routines. Certainly, I can't go back to my apartment. I'll have to find another roost."*

Teddy had often visited him and showed concern since he had been wounded in Guatemala, but Den wouldn't consider calling Teddy for help. The man who tried to kill him might be waiting at Teddy's apartment building. Moreover, Teddy, too, was suspect. He was part of Aegis.

Den could take no chances. "Well," he said to no one in particular as he continued walking down the side street, "the scalded cat hates all kind of water." It was his way of telling himself that he had to be doubly careful and could trust no one.

Den made no attempt to spend the night in a hotel or a motel. Someone could check hotel and motel late night registrations. He could be identified and killed before the sun arose. Den bought a newspaper and entered an all-night porno movie theatre.

If Red Dot was still looking for him, he doubted he'd look there. Den wedged himself into a seat, rolled up the newspaper and shoved it down the front of his shirt. Resting his chin on it, he tried to sleep. A casual observer, seeing his upright head, would think he was watching the films.

Chapter 14

The sun was up when, crumpled and unshaven, Den left the porno movie house. The smell of the place clung to him and he felt more than a slight need for a shower. His muscles objected to the cramping ordeal of trying to sleep in a dusty theatre. He wondered how other patrons could spend the entire night watching, over and over, the kind of court defined "free speech" spectacles he had dozed through.

As he walked from the theater, Den concentrated on deciding how to best protect himself from his unknown enemy. Undoubtedly, whoever fired that shot had watched him and knew the patterns of his daily movements. The man knew where Den lived and had rented an apartment across the street. Only one thing was absolutely certain. The man who fired that shot would try again.

Den had to find a safe place to sort things out. He needed help, but he had no close personal friends in Washington. Who could he turn to? Who could he trust? Then the perfect name came to mind. Ferdie Robbins.

Ferdie Robbins didn't socialize with business associates. If anyone in the CIA asked Ferdie for an out-of-office meeting, Ferdie would find an excuse to say "no". He might answer with: "I'm having an attack of appendicitis and must go to the hospital immediately" or something so equally ridiculous that it would be abundantly clear Ferdie wasn't interested in any kind of meeting.

Ferdie avoided being seen in public with Agency associates or, for that matter, with anyone in the CIA. People might wonder what they were talking about. Ferdie feared they would all wonder why the chats weren't happening in the offices at Langley. They would speculate. Was he passing secret or confidential information to them? That sort of speculation could lead to trouble and Ferdie didn't want any kind of trouble.

Den was well aware of Ferdie's obsession for secrecy. He recalled the dark and nearly deserted Arlington lounge Ferdie had selected for the place of their only out-of-office meeting. An assassin would never think Ferdie Robbins would expose himself to the danger of shielding anyone who might, at any moment, be murdered. Ferdie's apartment would be a perfect hide-out.

Den knew it would require some convincing to get Ferdie to let him stay with him while he developed the best plan for staying alive, but Ferdie had trusted Den and had helped him learn the facts about Mick McCarthy's death. Perhaps he would help him again.

As Den walked to the nearest public telephone booth, he made a plan calculated to overcome Ferdie's super-cautious personality. He had no intention of explaining his problem over the phone. That would frighten Ferdie. Den would say nothing except that he needed transportation. He'd ask Ferdie to pick him up. Nothing more.

* * * * *

Ferdie admired Den. He was sure it was Den who gave Jacobson the beating. Ferdie liked to think he had a hand in giving the man that long overdue bit of repayment for his many past sins. As far as Ferdie was concerned, the administering of the beating was a good reason to take a chance and again meet with Den.

Ferdie drove to the bus stop shelter where Den waited. He stopped his car and unlocked the doors. Den got into the front seat. A night sleeping in a dirty, evil smelling, third-rate all-night movie house is not a beauty treatment. As he sat beside him, Ferdie thought: "*My God, he looks terrible.*" What he said was "You look good, Den. What have you been doing?"

"Thanks. I look like hell and I know it. Let's go some place where we can talk."

"We can go to your apartment?" Ferdie suggested.

"No we can't. Let's go to yours."

After noticing Ferdie's expression, unmistakably announcing his complete disapproval of the suggestion, Den lied. "I've had a fire."

Then he told the truth. "I need your help."

Ferdie drove to his apartment building. He was uncomfortable, but relieved when no one was in the elevator or in the hallway to see the two of them together. Safely inside his apartment, there were sincere overtones in Ferdie's voice when he said "I expected you'd return from Guatemala by commercial airline. When I made the arrangements to send the jet to pick you up in Dallas, I knew something was wrong and I was worried. I can't tell you how relieved I was when I found out your wounds weren't serious. Are you OK now?"

Den was completely unprepared for Ferdie's unintended disclosure. He was more than merely surprised. He was startled. He experienced a shock of recognition. He didn't show any of it. Instead, he quite calmly asked: "Thanks for your concern. I'm fine Ferdie. And thanks for the transportation from Dallas. Did you schedule an Agency jet to take me from Belize to Washington?" Ferdie slowly shook his head from side to side.

At that moment, some of the puzzle's pieces came together. One of Den's scenarios had just been confirmed - unmistakably confirmed. No provision had been made for his return from Guatemala. Operation Ocelot was designed to kill him. It was supposed to end with him lying dead on a dirt road, next to the bodies of Guatemalan students who protested against the Junta.

The face of his enemy was now clearly revealed. It wasn't Chileans or drug lords or the Guatemalan Junta. Teddy and Jacobson and Aegis were the ones who planned Operation Ocelot. They were the ones who planned to kill him on that Guatemala back road. They were the ones who tried to kill him in his North Hancock Street apartment. They were the ones who would again try to kill him if they got another chance.

Ferdie's discomfort grew as Den's expression changed and he became silent. Something he said caused Den to react in a peculiar manner. Why did Den want to know if transport from Belize to Washington had been ordered? Ferdie's discomfort took a big leap when Den abruptly said: "I'm going to have to trust you, Ferdie."

Those words rang a warning bell. For Ferdie, ignorance was more than bliss. It was safety. He had a rule he seldom broke. It came from the axiom: Hear no evil, see no evil, say no evil. Ferdie adopted the adage, but he substituted the word "nothing" for the words "no evil". He didn't want to know whatever Den was going to tell him.

The hair rose on the back of his neck when Den said: "There is a secret organization inside the Agency. It plans and carries out assassinations."

Ferdie's backbone straightened. Noisily and involuntarily, he filled his lungs. His eyes snapped wide open. Ferdie started to object. "I don't want to hear…" he began and he backed away from Den.

"Listen to me," Den said as he grabbed Ferdie's arm to keep him from running. "I was sent on a mission to assassinate a terrorist in Guatemala." He couldn't bring himself to tell Ferdie he had been involved in killing students. "The people who sent me tried to kill me. They want to keep me from ever telling what I know. I survived their Guatemala ambush. Last night they tried again. They missed me by inches. These people want to kill me, Ferdie. They want to kill me."

Den could feel Ferdie stiffen. He was almost rigid. Den told him what had happened in his North Hancock Street apartment.

"I don't know if I can be of any help," Ferdie said in a voice a full octave higher than usual. Oh, how he wished he hadn't answered the phone when it rang that morning.

Relaxing his grip on Ferdie's arm, Den said: "The people who are trying to take me out are a secret group, buried inside the Agency. They have power. They're too big to fight. They'll get me if I give them half a chance."

The outline of a plan was already forming in Den's mind. He wouldn't tell Ferdie about his intentions. He wouldn't tell anyone about them. Besides, Ferdie wouldn't want to know.

"I've got to get out of here, Ferdie," he said. "I've got to get out of Washington and I need your help. I need a new identity."

Ferdie Robbins, prudent, discrete, circumspect and cautious, had the chance to do what he had only dreamed of doing. He wanted to experience a reckless plunge into the dark world of danger. He swallowed hard and was surprised and just a bit frightened to hear his own words: "I'll help. What do you want?"

"I'll need a driver's license from Pennsylvania," Den answered, "and a passport in the same name. I'll also need a second driver's license and a passport with a different name. Use an Idaho address on that one. That should be enough. Can you do it for me?"

Ferdie's answer was indirect. "Do you want the passport photo to show a moustache? Or a beard? How about the driver's licenses?" Den was relieved. Ferdie was aboard and if anyone could keep his mouth shut, that man was Ferdie Robbins.

* * * * *

It was a pleasant, late autumn, Indian summer day inside the Belt Line. It was noon. The parks were filled with people enjoying the last good days of the season and dreading the onset of winter. Some of them were eating lunch. Others were walking and swinging their arms. It was a part of a noontime exercise routine designed to give them the impression they were doing something good for their health.

No one shared the bench occupied by a man with a battered suitcase. He was wearing mismatched, ill-fitting clothing and looked like he hadn't shaved in more than three days. A car drove past and threw a McDonald's paper bag out the window. It landed near the curb in front of the man. He picked it up and looked inside, probably hoping to find a French fry or two that had been overlooked. Disappointed, he took the bag to one of the park system's trash containers and tossed it inside.

Ferdie had mixed feelings about his decision to help Den. When he threw the McDonald's package from his auto and drove from the park, fearing he might have been followed, he had enough "danger" for the rest of his life. He was relieved and comforted by Den's promise to ask nothing more of him.

Den was equally relieved and comforted by the fact that he wouldn't have to put up with Ferdie's almost lunatic secretive reclusion. His cloak and dagger scheme to pass the new identification papers to him wasn't really necessary.

No one noticed Den retrieving the documents Ferdie had stuffed into the McDonalds bag. Ferdie had done an excellent job. The

Pennsylvania driver's license named its owner as Ernest Adams. The vital statistics were reasonably accurate. The photograph on the license was a work of art. It showed a man of such bland and unremarkable features that someone who once saw the photo would have a hard time picking Den out of a police line-up.

Still, a traffic cop would have no trouble matching it with Den's face, providing he was wearing the dark horn rimmed glasses shown on the picture. With his customary thoroughness, Ferdie attached the glasses to the license and passport.

The pictures in the other passport and in the Idaho license showed another Den. It was close enough to make him identifiable, but not too specific. They were of the same quality as the Pennsylvania documents and didn't require him to wear glasses.

In the park restroom, Den exchanged his Goodwill bum-like ensemble for the respectable clothing he carried in the old suitcase. He shaved and taxied to a Langley commercial district. He found an alley dumpster and got rid of the suitcase and its contents. Then he walked to a bank where he cashed in his CDs and cleaned out his savings and checking accounts.

* * * * *

During the three days Den lived in Ferdie's apartment, he kept the promises he had made. He didn't leave the apartment. He didn't make a single phone call. He didn't stand close enough to a window to be seen from the outside. They were easy promises to keep. Den shared Ferdie's fear of discovery.

An almost palpable sense of impending danger had been Den's constant companion since the moment the bullet shattered the window of his apartment and passed only inches above his head. It was now perfectly clear that someone inside the Aegis organization had ordered his murder. He remembered Teddy Smith's near obsession with the necessity of keeping the existence of Aegis concealed and unsuspected. The knowledge of its existence, he had often repeated, could lead to disaster for the people in the conspiracy

People inside Aegis feared he would talk. That fear would be reason enough for them to try to completely terminate his ability to consciously or unconsciously expose them. Certainly, they would look for him and if they found him, they would kill him. Den had to make sure they didn't find them. His immediate concern was to get out of Washington.

While he stayed in Ferdie's apartment, waiting for the new identification documents, Den had time to look for other ways to protect himself. He would be safe if Aegis was destroyed, but how could he destroy it. If he told what he knew to one or two of the CIA's top guns, they might decide to protect the Agency by engaging in a cover-up.

Worse, they might be part of the Aegis conspiracy. Then cover-up was sure to follow. In either of those cases, warning CIA people of the presence of Aegis would offer no guarantee of protection and, he feared, the warning might lead an assassin to him.

Den considered going to the media - to the Washington Post or to some TV news talking head. If any one of them had the story and knew others in the news business were privy to the same revelations, everyone would rush the story into publication. Nobody in the news business would ever consider running the risk of being late with the news, be it real or be it pure figments of media imagination. There would be no possibility of a cover-up.

But Den could not go to the news media. If he publicly unmasked Aegis, the assassinations of del Valle and Montoya would become known. So would the murders of the Guatemalan students. If he used the media to expose Aegis, he would also expose himself as an international hit man.

Congressional immunity from prosecution might offer some protection within the United States. Outside the United States was another matter. Guatemala would want to extradite him. Surely it would demand that he be brought to Guatemala to face justice for the murders he had committed inside that country. The CIA and the State Department have never been on friendly terms. The State Department would happily embarrass the Agency by pressing the Administration to send him back to Latin America for trial.

If Den went public and destroyed Aegis, he would be trading the risk of being killed by them for the risk of being killed by a firing squad in Guatemala. Public exposure of Aegis, he concluded, was not an option. Den could think of only one other way to survive. It was the alternative he began to plan during his first minutes in Ferdie Robbins' apartment.

He would find a temporary sanctuary and hide there until he found a perfect way to vanish. Then the man known as Den Clark would disappear from the face of the earth and, simultaneously, another man with another name would materialize in a place distant from previous association.

Den believed Aegis had to be composed of perhaps as many as twenty or possibly thirty people all located near the Belt Line. He knew they would initiate a search for him in the Washington area. They'd probably check the passenger lists of the various flights leaving nearby airports. They'd interview anyone who knew him.

Only one person had information and, if he were even questioned, Den was sure Ferdie Robbins wouldn't talk. Den would do his best to leave nothing for his pursuers to discover.

Aegis could undertake an effective search in the Washington area but he doubted they had the manpower to engage in a nationwide pursuit. They might have enough influence to get the FBI to quietly look for him. Even if the FBI got involved in the search, tracing the movement of a man who used bus transportation would be difficult. At least, it would be time consuming. Distance from Washington would remove him from immediate danger and it would give him time to seek longer-term safety.

After Den closed his bank accounts without incident, he went to a Greyhound station and bought a round-trip ticket to Philadelphia. There are a lot of used car dealers in Pennsylvania. Den planned to buy a vehicle from one of them. He would use the name Ferdie Robbins had selected for the bogus passport and Pennsylvania driver's license.

Given enough time and some good luck, Aegis might be able to follow him from Washington to Philadelphia. There, Denver Clark would again disappear and they would face the problem of discovering his new identity. To find Ernest Adams, the name appearing on Den's

Pennsylvania auto registration, they would have to check the identity of everyone who bought a car during the time he was suspected of being in Philadelphia.

If they found the record of a vehicle title transferred to Ernest Adams and if they found Ernest Adams did not exist, they might guess it was Den Clark's fictitious identity. Even if they guessed it and could discover the vehicle's license plate number, they would have the problem of finding where he had gone. By the time Aegis traced his movements from Philadelphia, Den would no longer be Ernest Adams. He would be in yet another place with yet another identity.

* * * * *

During November and December, Arizona is a popular refuge for people who believe northern states are not fit for human habitation during the period between the close of the deer hunting season and the opening of the fishing season. A stranger living alone in some small desert town would attract more attention than a wintertime visitor in a more populated center.

A man could blend into the streams of tourists who, every day from fall to spring, enter and leave the larger Arizona cities. If a man wanted to hide in Arizona, Phoenix or Tucson were the best destinations. That is where Den decided to look for the temporary sanctuary he needed.

Tucson had an advantage over Phoenix. Gigi Grant lived there. Den trusted her. It was a trust that was built during the months they shared their lives. He was certain he could safely confide in her. Surely, she was not a part of the Aegis network. Cold logic confirmed what his emotions wanted him to believe. If she was a part of Aegis, there would have been no attempt to send her to some CIA back-of-the-moon station. Aegis would have protected her from that kind of treatment.

Den's decision to go to Tucson had an additional motivation. He cared for Gigi, more than he had cared for any other woman. He wanted to go to Tucson because he wanted to see her again.

Den convinced himself contact with Gigi did not expose her to the dangers he faced. Neither Teddy Smith nor anyone else in the Agency knew he and Gigi had even communicated since the few months they spent together at the Kent School. Only Ferdie Robbins knew he had met with her the night before she quit the Agency. No one knew what she told him about Jake Jacobson. Aegis had no reason to believe he would go to her.

Den planned a single meeting with Gigi. He'd tell her about Aegis and the attempts on his life. He'd tell her he needed time to plan a perfect disappearance. He'd ask her to help him find a place where he would, at least for a few weeks, be safe from discovery. Then he would vanish from her life.

Chapter 15

It is possible to drive from Philadelphia to Tucson in three days. In a second hand Chevrolet pick-up truck, it's easier to do it in five. The leisurely pace suited Den. He wanted time to think and to plan. He was safe for the moment and he was able to focus his attention on matters other than avoiding the immediate danger of being murdered.

Den looked back at Operation Ocelot with dismay. He berated himself for acting like an imbecile. He should have known that Guatemalan Colonel wouldn't have the guts to try to kill a CIA agent without Langley approval. He should have recognized Teddy Smith as a consummate con artist.

"All those expressions of interest in my well being? All that drivel about the Guatemalan Colonel going off half-cocked? Just bullshit. A dangerous terrorist leader in the Guatemalan hills? How could I have been so naive," he thought.

"The Agency knows what's happening in Guatemala. If there's a terrorist cell down there, they know it. If they ever heard so much as a rumor about one, they would damn well quickly get first hand information about it. That's their business - collecting first hand information. They wouldn't take the word of some Guatemalan army hit man. Teddy lied to me about Ocelot. He knew there was no terrorist cell. He knew Rodriguez wanted to kill students. He knew I wasn't supposed to get out alive."

With the 20/20 vision of hindsight, Den wondered how he could have been so gullible. On his way to Arizona, he accused himself of being a damned fool and put himself on trial. He was more than the defendant. He was also the prosecutor, the judge and the jury.

As the prosecutor, he argued the case against himself. He was forced to admit his inner voice had, long ago, given him fair warning.

He had elected to disregard it. That decision led him to unjustifiable killings on a lonely Guatemalan road.

Had he thought for a moment, he should have realized a scattering of cocaine, a phony passport or a discarded cap couldn't convince anyone that the murder of some anti-Junta university kids was a drug transaction gone wrong. It wouldn't have convinced Teddy.

Anyone with the brains of a rutabaga, Den was forced to admit, would know the best insulation to protect Colonel Máximo Rodriguez from the charge of death squad murders would be the body of a dead gringo - the same one who had holed up in a fancy hotel and damn near advertised in the newspapers for cocaine. "*I should have seen it coming,*" Den thought. "*It just never occurred to me. It never occurred to me that I was expendable.*"

There was no way for him to excuse himself. Acting as the jury, Den found himself guilty of the charge of being a fool. All he could do in his own defense was to promise it would never happen again.

As his own judge, Den took pity on himself. He withheld sentence, put himself on probation for the rest of his life and warned him. If he ever again acted like a damned fool, his probation would be revoked and he would be sentenced to death.

That sobering thought emphasized his continuing jeopardy. Escape from Washington did not end his peril. Important people in the CIA wanted him dead. If Aegis wanted to remain concealed and continue its clandestine operations, it couldn't let him live. He had to be permanently silenced.

Aegis found Humberto del Valle in rural Chile. It seemed probable he was found because someone within his circle of friends, by purpose or by mistake, let something slip. Someone gave out a clue that led Aegis to the place where del Valle was hiding.

If Den stayed in the United States, sooner or later, someone would discover his identity. A CIA associate, a one time SEAL companion, a friend from his past - someone would recognize him and by luck or by design, someone in the Aegis organization would learn where he was hiding. Long term concealment within the United States would be risky.

The possibility of his casual identification would be reduced if he went to a place where no one knew him. He had to move out of the United States to some country where the chance of the discovery of his true identity was minimal. Even then, he would live with the constant fear of someone recognizing him. He would spend the rest of his life like Humberto del Valle, wondering when he would see a stranger approaching with a weapon in his hand.

* * * * *

As Den drove west, the search for him in the Belt Line terminated. The men who looked for him couldn't find as much as his footprint. In the CIA complex at Langley, Jake Jacobson was seated in the chair in front of Teddy desk. "What do we do now?" he asked.

Teddy shook his head. "The toothpaste is out of the tube. How in hell did he get away?" Jake made a gesture, arms in front of him and palms up. It was a prelude to an explanation, but Teddy wasn't looking for an answer to his question. Still shaking his head and ignoring Jake, he went on: "He's loose and he knows we are behind the apartment shooting."

Jake looked puzzled. "How do you know that?"

"If he wasn't on to us, he would have called me and asked for help."

"You think he's no longer in Washington?"

"I'm not sure, but I think he's gone. I don't think he'd stick around, knowing we were the ones who took the shot at him. I've already run a check on the people who took outbound flights from Reagan and Dulles and all other area fields. Every passenger is legit. Den Clark didn't fly out of here. His car is still in his underground parking space at his apartment building. I suspect he took a bus, but that's only a guess."

Teddy leaned back, his head resting on his interlaced fingers. He could imagine Den's reaction to the failed attempt to kill him. Initially, it might be fear. Ultimately, it would be anger. Den's anger could produce results Teddy preferred to avoid. He hoped his guess was right and Den had left town. He didn't want him in Washington, planning a revenge that might take the form of a midnight bullet. Jake had failed. Teddy knew Den wouldn't fail.

"It's been nearly a week now," he said. "That's a good sign."

Jake was surprised. "A good sign?"

"Yes, it's a good sign. If Den wanted to blow the whistle on Aegis, he would have done it already. We're safe as long as he's quiet. There's no point in embarking on a search for him. He's gone and we don't know where to look. If he's going public, he'll do it before we can find him. Let's hope he has good reason to keep his mouth shut."

Teddy had no intention of continuing the search for Den Clark. Jake wasn't happy with that decision. He wanted another chance to kill him. "He might keep quiet," Jake agreed, "but he might talk." Jake emphasized the words "might". "Do you think we can run that risk?" he asked.

"Den Clark holds the ax and our heads are resting on the block. He can use that ax today or tomorrow or whenever he chooses. Is it safe to think he'll never use it? If you turn me loose, I'll track him down and when I find him, I'll take care of him."

Teddy expected Jake wouldn't like the decision he had made. He knew Jake hated Den and Den had no reason to harbor kind feelings toward Jake. He suspected Den knew about Jake's involvement in Agent McCarthy's death. That had to be the reason Den gave him the beating and sent him to the hospital. Teddy knew Jake wanted revenge and he believed Jake wouldn't be satisfied until Den Clark was dead.

Jake's animosity toward Den was clear enough. He pressed Teddy to use the double ambush scheme and it was concealed within Operation Ocelot. He pushed the plan to kill Den while recuperating in his apartment. Now, he wanted to find him and kill him. The pattern was obvious. Teddy knew just how much Jake wanted Denver Clark to die.

Jake wanted another chance to fulfill the promise he made to himself when he lay in the hospital bed recovering from his beating. Teddy wouldn't give it to him. Instead, he told him: "You had your opportunity. You did more than miss. You gave him a warning. Den is smart and now he's wary."

Jake began to remonstrate and Teddy silenced him with a wave if his hand. "I'll give you another scenario, Jake. Neither one of us has an idea of where Den is, but let's say you find him. Den might find you, too. Then you might get dead. Or Den might disappear again before you could..." Teddy paused for a second before adding with just a touch of sarcasm, "take care of him. We don't want to spook him into sending an anonymous letter to the Director." He paused for a second and then added: "or to the Washington Post."

It didn't take a genius to understand Jake was capable of telling any kind of lie if it resulted in Den Clark's death. Jake's obsession with killing Clark had put his own credibility in question. Teddy's concern was growing. He wondered if, in fact, there was a man named Abdul. Jake might have pocketed ten thousand dollars and told him a fairy tale about the terrorist's agreement to replace Den. Teddy had to be sure there was an Abdul and, if so, was he going to work with him and Jacobson.

"I'm going to say this just once," Teddy said to Jake. "Forget about Den Clark. I'll handle that problem. You've got other fish to fry. Making sure we have a solid replacement for Clark is your first job. I want you to bring Abdul into Mexico. Let me know as soon as he arrives."

Teddy dismissed Jake, saying he had a number of matters requiring his attention. An unhappy Jake left his office. Teddy watched him leave. He slowly shook his head. *"Problems come in bunches,"* he thought.

Teddy didn't know if his greatest danger lay in Den Clark or in Jake Jacobson. Jake's planning of clandestine operations could only be characterized as excellent. He had a knack for misdirection and duplicity. Those Machiavellian qualities were as valuable as they were rare. Jake's scheming abilities, however, didn't blind Teddy to his defects.

Teddy was a pragmatist. He would cooperate with the devil himself if he saw an advantage. Jake was clever, but he wasn't able to manage his ego. Jake carried grudges. Jake would destroy a man he didn't like. The quality of the man's work meant nothing to him. If the report Henry Putnam showed to Teddy was characteristic of Gigi Grant's work, an excellent officer was lost when Jake forced her out of the Agency. Jake's obsession with destroying Den was an example of his ego taking control of his brain.

Other defects were equally troubling to Teddy. Jake Jacobson was not burdened by any sense of loyalty to anyone or anything. Jake was motivated by self-interest. Jake's downgrading of associates in the Projects Branch was his way of eliminating competition and insuring his own elevation to Teddy's position when, and if, the time came. The ways Jake tried to curry favor were unambiguous. Jogging with him came to mind.

Jake was not trustworthy. Teddy had no solid proof of it, but he had no doubt of it. In his bones, he knew Jake would turn on him if by doing so he could save his own hide.

If he had it to do again, Teddy would not rescue Jake from the expected effects of his Syria insubordination. He would leave him in Damascus to stew in his own juice. If he had it to do again, he would not adopt the double ambush of Operation Ocelot. But Teddy had no H. G. Wells machine to carry him back in time and allow him to correct his errors. He had to play with the cards he held. He knew he'd have to deal with Jake sometime.

Teddy damned Jake Jacobson. If he hadn't screwed up, Den would be dead. Of course, Den had gone underground. There was no point in looking for him. He'd be very hard, if not impossible, to find. Sooner or later Den would break cover and when he did, Teddy would deal with him. As long as Den made no waves, Teddy would sit tight.

Teddy hoped Den would keep his mouth shut. If he didn't - if he scattered a bunch of anonymous tips to congressmen or newspapers - Teddy would be in for some heavy weather. He had already planned to throw Jake to the dogs, but he looked for another plan. It's always best to have more than one string on the violin, just in case the first one breaks.

* * * * *

Later in the afternoon, the Deputy Director gave Teddy Smith five minutes of his time. Anyone else would have been shunted off to someone further down the chain of command, but Deputy Director Cullen Brewster appreciated Teddy's reputation and always had time for him.

Teddy engaged in no small talk. "Thank you for your time," he said as soon as he entered the Deputy Director's office. "I'll come directly to the point. We have a rogue agent in Clandestine Services. I believe the matter should be treated with the utmost discretion. You should understand the full extent of the problem."

"Continue," Deputy Director Brewster said, taking Teddy's warning as calmly as if it were the morning weather report.

"One of our agents, Den Clark, was sent to Guatemala to investigate drug production and trafficking. You may recall he recently returned unexpectedly. He had two gunshot wounds."

The Deputy Director nodded and said that he was aware of the mission and the agent's early return to Langley.

"I'm sure you are also aware of the request for assistance made by Colonel Máximo Rodriguez - the request that was quickly and firmly denied."

Again, Brewster merely nodded and Teddy continued.

"You've seen the reports of the drug-associated shootings of some Guatemalan students. Of course, we all believe Rodriguez arranged them since the killings so closely coincided with the request the Colonel made of us. It is my belief that Clark was bribed by Colonel Máximo Rodriguez to kill those students."

The Deputy Director lifted his chin a few millimeters and, for only a second, his eyes opened just a bit wider, indicating an increased degree of interest. For Cullen Brewster, it was a display of emotion seldom shown. "Continue, please," he said.

"Last week, I scheduled Clark for a face-to face in my office. He didn't appear. I instigated a search. His apartment has been abandoned. No one has seen him. No one knows his whereabouts. We checked with all his known associates, the area hospitals and police records. Nothing. Nothing at all. Den Clark has disappeared.

"It is possible this matter may come to light and the Agency could be improperly criticized. We have reason to suspect Clark may have been involved in other killings as well. Due to the sensitive nature of the matter, I thought a verbal report might be more convenient that one in writing."

The Deputy Director showed no reaction. After a few seconds he asked: "How do you propose to handle the situation?"

"We could alert our off-shore stations. Clark may have already left the country, but I doubt it. I'd guess he'll stay hidden in the States for a while. When things have quieted down, he'll, withdraw his nest egg from some Swiss bank account and, again, vanish."

"Then we must find him before he leaves the country," Cullen Brewster said.

This was not what Teddy had in mind. He did not want any search, foreign or domestic, to be ordered. A search could cause Den to protect himself by going public and that could end in the demise of Aegis and anyone associated with it. Teddy sat quietly and made no comment. The Deputy Director read Teddy's silence as disapproval. He digested Teddy's lack of enthusiasm. After a momentary pause, he added an alternative: "Or, we can do nothing."

Now Teddy smiled. "That's very wise, sir. I never thought of that. As usual, your suggestion is well founded. I certainly agree with you. The worms are still in the can. There is no reason to risk opening it. If the man feels safe and ends up retired in a house on the French Riviera, nothing will ever come to light. If something does surface, there should be no hint of possible CIA involvement in any of Clark's murder for hire machinations."

Without changing his expression, Cullen Brewster again nodded his head. Then he stood up and Teddy turned and left the room.

Back in his own office, Teddy's mood was bright. He hoped Den would just disappear and keep his mouth shut. If he remained silent, there would be no problem and everything in the garden would be lovely. If Den tried to expose Aegis, certainly nobody in Langley, from the Director on down, would admit to CIA sponsored assassinations. Any suggestion of Agency involvement in the deaths of del Valle, Montoya or the Guatemalan students would be strenuously denied.

Teddy had set the ground work for the Agency's defense. Cullen Brewster would admit Clark had once worked for the CIA. He would describe him as a rogue operative who vanished when suspected of criminal activity. He would admit Clark may have hired out as a private assassin and got paid a bundle to kill the enemies of whoever would pay his fee.

Joselito Montoya's drug lord successor as well as Colonel Rodriguez and some unidentified father of some murdered Chilean student all had the means and the motives to hire Clark's service as an assassin. Anything Den might say about a secret organization within the CIA would be dismissed as nonsense. Finally, if the heat got unbearable and a scapegoat was needed, there was always Jake Jacobson.

Teddy smiled. He had covered all the bases. He made detailed notes of what transpired in Deputy Director Cullen Brewster's office. The Deputy's suggestion of off-shore searches and, subsequently, of inaction were not mentioned. If Teddy was accused with collaboration in the Guatemalan deaths, he would have a written record showing he had advised the Deputy Director in a timely fashion. Brewster would have to take the heat. The Clark Affair no longer required Teddy's attention.

* * * * *

In the days immediately following the Revolutionary War, the Brewster family did not join fellow Massachusetts Tories in their migration into pro-British Canada. They remained in Boston, facing the criticism of Hancock, Revere, Adams and others who had supported the patriots. The Brewster family stayed and continued to quietly build their already considerable assets as well as their reputation for philanthropic endeavors.

Through the years, the Brewster family occasionally produced a black sheep, but, in both number and percentage, far less than social statisticians would project. Banking, international trading, and venture capital investment were the family's favored business occupations. Each generation advised their children to eschew both politics and any kind of involvement in government. That advice was usually followed.

As a child, Cullen Brewster was fascinated by stories of the World War II espionage. The failures of intelligence that led to Pearl Harbor, the breaking of codes that led to the success of the Battle of Midway, the work of the agents who parachuted into France and Yugoslavia, the clever manipulations that misled the Nazis prior to the invasion at Normandy - those were the stories he adored. In spite of family opposition, as soon as he finished his education, Cullen Brewster looked for and found a position in the CIA.

In many ways, he was a typical product of his class. Educated at private schools, he received a degree from Yale and continued his studies at Eton. Unlike most of his classmates and all of his progenitors, Cullen Brewster was a Phi Beta Kappa. His college friends and the men he knew through family social and business associates connected him with some of the most powerful people in the country.

Brewster made no compromise with present day dress practices. He was always impeccable dressed and never appeared in his CIA office without a boutonnière in the lapel of his invariably dark and carefully tailored suit. His only idiosyncrasy appeared to be his custom of wearing bow ties.

The people in the Agency who referred to him as "that patrician son of a bitch" were those who disliked his accent, his dress and his soft-spoken, superior manner. They weren't aware of the depth of his experience, his acute analytic capacity or his almost uncanny ability to accurately determine the "why" behind a growing problem, his ability to forecast the probable "what next" and the practicality of his proposals of "what to do about it".

Cullen Brewster carried more weight in the Agency than was suggested by his title - Deputy Director of the Directorate of Operations. His judgment and his advice were recognized and appreciated by those who were responsible for advising national security people. When Deputy Director Cullen Brewster spoke, the Director listened. Brewster took great satisfaction in accomplishing the tasks assigned to him. He was comfortable in the position he occupied. When offered opportunities to advance up the chain of command, he politely and consistently refused.

Chapter 16

As directed by Teddy, Jake contacted Abdul. The message told the Jordanian to come to Monterrey, pick up a package at the Fed-X office and wait for Jake to contact him at the Nuevo Mundo Hotel. Teddy's instructions were given to Jake simultaneously with the announcement of his decision to terminate the search for Den Clark and the rejection of Jake's offer to find him and kill him.

Since the meeting in Teddy's office occurred only as few days after Jake's failed assassination attempt, all of these events were inter-related and it didn't take a Ph.D. to figure out what they meant. In plain English, Teddy's confidence in Jake took a back-step when he screwed up his attempted assassination.

Teddy's suspicion that Jake would lie to him if it helped get his approval for killing Den had been strengthened. He had growing doubts about whether Jake told him the truth when he reported Abdul's agreement to take Den's place.

Jake fully understood Teddy's state of mind. He knew his future in the CIA depended upon Abdul's appearance in Monterrey. If Abdul rejected his proposition and elected to stay in Syria, Jake had to make a difficult decision. He could tell Teddy he failed in his Damascus mission and admit he had been double-crossed (again) by a terrorist who now had ten thousand dollars of CIA money or he could tell him Abdul was unable to go to Mexico because he had been killed in some Israeli operation.

He leaned toward the second alternative, but it gave him little solace. Even if the lie couldn't be disproved, it would probably fail to convince an already skeptical Teddy Smith. The lie would do nothing to rebuild Teddy's opinion of his honesty. Teddy's growing suspicions would be enough to destroy Jake's future in the CIA. If Abdul stayed in Syria, Jake would have to choose between being considered either an incompetent or a liar. Perhaps, he would be considered to be both.

* * * * *

In Mexico City, immigration officials didn't raise an eyebrow when Abdul, using a Jordanian Passport, entered the country. A day later, in accordance with Jake's instructions, he was in Monterrey. As directed, he went to the Hotel Nuevo Mundo where a room on the third floor had been reserved for him. The rooms on the first floor of that long ago constructed building catered to prostitutes. The second floor was reserved for transient guests and the top floor - the third - was high enough above the street to get away from some of the noise and smells. Its few occupants were longer-term residents, people with limited resources and no place else to go.

Abdul followed Jake's instructions. He went to the Fed Ex office and retrieved the package that awaited him. He wondered if the package was a disguised bomb. Abdul had not dismissed the possibility of a CIA plot to kill him or perform some other act of perfidy. In the municipal park across the street from the Nuevo Mundo, he gave a boy ten Pesos and told him to open the package. Watching from a safe distance, Abdul was relieved when there was no explosion.

The package contained the book entitled: The Complete Works of William Shakespeare. It was bound in plastic that looked quite a bit like quality leather. Abdul's interest in Shakespearian plays and sonnets was limited to the point of being non-existent, but he was pleased to receive the volume. Back in his room in the Nuevo Mundo, Abdul removed the one hundred dollar bills interspersed between the book's pages. He counted them twice. As promised, there were one hundred of them.

When the Fed-X office confirmed the delivery of the package containing the book, Jake was relieved. At least, Abdul was in Mexico and hadn't disappeared with the money given him in Damascus. Now it remained to be seen if he would run after taking the second ten thousand dollar payment.

Jake reported Abdul's arrival in Monterrey and Teddy dampened his suspicions. He only dampened them. They remained in the back of his mind. Teddy had been comfortable with Den. He was smart and tough and capable and, equally important, he was dependable. The only knowledge Teddy had about Abdul was the sketchy information Jake provided and Teddy wasn't sure Jake's information was reliable. Working with an Arab terrorist didn't inspire much confidence.

Teddy wished he could rely on the accuracy of Jake's reports as much as he had been able to rely upon the ones he received from Den. The best way to test Abdul's reliability was to give him a job and see how he performed. Teddy wasted no time.

He told Jake to go to Monterrey, give Abdul an assignment and stay with him until he had finished it. Then he wanted a complete report of the terrorist's competence. As far as a target was concerned, Teddy told Jake to pick someone - a drug smuggler, a corrupt Mexican policeman, anyone. The target was not important. The way Abdul behaved was important.

Jake was in a pleasant mood when he sent a coded message to Abdul announcing his arrival in Monterrey. He had already selected a target. It was Gigi Grant. In Damascus, Jake had asked her to keep him out of her report of Mick McCarthy's death. He even promised to pay her. She refused, called him a detestable scoundrel and hoped he got burned. Now that bitch would pay for her insolence

Jake remembered Den was in Langley when Grant was recalled for re-assignment. Within days, Clark gave him that humiliating beating. Jake felt those nearly simultaneous events had to be connected. He suspected Grant might have told Clark of his involvement in Mick McCarthy's death. Whether or not his suspicions were correct wasn't important. It would be prudent to permanently close G. G. Grant's mouth. Soon it would be pay-back time.

In marking Gigi for assassination, Jake considered the potential of creating a serious rift between Teddy and himself. Teddy might not be comfortable with the killing of a one-time CIA agent. Teddy would probably correctly assume the purpose of selecting G. G. Grant as Abdul's victim was to further conceal Jake's involvement in the death of Agent McCarthy. When Jake reported back to Teddy with the results of Abdul's work, Teddy might ask him to justify his decision to make her the target.

Teddy agreed to kill Den Clark in Guatemala only after he had been convinced Den was a danger to Aegis. That gave Jake the key to the way he would convince Teddy of the advisability of Grant's elimination. Jake was prepared for Teddy's questioning.

He would remind Teddy of Grant's assignment to the Damascus Station. She had to be acquainted with Abdul's activities in Syria. *"She probably would be able to identify Abdul and tie him to me. Grant had no reason to be sympathetic to me, to you, or to the CIA. She knew enough to cause trouble and the kind of trouble that could easily become a threat to Aegis."* Those were good reasons for her elimination.

"Besides," Jake thought, *"Teddy said I could select the target. And suppose he does object. It will be a fait accompli. What can he do about it? He can't hurt me. I've got too much on him."*

* * * * *

In Monterrey, Abdul had twenty thousand American dollars. Abdul presumed the announcement of Jake's arrival in Monterrey meant the CIA had work for him to do. It meant Jake would give him more money. It would be half of the cost of an assassination. Of course, he could fly back to Damascus right now, but why should he leave Mexico? So far, his casual association with the CIA had been a very profitable business.

Certainly, none of his compatriots in Syria could fault him for getting as much money as possible from the CIA, especially if he killed the Agent who delivered it. Abdul decided he would wait for Jake. Whether or not he had more dollars to give him didn't matter. Abdul would complete the plan he made in Damascus. He would kill Jacobson and return to Syria.

Abdul enjoyed a pleasant morning seated in the sun in the middle of the municipal park where he could watch the entrance to the Nuevo Mundo Hotel. He sat and waited for the arrival of Jake Jacobson. In the warm sun, he thought about the naivety of the proposition he had received.

He had spent his life fighting for the creation of his Palestinian homeland and the eradication of the Jews. Jacobson expected him to move half way across the world and work for the Americans. They were the ones who helped the Jews throw the Palestinians out of their homeland. They were the ones who armed and protected them.

On the other hand, life in Mexico, he conceded, was peaceful, certainly more peaceful than life in the Near East. Political murders were relatively rare. There were no armed battles between religious sects - no suicide bombers - no Israeli airplanes dropping missiles on automobiles or homes - no exploding rockets. He thought about the goal of driving the Israelis into the sea. It had been a bloody fight for decades and decades. That fight would continue, but each of the past prospects for success had ended in frustration.

Abdul could see an advantage in disappearing into the New World and leaving the endless Near East struggles behind him. Perhaps, after all, Jacobson's naive proposition had some merit.

* * * * *

The flight from Dallas to Monterrey arrived in mid-morning. Jake deplaned and passed through Mexican customs. He went directly to the Nuevo Mundo Hotel and was disturbed when Abdul was not in the room reserved for him. Jake hoped Abdul was having lunch. He would have to wait for him to return. Jake left the Nuevo Mundo and, for a few minutes, stood on the sidewalk in front of the hotel. He crossed the street, to the park and found a conveniently placed bench. He sat and waited for Abdul.

From his place in the center of the municipal park, Abdul saw Jake Jacobson enter the Nuevo Mundo hotel and re-emerge a few minutes later. He watched Jake wait in front of the building and then cross the street and sit on the park bench facing the hotel.

From his position behind him, Abdul watched for some hint of a trap. Jacobson appeared to be alone. At times he appeared to be nervous, glancing at his wristwatch and, from time to time, standing and looking around. Obviously, he was waiting for Abdul.

It was a temperate and sunny afternoon in Monterrey. Jake's frame of mind did not reflect temperate or sunny speculations. He was not happy. The longer he sat on that bench, the more his unhappiness grew. He had reason to be unhappy. He promised Teddy Smith he would secure the services of a capable assassin. Abdul could not be found in the Nuevo Mundo.

If he had returned to Syria it would be hell to pay. It would be crystal clear he had misled Teddy. Jake preferred the term "mislead," but he knew Teddy would use the word "lied" It would also mean twenty thousand dollar of CIA funds had vanished. There would be no way Jake could disguise those gloomy disasters

The growing possibility of their occurrence occupied his thoughts. *"You can't trust these goddamned Arab rag heads."* Abdul double-crossed him in Damascus. He could easily double-cross him again. If Abdul took the latest payment of ten thousand dollars and returned to Damascus, Jake would have to face some very loud and disturbing music.

It would, at the very least, destroy his relationship with the man who protected him. The people who were his competition for advancement within the CIA would no longer fear him. Teddy would probably demote him. Worse, Teddy might can him. The possibility of being fired led Jake to recall his other failures.

Teddy wanted to scrap the second ambush hidden within Operation Ocelot. Jake talked him out of it. He convinced Teddy the death of Clark afforded important protection of Aegis, but Den survived Ocelot. Now there was another instance of him being present in a place where an assassination occurred. It was another "coincidence" to attract the attention of some CIA internal security analyst. The protection Jake had planned for Aegis evaporated and was replaced by a newer danger. It became necessary to remove Clark before he talked.

If that wasn't enough, Jake botched the attempt to kill him. He thought he had Clark in the crosshairs when he squeezed the trigger, but the bullet destroyed nothing more than a window and Jake's own beliefs that he was a capable killer. Jake's missed shot moved Clark into a position where he became an even larger threat of Aegis exposure.

Clark certainly knew it was Teddy Smith and Jake Jacobson who were behind the attempt on his life. That added another dimension to Jake's concern. Den Clark might look for revenge and decide to come after him. The thought of it was more than merely disquieting. To make matters still worse, Teddy no longer gave any indication of interest in actively pursuing Clark. He showed no interest in wanting to kill him.

Jake had no cause for joy. Things were not going well for him. If, as he suspected, Abdul was on his way back to Damascus, Jake's future looked bleak, indeed. In spite of the beautiful day, Jake sat on the bench in the Monterrey municipal park in a somber and dejected mood. He again looked at his wristwatch. He'd been watching the entrance to the Nuevo Mundo for nearly an hour. *"How much longer?"* he wondered.

Trying to lift his own spirits and grasping at straws, Jake created convenient explanations for Abdul's absence. The hotel and Abdul's room are not attractive places to spend the day. Abdul could be expected to spend as much time as possible away from it. He could be sight-seeing, or doing something else. Maybe he mis-read my message. Maybe he thinks I'll arrive tomorrow. Maybe he is taking a long lunch. But Jake could not erase the thought that he had been deceived again.

In desperation, he decided to wait until midnight. If Abdul didn't appear by that time, he didn't know what he was going to do. Jake was roused from his brown study when, from close behind him, someone spoke. "It is good to see you again."

Chapter 17

Jake's muscles involuntarily tightened and his head snapped in the direction of the words whispered into his ear. He saw Abdul standing behind him. After his initial surprise, Jake regained his composure and felt only relief. Again, the world was good. "You are a cautious man, Abdul," he said. "That speaks well of you. Prudence is an essential element of our business."

Abdul and Jake exchanged perfunctory and brief pleasantries. They left the bench and walked toward the center of the park where there was less pedestrian traffic and they could talk without being overheard. Abdul said nothing. Jake began the conversation.

"We both know you will never trust the CIA and we both know the CIA will never trust you. Still, we have mutual interests making it possible for us to work together."

He looked at Abdul who nodded. This was a disarming statement. It spoke a clear and obvious truth. There was no attempt at subterfuge, no obviously misleading flowery comment. It was a simple statement of fact.

Abdul broke his silence. "It is nice when, as you Americans often say, 'the cards are on the table'. You want me to kill your adversaries. You have already invested many dollars without asking anything of me. This tells me how much you need me. I have taken your money and come to your hemisphere. This tells you I am interested. It also tells you I am motivated by the money you will pay."

Now it was Jake who nodded. "It is not necessary for us to throw our arms around each other and cover one another with warm, moist kisses. As long as we perform services for each other, we can work together. I will be your conduit to the Agency and I hope you will always speak as openly and frankly as now."

"I hope you will treat me with the same candor," Abdul answered and then added, "and I share your skepticism." They looked at each other for a second. Then they both smiled. Then they both nodded.

"A good beginning," Jake observed. "We have found common ground. Now it is time to take the next step."

"You are telling me you have an assignment." It was a statement, not a question.

Jake told Abdul it was more than an assignment. It was an Agency test. He would be asked to enter the United States illegally, find his target, make the kill and then return to Mexico. Abdul was surprised when Jake told him he expected the assassination to take place within 72 hours. He was accustomed to spending days and sometimes weeks in watching a target while he planned the time and place for his death. The CIA was not going to give him that luxury. He would enter no objection. It was an opportunity for him to prove his worth.

Abdul asked Jake for a description of the intended victim. He wanted to know how he would identify him. What was his name? What was his business? Where did he work? Where did he live? Did he have bodyguards? Did he have a daily pattern to his life?

Then Abdul received another surprise. Jake told him his target was a lawyer living in Tucson. Her name was G. G. Grant.

"Ah. She's the woman who was the CIA agent in Syria."

"Do you know her?"

"Know her? No. We knew the names of all of the CIA people in your Damascus cell, but I didn't know her. I may have seen her once or twice. I don't recall. No. I don't remember her."

"She's no longer in the Agency," Jake said and, again, Abdul interrupted him.

"So, she knows too much. So, she has to be silenced. So, the CIA wants to purge itself of a potential embarrassment. The Central Intelligence Agency doesn't like to be embarrassed. I will have to remember not to become an embarrassment."

"I always remember it," was Jake's cynical response to Abdul's cynical comment.

Jake gave Abdul a description of Gigi Grant. He gave her office address and the license number of her black Cherokee Jeep. Abdul interpreted the lack of more specific information to the CIA's interest in testing his ingenuity. He didn't understand it was only a reflection of Jake's lack of specific knowledge.

Jake instructed Abdul to make no attempt to pass through U. S. Customs at Nogales. He gave him the name of a "coyote" operating out of a rural finca ten miles to the west of Mexican Nogales and close to the border. The coyote would take him into Arizona a few miles from a place called Flores.

Flores was little more than a saloon, a general store, a gas station and a few buildings. An automobile would be parked behind the gas station. Jake gave Abdul a key that would fit the ignition and told him to drive to Tucson and call him when he arrived. After giving him a telephone number and an envelope containing half of Abdul's promised compensation, Jake wished him good luck and left the park.

Jake's visit to Monterrey may have begun in an atmosphere of discouragement, but it ended with pleasant optimism. It looked more and more like Abdul may have decided to work with him and Teddy. Time would tell. If he killed Grant, Jake's promise to find a replacement for Den Clark would be validated and his standing with Teddy would not be injured. At the same time, he would get rid of the Grant woman - one of the few people who knew his Damascus history. If, after killing her, Abdul disappeared back into the Near East, Jake couldn't care less.

As he looked for a taxi to take him back to the airport, Jake was satisfied. He had avoided damage to his reputation. His position with Teddy was secure. Soon, G. G. Grant would be dead. Den Clark was the only problem yet to be resolved.

"*Damn Teddy!*" Jake thought. He seemed to be willing to take the chance Den would keep his mouth shut. He wouldn't let Jake track him down. Every passing day brought Jake more anger and an even deeper desire to kill Clark. Jake had been patient. It looked like he would have to continue to be patient.

* * * * *

From his room in the Nuevo Mundo, Abdul watched Jake enter a taxi and begin his trip back to the States. As soon as the taxi disappeared from sight, Abdul opened the envelope Jacobson had given him and counted the seven thousand five hundred dollars it contained.

He thought of his early years in a Palestinian refugee camp - poverty - the indignities of dependence on Hezbollah charity - hunger - less to eat than an Israeli house dog. Now he had well over twenty-five thousand dollars and the promise of another seventy-five hundred when the Tucson lawyer was dead. If one of his Damascus jihad leaders told him to kill the woman when she was stationed in Syria, he would have done it without compensation

It was less than a few weeks since Abdul met with Jacobson in Damascus. At that time, Abdul believed Jake made the contact because the CIA was planning assassinations in the Near East. He thought the Agency wanted a Moslem assassin to enter Moslem territories and kill Moslem leaders - the men who believed as he did. The West slandered them with the name "terrorists". He would call them "freedom fighters".

When he was directed to come to the Western Hemisphere, Abdul expected to be asked to kill a fellow Moslem who lived in America. Perhaps, someone who raised funds for Palestinian causes. Perhaps, it would be a freedom fighter sent to the United States to organize bombings. Abdul would not hesitate to kill Christians or Jews, but it would be impossible to kill fellow Moslems who supported jihad.

Abdul recalled his initial reactions to the CIA proposal. When he was called, he would fly to Mexico. He'd take the second ten thousand dollars that had been promised. He would agree to kill whoever Jacobson named and collect the one-half advance payment. Then he would kill Jacobson, warn the intended victim and quickly return to Syria.

That plan was jettisoned when Jake told him his target was not a Palestinian compatriot. It was an American. Not only that. It was an ex-CIA agent. Abdul sat on the edge of the hotel room bed and ran his fingers over the crisp edges of the bills. He liked the feel of them. Why, he asked himself, shouldn't he at least consider staying in Mexico and working for CIA money? Perhaps he wouldn't be asked to kill Moslems. Perhaps he would only be called upon to kill ex-CIA agents.

He could live in Mexico and still favor jihad. He could always refuse any CIA assignment if it was offensive to him. A new, well-paying job on this side of the globe was attractive. He would live well. He could have good Western clothing, good food, a good place to live - perhaps in an apartment building. Then, ashamed of himself, he broke his reverie.

"No," he said aloud. "No. The Americans and their CIA can never be trusted. The greatest danger exists when you feel secure. I will work with Jacobson, but I must never trust him. I promise myself I will always be ready to take his money and kill him." He spoke those words aloud in an unsuccessful attempt to quiet the re-occurring thought that he should leave his Near East life behind him and begin a new life in a new world.

Abdul packed his suitcase and prepared for a trip to Nogales and a meeting with the coyote named Carlos Montenegro.

*   *   *   *   *

During his early teens, Carlos Montenegro lived in Nogales, Sonora, across the border from Nogales, Arizona. He managed to survive through petty thievery. If he had been a more successful thief, he would not have spent five years in a Mexican prison. Five years in a Mexican prison gives a man not only opportunity, but also good reason to reflect on the course his life has taken. The young man had time to plan his future.

Some Mexican prisoners were attracted to the drug business. It was an occupation with good financial reward, but Montenegro knew the people who trafficked in narcotics fought among themselves. They had no prejudice against killing one another or killing anyone else who might be standing nearby. It was a violent business.

Montenegro was not averse to killing someone, but he did not like the possibility of someone killing him. He was careful to avoid risks that could end up in his own death. Those risks, he thought, were much too great if one was engaged in the drug trade.

During his time in prison, Montenegro also learned men were paid to lead people across the Arizona border. Such men were called "coyotes". Guiding undocumented persons into the United States was less profitable than the drug trade, but the risk of being killed or being caught and sent to prison was low. Carlos' own experience convinced him the potential of being returned to prison was almost as frightening as the potential of being shot and killed.

The risk of imprisonment in the coyote business was low. The Mexican policía didn't assign a high priority to interfering in the business of human exportation. On the United States side of the border, if a man was apprehended while smuggling illegals into the country, there was little chance of criminal prosecution. Usually the coyote, along with the undocumented immigrants, was simply sent back to Mexico.

Carlos Montenegro would be satisfied with the life of a coyote. He decided to discontinue his occupation as a marginally successful thief and dedicate himself to the profession of smuggling undocumented Latinos into the United States. As soon as he was released from prison, he returned to Nogales and began his new profession.

It was a simple matter for Montenegro to lead Latinos to the Arizona border. On those few occasions when apprehension by the United States Border Patrol became a danger, Carlos Montenegro immediately abandoned his charges and hurried back into Mexico. Left to fend for themselves, some of the illegals were caught and deported. Some of the others, avoided capture by the "migrantes", but, unable to decipher the maps Montenegro supplied, they wandered in the Arizona desert until they died of thirst or exposure.

Sometimes a different kind of "undocumented" would appear at Montenegro's finca. These people weren't looking for jobs in the United States.

It was easy to recognize them. The way they dressed and the way they spoke distinguished them from the people who were looking for work in the United States. They usually carried more than a modest amount of money with them. This other kind of client had good reason to avoid the possibility of being identified as they returned into the United States.

A gringo aviator, named by the Drug Enforcement Agency as a narcotics trafficker, brought money with him when he hired Carlos Montenegro to take him back into the United States. The gringo never got into Arizona. He was killed at the border. The money he carried paid for Montenegro's finca - an adobe building and a few sheds located on a hectare of land outside of Mexican Nogales.

Another felon, a bank embezzler who absconded into Mexico, wanted to quietly return to his country. He, too, died at the border. A part of his money was used to purchase Montenegro's truck.

As the volume of illegal immigration into the United States expanded, so did Montenegro's business. He hired a peon to lead the emigrating Latinos into Arizona. Montenegro's own personal coyote services were offered only to those who appeared to carry money with them. Montenegro's prosperity was a monument to his ability to determine who had money and to his ability to persuade them to follow him to some remote spot near the United States border.

* * * * *

The sun was beneath the horizon when Chico Cisneros finished his supper of beans and rice. He recognized the sound of the automobile that was approaching the adobe ranchito where he lived. They were made by his patrón's truck. Chico removed the dishes from the table and wiped its surface with his sleeve. Then he stood against the wall and waited.

The engine stopped, the truck door slammed and, soon, Carlos Montenegro entered the building. He was with a man who was going to Arizona. That man was not the usual kind of "bracero" Chico would take to the border. He didn't look like a peon worker. He was wearing good shoes and the kind of clothing gringos wear. They looked almost new.

Chico liked being a coyote. It was easy work and it provided him with good food and a comfortable place to live. However, he disapproved of the killings that occurred whenever the patrón took a prosperous looking client toward the United States. Chico hoped he would be allowed to lead the well-dressed stranger to Arizona. That would mean the man would live.

Though Chico suspected he knew the answer, he still asked: "Quiere que manejo la máquina?"

"No," Montenegro answered: "No. Yo lo haré."

The stranger was wary and suspicious. He stood in a place where he could see Chico, Montenegro and the room's single open window. His eyes constantly watched all three. He had a hard and humorless look about him.

"What were you saying?" he demanded.

"He asked me if I wanted him to drive the truck," Montenegro quickly answered. "I told him I would do it. You should learn to trust, my friend. Surely the ones who sent you must have told you I am an honorable man. I would not trick you. Have confidence. Soon you will be safely inside the United States. Come. Let us have a tequila and relax."

"I do not drink alcoholic beverage," was the man's curt reply.

A few hours later, Montenegro turned off the truck's headlights and drove the last mile of the trip by the light of the moon. He stopped and, with the aid of a flashlight, pointed to a spot on a hand drawn map. "We are here." He moved his finger a few inches to a dot identified by the word "Flores". "Here is where you want to go. Here is the trail." Montenegro pointed to a broken line on the map. "It is on the other side of the frontera. Not too far away. Follow it to the east. The east is that way," he said, gesturing in the darkness of the night.

Montenegro and his passenger left the truck and Montenegro continued his instructions. "Arizona is very close. It is in that direction," he said as he waved his hand to the north. "The trail you look for runs parallel to the frontera. It is less than a kilometer beyond it. You can't miss it. Just keep heading north until you find it. Then walk to the east. It will take you into Flores. Now, let's wait here for a while. It is best to cross over when the moon is behind the clouds."

The men leaned against the truck's fender. The stranger had paid Montenegro with new United States one hundred dollar bills and Montenegro was sure he had more of them. He intended to kill him, but the "illegal" was cautious. He never turned his back to Montenegro. Moreover, the man was armed. More than once,

Montenegro saw the butt of the pistol the man carried in the holster under his arm. Montenegro broke the silence.

"You have a holster and a pistola under your jacket. Do you think that is wise? If the "migrantes" - the American Border Patrol - find you with a weapon, it could mean trouble for you. If they catch an unarmed man, they usually send him back here without making any fuss. But, if you carry a pistola … I don't know."

The well-dressed man was silent. After a few moments, Montenegro continued. "It would be best if you leave the pistola here in Mexico. You can always buy another one in Arizona. They are easy to buy."

Silence.

"I think you should listen to me, my friend, I don't want you to get into trouble when you are in Arizona."

The passenger shifted his weight and unbuttoned his jacket. "I believe I will keep it with me. Would you like to see it?"

"Oh yes. I would very much like to see it."

The passenger removed the Beretta from the holster under his arm and handed it to Montenegro who weighed the weapon in his hand. "This is a very nicely balanced gun, my friend." Then Montenegro quickly pointed the pistol at his companion's head and pulled the trigger.

Instead of an explosion, Montenegro heard the click sound of a firing pin hitting an empty chamber. Then he was spun around and a knife was drawn across his throat. He fell to the ground, the severed pulsing veins of his neck spurting blood onto the desert sands. Soon, he was dead.

The stranger picked up the Beretta, took a clip filled with fourteen 9mm Parabellum rounds from his pocket and slammed it into the weapon's empty handle. He wiped the blood from his knife on Montenegro's shirt and returned it to the sheath beneath his jacket. Without looking back, he walked north into Arizona.

* * * * *

Chico Cisneros sat at the table in the adobe building until the sun had risen. His patrón had not returned. He followed the tire tracks of Montenegro's truck, hoping to discover what had happened to make him so late. When Chico arrived at the scene and saw Montenegro's body, he removed his ring, wristwatch, wallet, shoes and belt. Then he took the shovel from the truck, dug a shallow grave and buried the body.

As he drove back to the adobe building, Chico wondered what he would do. If he stayed at the finca, he would need money for food and gasoline. Perhaps people would continue to come to the finca looking for a coyote. Perhaps they would pay him to be their guide. How much should he charge for taking people to the Arizona border?

Chapter 18

By the time he left New Mexico and crossed into Arizona, Den had reason to believe he had left no scent for his enemies to follow. The preoccupation with the danger threatening him in Washington began to be replaced by a sense of relief. He was safe from any immediate threat of violent death.

Thanks to Ferdie, Den had the protection of false identification papers. The Pennsylvania forgeries gave him a credible new identity. He used it when he bought the Chev pick-up. He would use it for only a few weeks. As soon as he had found the way to completely vanish from any possible Aegis radar screen, he would adopt the one appearing in the Idaho passport and driver's license. In the meantime, he would have time to plan his permanent disappearance. He would have time to plan his new life.

The desire to identify and find the people who were responsible for the attempts on his life had been a secondary preoccupation when he was leaving Washington D. C. Den's feeling of qualified security brought with it an increasingly strong demand he make someone pay for those attempts. Aegis was an organization. He couldn't take the kind of revenge he wanted by attacking a faceless committee. He wanted names.

He wanted to know who said: "Let's send Den Clark to be killed in Guatemala." He wanted the name of the man at Langley who ordered his murder. He wanted to know who shot at him in his North Hancock Street apartment. These were the men who would be the object of his vengeance. So far, Teddy Smith and Jake Jacobson were the only members of Aegis he could identify. Surely, there were others, but who were they?

The word "dislike" didn't begin to describe Den's feelings toward

Jake. "Detest" was more accurate. Jake's involvement in Mick McCarthy's death, his responsibility for Gigi's resignation and his planning of Ocelot were more than sufficient reason for Den's feelings. He carried his contempt for Jacobson as a man might carry a wristwatch. He might not always be fully aware of it but it was always there.

Teddy Smith was a different matter. Den believed him when he said Aegis secretly undertook the extraordinary measures of assassination when necessary for the protection of the country. Teddy wasn't a contemptible, spineless sneak like Jake He was a consummate deceiver and an artful liar. He had succeeded in manipulating Den, using him to kill a bunch of kids - an indefensible act.

Teddy may have conceived Ocelot and Jake may have devised it, but Den didn't think Aegis would let men like Teddy and Jake make the final decisions to execute such plans. There had to be someone else, someone who approved Ocelot and signed his death warrant. That unknown someone ordered the shooting in his Arlington apartment. Den wanted his name.

* * * * *

The building was set back from a well-traveled street bringing traffic into a newish commercial section of Tucson. It was an attractive, but modest sized, one-storey office building. Its lobby opened onto two business suites. One of them was occupied by a realtor and the other by the Law Offices of G. G. Grant.

Gigi had been in Tucson for less than two years. Beginning a profession like the practice of law in a place where an attorney is unknown and has few friends takes courage and, usually, support from an understanding banker. Furniture, a library, office machinery, rent and food all require funding.

G. G. Grant didn't lack courage and she was able to find an understanding banker. After a half-hour's conversation, he recognized Gigi as a smart, dedicated woman who would surely create a successful practice and be able to repay both principal and interest. To further guarantee her success, the banker sent Gigi her first client. It was his secretary. She wanted (and certainly needed) the services of a divorce attorney.

As in most parts of the country, there were plenty of divorces in the Tucson area. Before Gigi secured the divorce decree for the banker's secretary, another client appeared. She was a teller from the same bank. During the ensuing months, Gigi established a good reputation in matters of Domestic Relations.

Family Court Commissioners liked her common-sense approach to property division matters. Guardians Ad-litem liked the way she approached child custody questions. She was competent. She was thorough. She didn't try to fool them and it was very hard for anyone to fool her.

The number of her representations in divorce matters grew steadily. So did the associated work of preparing new wills for recently separated clients and managing their real estate transactions. Gigi was developing a prosperous practice.

In most divorce actions, experienced lawyers usually have a good idea of how the issues commonly involved in domestic disputes will be resolved by judges and Family Court Commissioners. The settlements of property disputes, support payments and child custody questions follow patterns and good lawyers can negotiate realistic agreements - if their clients are amenable to reason. That's a big "if".

Too often, divorces become particularly nasty and difficult for client and attorney alike. Combative parties both insist on trying to tear the skin from their erstwhile partner's behinds. They are capable of engaging in all kinds of psychological warfare. When the stress of managing a difficult divorce action became too burdensome, Gigi Grant would take a time-out.

She'd drive out into the desert and walk, enjoying the peace and beauty of the surroundings, finding occasional footprints of javelina or being surprised by the explosive flight of a covey of Gambel's Quail. Her stress, like morning mist, would slowly disappear.

During these desert interludes, after office problems had faded, Gigi's thoughts usually returned to a less immediate, but still unforgotten disappointment - her experience in the CIA. She remembered how happy she had been when, a year out of law school, she left a Phoenix law firm in favor of a chance to become a CIA intelligence analyst. She had expected so much. She had been so disappointed. She was not prepared for the office politic atmosphere that permeates government agencies. The bureaucracy had strangled her enthusiasm for CIA work.

Of course, Jake Jacobson was a part of her thoughts. Her frown would deepen when his lies and deceits were remembered. That frown would begin to lighten when she remembered how Den Clark had sent him to the hospital. At least a kind of wild justice had been delivered. Then she would think about Den.

She'd remember the fun of their affair. She would wonder where he was. She would wonder what he was doing. After the catharsis of her desert retreats, Gigi would return to Tucson refreshed and ready to again do battle for (and sometimes with) her pugnacious client.

Johnson v Johnson had not been an easy divorce action. From the moment the Summons, Complaint and Order to Show Cause were served, each of the opposing parties became increasingly belligerent. The acrimony was intense and would not subside. Petitioner and Respondent each insisted on unreasonable demands. Compromise was a term neither party was willing to understand. It was a long and strenuous battle.

Johnson v Johnson got very nasty. Gigi finally told her client if she wanted to fight so badly she should remain married. It didn't do any good. The bitter, malicious and spiteful confrontations raged on and on. After endless Orders to Show Cause and hostile, but pointless battles, a Final Hearing ended late one afternoon and a Divorce Decree was issued. Johnson v Johnson was over.

A burden had been lifted from her shoulders. Gigi felt like a slave who had been liberated. She returned to her office, ready to give the good news to Charlotte.

Charlotte Novitski and Gigi Grant were a good secretary/lawyer team. They understood each other. They liked each other. They shared the same slightly off-beat sense of humor. They even shared the same general physique. When Charlotte went to the courthouse to file documents, she was occasionally mistaken for Gigi. Charlotte was secretly pleased by the mistake even though she was sure it was based mostly on the fact that both were honey blondes.

Charlotte called Gigi "Boss" and when the Boss agonized, she agonized. Charlotte hoped Johnson v Johnson was finished. It had been the cause of a lot of unnecessary trouble - like the time things looked like they were returning to an even keel and then the Respondent brought his girl friend to sit in on a Hearing. It produced the explosion he had maliciously planned.

After what Charlotte earnestly hoped would be the final Final Hearing in Johnson v Johnson, Gigi came back to the office, looking very tired. Charlotte asked: "Is it over, Boss?" Gigi smiled an exhausted, faint smile and nodded.

Charlotte smiled. She, too, was relieved. "I'll bet it's time for some desert R and R."

"Your crystal ball is working well. I need a couple days off. Any appointments for tomorrow or Friday?"

If there were none, Gigi would be free for Thursday, Friday, Saturday and Sunday. She'd have plenty of time to relax in the desert as well as time to attend to the cleaning, the shopping and the rest of her regular domestic weekend jobs.

Charlotte picked up the two files already lying on her desk and followed Gigi into her office. The diplomas and certificates hanging on the wall proved the Boss belonged to a number of professional associations, received a Doctorate in Law from the University of Arizona, was admitted to the Arizona Bar and authorized to practice before both Arizona and Federal Courts.

Those official looking framed documents were hung behind Gigi's desk in order to impress the clients who had to face them when they sat before her. The pictures hanging on the other three walls were the ones Gigi could see when she was seated at her desk. They were landscapes and peaceful desert and mountain scenes.

Charlotte put the calendar and the two files on Gigi's desk. "Friday is clear," she said. "You have two appointments for tomorrow. One is at ten and another at three." Gigi looked at the folders Charlotte had prepared. The lady scheduled for the three o'clock appointment was a new client. It was another divorce action and Charlotte, with her usual efficiency, had completed the preliminary interview report form.

The new client had been married for over twenty-five years. There were no minor children. The lady denied any suggestion of domestic violence or alcoholism. "This one can be postponed," Gigi said. "She may have made up with him already. If not, a few more days shouldn't make any difference." She looked up at Charlotte. "Would you call her and re-schedule? And make her promise not to kill him before Monday."

Gigi didn't waste time with people who wouldn't give the reason for wanting to meet with her. The last such appointment Gigi allowed herself to schedule insisted on absolute secrecy and then whispered that the Governor and the Sheriff were conspiring to have him kidnapped by aliens from outer space.

Charlotte's file notes concerning the ten o'clock appointment were brief. The man wouldn't divulge the reason for making the appointment. As Charlotte had suspected, Gigi wouldn't meet with him. "Would you call this one and tell him I've been called out of town, unexpectedly, and may not be back until the end of the millennium?"

"Sorry, Boss. No can do. He gave no address and no phone number. He didn't even give me his name. All he said was he wanted to talk about Jake, whatever that means."

"*My God*," Gigi thought. "*It's Den!*" She looked down at the nearly blank folder and made one of the easiest decisions of her life. "O.K." she said. "I'll take the ten o'clock. It might be interesting."

Charlotte gave her a quizzical look. She knew Gigi didn't talk with clients until she knew the subject matter of the interview. Why would she bother to take this one? Something was up. All the signs were there. Gigi avoided looking at her. She acted a bit too casual. Charlotte's suspicions were confirmed when Gigi, recognizing her secretary's obvious skepticism, said: "Just do it."

Gigi knew it had to be Den. He had to be in Tucson. She could understand why he left his cryptic message. If he were on an assignment, he couldn't announce his name or location to anyone. Did he want to talk about Jake? Of course not. She knew Den wanted to see her. Gigi relaxed in her chair and forgot about Johnson v Johnson.

Chapter 19

In the 1960s, the army created the Green Berets and the navy began to train SEA/AIR/LAND units. They became known by their acronym, SEAL, and were a result of President Kennedy's repeated interest in establishing a military strike force trained to rapidly response to dangerous threats and capable of operating as a specialized unit to enter the enemy's territory and strike suddenly and effectively at designated targets. Both SEAL and Green Beret forces often proved their value.

The intelligence community needed the capability to quickly collect information and analyze the degree of danger present in changing conditions in various parts of the world. Stale intelligence can paralyze analysis. Unlike the army's Green Beret and the navy's SEAL programs, it took decades for the CIA to establish the Sherman Kent School for Intelligence Analysis. The school was created for the purpose of training CIA people to produce more accurate and complete intelligence services.

* * * * *

When Gigi Grant became a part of the CIA, she was sent to the Kent school for its 22 week Career Analyst Training Program. At the same time, Den Clark, fully recovered from his Gulf War wounds, came to study there. During his first indoctrination meeting with the others who would receive the training, Den Clark heard Gigi Grant laugh. He turned, saw her smile and was attracted to her.

The following morning he saw her again. She had taken juice and coffee and toast from the cafeteria's selection. She moved to an uncrowded part of the room and transferred her breakfast from tray to table. As she sat, she heard a man say: "You're G. G. Grant." She turned and saw Den standing behind her. He held a tray of food. Before she could say anything, he placed his tray on the table, began to sit and asked if he could join her. She said "yes". She didn't really have an alternative. That was how it began.

Gigi's first impression of Den Clark was not favorable. She had been hit on too many times not to be wary of men who sought her out. This one's obvious self-assurance made her cautious. *Watch out!*, she told herself. She suspected Den was one of those "Hello, thank you, good-bye." types.

"I'm Den Clark," he said. "I'm here for Kent, too. I saw you yesterday afternoon at the indoctrination meeting."

Gigi acknowledged her name, nothing more. Den recognized her reticence and told her she was safe - he didn't bite. By the time they finished their light breakfasts, Gigi felt more comfortable with him and Den had confirmed his suspicion. She was someone he wanted to know much better.

During the first five weeks of the Analyst Program, Den and Gigi spent free time together. They attended National Symphony programs and enjoyed dinners together. They visited the Smithsonian, the National Gallery and various monuments sprinkled around Washington. Conversation became easier and more personal.

Den told Gigi of his early years in Bogotá, his service in SEALS and his hope and expectation to move from the Directorate of Intelligence into the Directorate of Operations. He wanted to be a covert operator in Latin America. His experience as a SEAL and his ability to fluently speak Spanish, when supplemented by the CIA's Career Analyst Program, gave him what he thought were superior qualifications for the work he wanted.

Gigi, obviously, was smart and well educated. Den was not surprised to learn she had been a practicing attorney before deciding to settle in Washington D. C. and pursue a career in the CIA. Den was surprised when she told him her undergraduate Major was archeology.

"By the time I left high school, I was sure I wanted to practice law," she told him one evening when they were relaxing in a dark and intimate bistro. "I took all kinds of English courses at the University.

Communication - written and spoken - is very important to a lawyer. But Archeology interested me and that was my Major. It's a strange parlay - law and archeology. I may have become the only lawyer in the country specializing in representing Egyptologists and mummies.

"If you were good enough as an undergrad, you might be asked to take part in an off-shore dig." She smiled when she added: "I was good enough," and she told him how she spent a summer in Iraq, collecting and classifying shards.

Gigi also reported her disappointment after being hired by a large Phoenix law firm. "It was like working in a factory - not my cup of tea. I thought about starting a private practice. However, the CIA interested me, too. So, here I am."

Neither Gigi nor Den spoke about another subject, but they both thought about it. They knew there was no future between them. Neither would voluntarily change their goals. A woman working as a CIA Analyst in Langley and a man assigned to covert projects in foreign stations had no business thinking about permanent arrangements. They were both sure their stars moved in different orbits. They avoided intimacy.

The second four-week portion of their training consisted of interim assignments. Because of his SEAL background, Den was sent to the Navy's Pacific Command Headquarters in Hawaii. It was part of the Kent School program designed to give CIA personnel experience in coordinating with military commands. Gigi was sent to the Amman Station in Jordan, probably because someone noticed she had experience with Arab cultures.

When that four-week period ended and they returned to Washington, their attitudes about their personal relationship changed. They missed each other. Though they knew they could have only a temporary relationship, they rushed to it. The first night of their return to Washington was spent exchanging that most intimate of gifts men and women can exchange.

Gigi and Den lived together for the time they remained in Virginia. When their Kent School program concluded, they parted. Gigi's first assignment took her to the Damascus Station. Den was assigned to Langley

Now, when sitting alone in her Tucson law office, Gigi would smile, remembering how their affair started and the passion and fun of its too short a life. She thought of the way it ended. There was nothing that could cast a shadow over her memories. No recriminations. No sorrow. No unfulfilled expectations. They held each other. They kissed. They said their "goodbyes". They went their separate ways, but they had forged a bond that neither then recognized.

Gigi recalled their last brief meeting in the Sheraton in D.C. It happened under the most trying of circumstance. Den had softened her disappointments and supported her when she most needed it. The warm renewal of their intimacies proved their shared feelings. She knew she was not alone.

* * * * *

The morning after the Final Hearing in the matter of Johnson v Johnson, a beep-beep-beep sound roused Gigi into semi-consciousness. Her arm appeared from beneath the sheet, found its way to the nightstand and silenced the alarm clock. For a few moments she struggled with a comforting thought. She could go back to sleep without seriously disturbing the movement of the planets through their celestial orbits. Life on earth would continue if she stayed in bed.

Her conscience won the battle. "Time to get up," it ordered. Gigi fumbled her way to the apartment's kitchen and turned on the coffee maker. Every evening before retiring, she readied the machine for morning use. She didn't want to have to measure coffee and pour water in the morning while still half asleep. She put half an English muffin in the toaster. When she had showered, dressed and returned for breakfast, she was fully conscious, the coffee was ready and the half muffin was still warmish. With the first cup of coffee, another day officially began.

One more housekeeping ritual to perform and she would be ready for the fifteen-minute drive to the office. She checked the cat's litter box. It was in a good-enough condition. She took what remained of a can of Friskies from the refrig, put it in the cat's dish, and filled the water bowl. Catastrophe had spent the night prowling the neighborhood. It was waiting, hungry and ready for breakfast, when Gigi opened the kitchen door.

Catastrophe looked up at her. Not wishing to appear to be too eager, it licked its paw, wiped at its whiskers a few times and then slowly walked into the kitchen, sniffed at the food, indicated it was marginally acceptable and began to eat. The cat chore accomplished, Gigi drove to work and to her anticipated reunion with Den Clark.

Charlotte suspected Gigi and the man with the ten o'clock appointment knew each other. That was the only explanation for the Boss meeting with him without knowing why he wanted to talk with her. When Den entered the Law Office waiting room, Charlotte could hardly contain her curiosity. That curiosity, however, went unsatisfied. Her requests for information - name, phone number, address - "for our client files" - were answered with a smile and a request - "Please tell Ms Grant her ten o'clock is here."

Gigi was standing behind her desk when Den came into her office. She didn't really know how to behave. She wanted to put her arms around him, but hesitated. Maybe he didn't share her wish. She knew she shouldn't just sit there and treat him with the impersonality that attended appointments with clients. Den's actions settled the matter. He came around the desk and hugged her. He didn't kiss her, but it was certainly more than a mere friendly embrace.

"It's so good to see you, Den. I've missed you. Where are you staying? How long will you be in town? What's happening in your life?"

Gigi knew Den. She could read the subtle nuances in the tone of voice and the postures of his body language. She recognized a tiny tentative quality in his conversation. At first she thought it was a sign of Den asking the same question she asked herself. Did the other one still harbor the same feelings they once shared when they attended the Kent school?

There was something else, too. Den avoided any reference to his work at the Central Intelligence Agency. It seemed odd. Even if he was on a sensitive assignment, it would be entirely natural for him to tell her, in general terms, of Agency gossip. Something seemed to be out of kilter. Gigi couldn't have guessed just how far "out of kilter".

Den had decided to tell Gigi everything about his association with Aegis. It would not be an easy conversation for him. He knew he loved her. He hoped she would understand he loved her. He hoped he would not destroy her love for him. He feared she might believe he had become little more than a cold blooded assassin. He knew he had to tell her this would be their last meeting. He intended to disappear and never return.

Den told her about his first meeting with Teddy Smith and his recruitment into the organization hidden within the Agency. Though he knew the assassinations were illegal and unapproved by the Agency, he believed Aegis was engaged in removing threats to his country. He was convinced it was work that had to be done.

After Teddy Smith arranged his transfer to the Clandestine Service, he expected to be sent to some station in Latin America where he would do the work of a covert operative. He expected to be occasionally contacted by the men who called themselves Aegis and asked to undertake an assassination project. Then he described how his work with Aegis was a journey to disillusion, anger and frustration. He told her how Aegis misled and used him.

Den had not expected to receive three Aegis assignments in rapid succession. Those three missions, he told her, offering only minimal protection of national interests. Gigi sat behind her desk, quietly listening as Den disclosed his assassinations. Gigi agreed Humberto del Valle was some kind of a monster. She also agreed he was no serious threat to the United States. Joselito Montoya's Bolivian cocaine cartel was an obscenity. It might be argued that drug trafficking represented some kind of a menace to the country, she conceded, but still...

Den reported how his confidence in the value of Aegis was strengthened when his mission to Guatemala was explained. He couldn't look at Gigi when he told her of his part in the killing of the students. He told her everything that happened. The Guatemalan Colonel's death squad attempts to kill him, Teddy's lies, Ferdie's proof that Operation Ocelot was meant to end in his death and finally, how he escaped from Washington.

Den berated himself for agreeing to work with Teddy Smith, for not suspecting the dark side of Aegis and for becoming nothing more than a murderer.

Gigi tried to soften the charges he made against himself. She told him there was no way he could have guessed the true Aegis agenda. Den only looked away and shook his head. He was unwilling to absolve himself from his responsibility in the murders on that rural Guatemalan road. He took a deep breath to compose himself before continuing.

Den was capable of exposing Aegis and Aegis could not run the risk of exposure. The people inside the conspiracy were well aware of the danger he presented. They would do everything possible to eliminate that danger. Den explained why he felt he had to remain silent. He finished his story by saying he needed a secure place to hide. He needed a few weeks to find a way to disappear so completely that Aegis could never find him. He told her he wanted her to know everything about Aegis "just in case".

Gigi remembered the way the report of her investigation into the death of Mick McCarthy had been re-written. She was only momentarily surprised by the existence of a hidden cell within the CIA. She might have anticipated Jake Jacobson being a part of the conspiracy. Gigi didn't question anything Den told her, but she caught her breath when she heard the words "just in case".

Gigi knew what Den meant. In spite of his efforts to disappear, Den understood he might be killed. Gigi didn't hesitate. She told him she would help in any way she could. After a moment's silence, Den reached over the desk and took her hand. He needed help, but he didn't want to expose her to any danger.

"Think long and hard before helping me, hon," he told her. "If Aegis thinks they can keep their secrets by killing both of us, they will do it in a minute. You've got to know that. It's a fact. I don't want anything to happen to you."

Gigi needed no time to reconsider. She knew what she wanted to do. Slowly, emphasizing each word, she said: "You need me, Den, and I need you. That's all there is to it."

Den and Gigi left her office together. She didn't introduce him to Charlotte. It was not an oversight. It was intentional. It would be best if no one knew Den was in Arizona.

In the parking lot, Den pointed to his second-hand pick-up truck. He told her Aegis might never learn he and Ernest Adams, the name appearing on the Pennsylvania Registration Certificate, were one and the same person. If they did, they would still have to find the truck and then find him. Gigi paid little attention to his words. She had a more important thought in mind.

"I know just the place for your stay in Arizona," she said. She got into Den's truck and showed him the way to McCord Court, a cul-de-sac in one of Tucson's residential districts. "Next apartment building. Go up the far driveway. Stop at the side door." Den did as directed. When he stopped, Gigi leaned across the seat, kissed him lightly on the cheek and said: "This is where I live."

Den followed Gigi into her first floor apartment. Passing through the kitchen and living area, he saw an open doorway leading from the living room. It opened into Gigi's bedroom. Without saying a word, Den entered it and put his luggage on the floor. Then he turned. Gigi was next to him. He kissed her.

It was the long sensuous kind of kiss they had enjoyed when they lived together during their Kent School training. Den moved his hands down her back until they cupped her buns. He pulled her close to him. She pressed her body tightly against him. Den moved slightly to the side. He gently took her left hand from his neck and moved it down below his belt. He moved his hand to her breast. His fingers remembered them. Their lips separated and, gently moving their hands, they looked at each other, smiling.

They unbuttoned blouse and shirt. Gigi raised her chin while Den kissed her throat and loosened her brassier. Then his lips moved down her throat, pausing at both pink areolas and now erect nipples. Gigi unclasped Den's belt before she sat on the bed, leaned back and encouraged him to kiss her stomach. She kicked off her shoes and Den pulled her slacks and panties down past her knees and onto the floor.

Den removed his remaining clothing and kissed her again, first on her stomach and then lower. They stayed in bed until after five in the afternoon. They were hungry. They would dress and go out for dinner.

Chapter 20

While Den and Gigi were driving to her apartment on McCord Court, Jake Jacobson sat in his Tucson motel room, watching morning television and waiting for Abdul's phone call announcing his presence in Arizona. He was becoming increasingly nervous.

Abdul was a cold fish. He seemed to have no readable body language. Jake never knew what thoughts were stirring behind his dark, unsmiling eyes. Jake's old concerns ran through his mind. Abdul's promises were worthless. Jake didn't know if he was on his way to Tucson or on his way to Damascus.

Jake reviewed a possible timetable. If Abdul had immediately left Monterrey for Nogales, he could have met with Montenegro, crossed the border and gotten into Flores sometime after sundown. He could have picked up the automobile at the garage sometime after midnight, perhaps by two, or three, or maybe four o'clock in the morning. It would take less than two hours to drive from Flores to Tucson. He could have been in town by six in the morning. Why hadn't he called?

Jake calmed himself by giving reasons why Abdul would be delayed. Perhaps it took more time to get to Nogales. Perhaps he had trouble finding the coyote. Perhaps Montenegro wasted a day before bringing him to the border. Perhaps it took more time for Abdul to get to the garage in Flores. Maybe the Border Patrol caught him. There was another possibility haunting Jake. It was the specter of a smiling Abdul flying back to Syria with a lot of CIA money tucked into his carry-on.

Shoes off, but otherwise fully dressed, Jake slumped in the chair beside the motel room table. The mid-morning Arizona sunlight shined through the window. He was nodding off when the phone rang. Jake turned off the television and picked up the phone, hoping it wasn't Teddy. It was Abdul.

"I'm here," he said and then hung up. Jake was relieved. Abdul had not jumped ship. Again, the fears that badgered him disappeared instantly. He told himself he had no cause for concern. Abdul was in Tucson and ready to kill Gigi Grant.

*   *   *   *   *

Abdul looked upon his first assassination assignment as an easy proposition. *"This is a CIA test of my abilities?"* he asked himself. *"It's not a test. It's child's play."* The project contained no foreseeable complications. Ex-agent Gigi Grant had no bodyguards or other special protections. She was unaware of the plan to kill her. He could walk up to her. There was no way she could identify him as a dangerous adversary. There would be no problem in killing her. *"Fifteen thousand dollars for this? I don't believe it."*

Abdul's plan was simple. He would go to the woman's law office and wait until she was alone. Then he would shoot her. He'd meet with Jacobson and collect the balance of his bounty. He didn't know what to do with the automobile. He'd return it to Flores or leave it somewhere in the desert unless Jacobson gave him different directions. He could be back in Mexico before the next sunrise.

After the brief call to Jacobson, Abdul checked the telephone directory for the address of the G. G. Grant Law Office. He looked at the note Jake had given him. It was the same address. He found the directory's city map and located the office. It was after eleven o'clock when Abdul drove his automobile onto the office building's black-topped parking area. Gigi and Den had driven from the lot in his second-hand Chevrolet pick-up only minutes before Abdul's arrival.

Abdul found Gigi's black Cherokee and compared the number on its license plate with the one Jacobson had provided. *"Her Jeep is here,"* he thought. *"Soon it will be the time when the Americans take their noon meal."* Abdul parked next to the Jeep. He was careful to straddle the painted line dividing the two spaces to the left of Gigi's Cherokee. It would keep anyone from parking between him and the Jeep and, at the same time would put about six feet between him and the driver's side door of the Cherokee.

When the woman came out for lunch, she would walk to the driver's side of her automobile. Abdul would point his weapon through his rolled down window and kill her. He wouldn't have to leave his car. He repeated the description Jacobson had given. The Grant woman was 5 feet 8 inches tall. She usually wore a business suit and no hat. She had light brown, almost blonde hair and weighed a hundred and twenty-five pounds.

Abdul watched the few people who entered and left the building. He saw no one closely matching Grant's description and no one approached the lawyer's Jeep. Abdul waited until a half hour after mid-day. Finally he concluded the woman would not leave for lunch. She must be eating in her office.

Abdul checked the magazine in his Beretta. He pulled back the slide, let it snap forward and a bullet entered the chamber. Then he returned the weapon to its under-arm holster and walked to the entrance of the office building. The lobby was empty. Abdul was alone. He went to the door with the identifying sign: Law Offices of G. G. Grant. He turned the doorknob. It was locked. He knocked at the door. No answer. He knocked again. No answer. He knocked once more.

* * * * *

After Gigi left the office with her ten o'clock appointment without bothering to introduce him or tell her where she was going or when she'd return, Charlotte Novitski was sure the two were old friends. She was equally sure they had been lovers. That made her smile. Her speculations ended when she remembered she had some work to do.

She typed out the few letters and status reports that had accumulated. She reviewed the monthly billings, noting the ones needing attention. She made a list of the dates and times and places and subjects of Gigi's upcoming court appearances. It was twelve o'clock when she was satisfied she was up-to-date with her work.

Charlotte locked the waiting room door, returned to her desk and unwrapped her lunch - a chicken salad sandwich, an apple, a diet soft drink and a homemade brownie. She finished her meal and was reading the novel she kept in her desk drawer when she heard the office door handle turn. It was followed by a knock.

"*Damn,*" she thought, "*If I'm quiet, maybe it will go away.*" A second knock followed. Then a third. "*Damn,*" she thought again and went to the door.

* * * * *

After his third knocking at the door, Abdul hear the sounds of someone approaching from the inner office. He heard the lock click and saw the doorknob turn. The door opened and a honey blonde fitting G. G. Grant's description informed him: "We are closed until one o'clock and are taking no more appointments until Monday. If you will call on …" Charlotte never finished the sentence. She hardly had time to see the man, standing only a few feet in front of her, was holding a gun.

Charlotte was killed instantly. The force of impact of the bullet knocked her over backwards. She fell into the office. Abdul closed the door, turned and calmly walked out of the building. He got into his automobile and drove until he found a McDonald's. A hamburger, French fries and a malted milk were a tasty lunch. He could get used to American cooking.

After finishing his meal, instead of calling Jacobson, Abdul went to the place where the restaurant's telephone directory was chained to the wall. He opened the yellow pages to the motel section and matched the number Jake had given him in Monterrey with that of a Tucson motel. He wrote down the address of the Sahuaro Inn and found its location in the directory's map.

Jake answered the knock on his motel door. He did not expect to find Abdul standing before him. Abdul said nothing. He walked past Jake, pulled the chair from the room's table and sat. He let Jake start the conversation. Did he have any trouble finding Montenegro? No. Was the border crossing easy? Yes.

Abdul's monosyllabic answers were somewhat irritating. Jake wanted information, but all he got were "yeses" and "noes" - no explanations, no embellishments, nothing else. He stopped asking questions and began to suggest how Abdul might approach Gigi Grant. Abdul held up his hand, palm outward, like a parent silencing a talkative child. "It is taken care of," he said. When Jake showed his surprise, Abdul smiled the smile of satisfaction. He had impressed Jacobson.

"You're sure she is dead?

"Of course."

"You're sure it was Grant?"

"Of course. Her Jeep was in her office parking lot. She fit your description. I killed her. Now, let's talk about another more important matter."

"And what might that be?"

"Money."

"Oh. The money. Of course. It will be sent to the Nuevo Mundo. I think you can expect it in four or five days."

Abdul opened the single button in the front of his jacket and leaned forward in his chair. The shoulder holster and the butt of his Beretta were visible. As was intended, Jake saw them.

"Ah, I see," Abdul said. "Now I understand. You want me to trust you. I should go back to Monterrey and sit patiently in that mildewed room in that decomposing hotel and wait for you to send my money." His sarcasm was pointed.

Jake met sarcasm with sarcasm. "Ah. I see," he mimicked. "Now I understand. You want me to trust you. You want me to take your word that Gigi Grant is dead. I shouldn't be allowed to confirm her death. I should pay for services without knowing whether or not they have been properly rendered."

Stalemate.

Abdul thought for a moment. Then he nodded, leaned back and re-buttoned his jacket. "Why don't we stay here and enjoy each other's company until the television reports of the evening news?"

* * * * *

Jake lay on the motel room bed. Propped up by pillows, he leaned against the headboard. A towel, draped over his chest, was meant to catch the dripping from the wedge of pizza he held in his hand. A half empty can of beer rested on the night stand beside him. Abdul was eating his second slice of the delivered pizza. He sat at the motel table sharing its surface with a glass of milk and the flat, opened carton that contained the uneaten balance of their pizza order.

At six o'clock, the KXTC news program appeared on the TV screen. The newscaster, trying his best to reproduce the sound and cadence of the voice of Ted Koppel, reported the international disasters and then turned to the local news. The death of Gigi's secretary was the lead story.

"Murder, most foul, has again visited Tucson. Charlotte Novitski, a secretary in the G. G. Grant law firm, was shot to death sometime this afternoon. Her body was found minutes ago by Darlene Hacker. Now let me take you directly to the scene of the crime where Sandy is waiting with an exclusive interview with Miss Hacker - live."

Then the announcer grinned broadly, obviously pleased with his station's technical ability. His fixed smile remained on the screen for a few seconds more. Then he said: "live" again and, finally, the connection was made.

"This is Sandy Wilson, your on-the-spot television reporter. I'm at the Grant Law Office building - the scene of the grisly murder that occurred sometime this afternoon." She moved to the side and shared the screen with an older woman.

"With me is Miss Darlene Hacker. She's the secretary of the Real Estate Office right next door to where Charlotte Novitski was brutally shot and killed." Sandy Wilson shoved the microphone in Miss Hacker's face, "Tell us, in your own words, what happened."

Miss Hacker wasn't prepared for what she originally thought might be a microphone blow to her nose. Her eyes widened and she stepped back half a pace. Regaining her composure, she spoke.

"Well, I was eating my lunch and I heard a loud noise from out here in the lobby. I came out and looked around, but nobody was here. Then, after work when I left for home, I saw something dark on the floor next to the law office door. It was blood. I opened the door and there was Charlotte, lying there on the floor. She was dead. I yelled and then called the cops. They told me I had to wait here. I want to go home."

Then the reporter asked her: "How did you feel when you saw all that blood and gore?"

Jake switched off the television set. He turned to a silent Abdul. "Are you sure she's dead?" he asked, sarcastically repeating the question he asked Abdul earlier in the afternoon. "Of course," he said, repeating the answer Abdul had given. "Are you sure it was Grant?" he asked in the same acidic tone. "Of course," he said, again repeating Abdul's answer. He walked to where Abdul was seated. He put both hands on the table, leaned toward him and said: "Abdul, we have a problem."

Chapter 21

As he drove from the Sahuaro Inn to Gigi's apartment, an agitated Abdul muttered to himself. She was the same size. She had the same color hair. Her car was in the parking lot. How was he to know it wasn't her? If Jacobson had given him a photograph there would have been no problem. It wasn't his fault. It was Jacobson's fault. His sloppy work meant the inconvenience of a twenty-four hour delay before his return to Monterrey.

Shortly after six-thirty, Abdul turned from Central Boulevard and entered McCord Court. Driving slowly, he found the street number of Gigi's apartment building. He continued on to the end of the cul-de-sac. Turning around, he headed back toward Central Boulevard. He parked close to Gigi's apartment building and remained in the car for a few minutes while he studied his surroundings.

He noticed there was neither pedestrian nor automobile traffic on McCord Court. He saw only residences and smaller apartment buildings. Except for the sounds of the automobiles on Central Boulevard, it was a quiet neighborhood. He left the car, turning up the collar of his jacket to obscure his face, and walked to the building with the address Jacobson had given him.

When he got to the driveway, instead of a black Jeep, an older pick-up truck was parked there. Abdul paused for a moment, questioning if he was at the right building. He took Jacobson's note from his pocket and confirmed the address. The number on the front door was the same as the number he had been given. This had to be the place.

Listening for signs of activity, he heard only muffled sounds coming from an open window in Gigi's kitchen. Abdul took the Beretta from under his jacket and walked down the driveway to the side door that led into the kitchen. If the door was locked he would break it down. He'd enter the room, shoot her and be done with it. Before he could get to the door, he heard the sound of it being opened.

A landscaper had planted ornamental evergreens next to the ground floor doorways of each of the rental units. Abdul slid behind the one that grew near Gigi's kitchen door. Holding the pistol next to his body, he flattened himself against the side of the building. This would be easy. The Grant woman would come out. He would shoot her. He'd walk back to the automobile and return to Jacobson's motel. The whole thing would take less than an hour.

Abdul was in for another disappointment. The kitchen's inner door opened. Through the still closed screen door, he caught a glimpse of a man, in stocking feet and unbuttoned shirt. He was carrying a shorthaired yellow cat. The cat stoically hung down from the man's right hand. It was willing to put up with this kind of insolent treatment because it was aware of the bowl of cat food in the man's other hand. The man pushed the screen door open with his left elbow. He put the bowl on the door stoop and dropped the cat, saying, "Out you go Catastrophe. Here's your dinner."

Abdul, not eight feet from him, held his breath. This couldn't be the right place. The woman he intended to kill wasn't married. Jacobson said she lived alone. The presence of the man and an older truck in the driveway instead of a newer Jeep meant only one thing. Jacobson was an incompetent. He had given him the wrong address.

If the man with the cat saw him, he would be able to identify him. Abdul would not let that happen. He hoped the man would turn away from him rather than toward him when he returned into the house. Abdul did not want to announce his presence with a gunshot, but it might be necessary. Noiselessly, he raised the Beretta and prepared to use it. He froze when he heard another voice coming from the interior of the apartment. "Den. Come, zip me up."

The man went back into the house without noticing him. When the inner door shut, Abdul exhaled, replaced his Beretta and, unseen, quickly returned to his car. He clenched his teeth in anger and wondered how could such a simple matter as the killing of an unarmed and unsuspecting woman get so complicated? It could have been so easy if Jacobson had given him a picture of the woman. It could have been so easy if he had given him the right address.

* * * * *

Den went back into the kitchen. He closed the door and for only a moment thought it was strange that the cat ran away from him rather than staying to eat the food he set out for it. Catastrophe was well aware of Abdul's presence behind the ornamental fir. Den was not.

After placing a kiss on the back of Gigi's neck, Den zipped up her dress. He assigned no significance to the sound of the car carrying a very angry Palestinian back to the Sahuaro Inn where he intended to berate Jake Jacobson for his stupidity.

Ten minutes later, Den and Gigi were ready to leave for dinner. Den saw a police car being parked in front of the apartment building. He watched as a uniformed patrolman and a man in plain clothes walked toward Gigi's front door. Then he heard the knock. He held his finger against his lips, warning Gigi to be careful and stepped into the bedroom, partially closing the door behind him.

"Why would the police come here?" he wondered. *"Could they be doing the work of Aegis? Could Aegis have already traced him to Tucson and to Gigi?"* It didn't seem probable, but it was possible. He took the revolver from his suitcase and returned to the door where he could listen to what was being said.

Den heard Gigi gasp when the detective told her Charlotte Novitski had been murdered at the Grant Law Office. Immediately, questions raced through Den's mind with lightning speed. *"Was it Aegis? Could Gigi be in danger? If it was Aegis, why would they kill Gigi's secretary?"* And then the alarm sounded. *"They will search the apartment. I've got to get out of here. Now!"*

In the living room, Gigi prepared herself for questioning. The detective, she guessed, had already studied the office appointment book. He knew Charlotte's scheduling for the day. Her story couldn't contradict it, but she had to be careful to keep Den completely out of the case. She decided to give long answers to the questions. She hoped it would give Den time to get out of the apartment before the detective began the search she was sure would be requested.

After a few preliminary questions, the detective asked Gigi to recount her activities and movements during the day. Gigi described her previous afternoon's return to her law office after the Final Hearing in Johnson v Johnson and her decision to take time off to recuperate. She took her time. She reported the two appointments Charlotte had made for that day and explained why one of them could not be postponed.

"This morning, I went to the office and waited for the ten o'clock appointment," she said. "The man never showed up. I waited until about eleven o'clock, maybe a bit later, and then came home. I've been here ever since."

By this time, Den had smoothed the bed, erasing any sign that two people had used it. He fluffed one of the pillows and put it in the closet. He took his toothbrush and shaving gear from the bathroom and stuffed them inside his suitcase. Satisfied that he had removed all traces of his presence, he quietly opened the window. Taking his luggage with him, he slipped out the building and into its narrow back yard.

* * * * *

Abdul was fuming by the time he entered the Sahuaro Inn parking lot. He jerked open the door to Jake's room, entered and the slammed it shut. Jake was at the mini bar, an opened can of beer in his hand. Abdul slammed the door with such force that Jake jumped and spilled some of the beer.

Before the echo died down, Abdul was engaged in his verbal assault, berating Jake for his incompetence, for being unable to give him a picture of his target and for purposely planning to expose him to capture by sending him to kill at the wrong address.

Jake calmed him and, after hearing his story, picked up the telephone directory. He turned to the Gs and, tapping his finger on the address of G. G. Grant, he showed it to Abdul. In contrast to the Jordanian's loud language, Jake spoke in subdued tones. "You are probably an expert in finding an oasis in the middle of some vast uncharted desert. How can you miss something as obvious as a street address in Tucson? Even a Jordanian imbecile should be able to do it."

Abdul became defensive. "I went to that address. I checked it twice. She must have moved. A man named "Ten" and a woman live there now. I should have guessed it when I saw an old truck in the driveway."

Jake began to show his exasperation. "Did it ever occur to that pile of Arab camel shit you call a brain that she might have been shacking up with some…" He stopped abruptly. "What did you say the man's name was?"

"Ten. She called him Ten."

"No," Jake thought. *"It wasn't 'Ten'. It was 'Den'. Den Clark is with her. I've found him. I've found the son of a bitch. This time he won't get away. This time, he's a dead man."* Jake hid his reaction to discovering the presence of the man whose existence tormented him. Now Abdul would kill Den Clark.

Aloud and in a calm voice, he explained: "I was the one who recommended you to some of the Agency's most important people. I said you were an experienced and reliable man. Was I wrong, Abdul? You have had two chances to perform and you have failed on both occasions.

"Now, matters have become muddled. You've screwed up twice. I'm going to give you your third and final chance. I'll settle for nothing less than the dead bodies of both Grant and the man called Ten. I expect you will kill them both very, very soon."

Abdul reservations about becoming a tool of the CIA had already slipped away. Now he saw the opportunity of easy CIA money slipping away. This man, Jacobson, had to be convinced he was a capable assassin. He had to be shown. Abdul would show him. Before the evening was over, Abdul intended to prove his ruthless efficiency beyond all doubt.

He arose from his chair, patted the Beretta in his shoulder holster and nodded. "I will do it. We will both go back to the woman's apartment. You will drive the automobile. When we get there, I will kill the woman and I will kill her lover. You will watch and see with your own eyes what I can do."

Abdul marched out of the motel room. A very unhappy Jake Jacobson followed him without comment. Jake did not want to be a witness to Abdul's murders. Planning assassinations was one thing. Being in the same room and watching a man like Abdul kill was quite another. Jake saw only one advantage to being present when Abdul killed. He would be sure Den Clark would see him before Abdul killed him. Den Clark would see him and understand the man he sent to the hospital was exacting his revenge.

Jake got behind the wheel and Abdul sat beside him. Neither spoke a word. When they left Central Boulevard and turned onto McCord Court, they saw another vehicle parked in front of Gigi's apartment. It was a police car.

Jake drove past the building. Through the apartment's bay window, he could see a uniformed cop and another man, probably a plain-clothesman. They were talking with Gigi. Both Jake and Abdul knew they were questioning her about the murder of her secretary.

The presence of the police was enough to scare Jake. He wanted to go back to the Sahuaro Inn. Abdul would have none of it. He had enough of delays. What should have been a simple killing had gotten out of hand. Jake had challenged him to perform and Abdul intended to meet the challenge.

Abdul insisted they wait at the scene and finish the work. If it meant killing more than two, he would do it. The presence of the police didn't bother him. He'd killed Israeli police and if American police got in his way, he'd kill them, too.

Abdul ordered Jake to drive past the apartment to the end of the cul-de-sac. He told Jake to turn the car around and park it facing Central Boulevard. If it became necessary to leave in a hurry, Abdul didn't want to be caught traveling in the wrong direction on a dead end street. From where they parked, Abdul had a good view of the front of Gigi's apartment.

"If the police leave without them," Abdul said, "we will walk into the house and you will see what I can do. If it looks like the woman and the man are going to enter the police car, you will pull in front of it before they can start. Block them off as fast as you can. Don't worry about witnesses. I will kill them all."

Jake caught his breath. This was not what he expected. He was in over his head and he knew it. He hoped the police would leave Den and Gigi in the apartment. The thought of cutting off the police car frightened him. The possibility of being that close to a firefight was unthinkable. Abdul showed no signs of stress. He was relaxed. He leaned back against the front seat, wiggled into a comfortable position and waited.

* * * * *

When Den left Gigi's bedroom, he closed the window from the outside and hid his suitcase behind the hedge that marked the rear edge of the apartment complex property line. Unobserved, he made his way along the hedge until he reached the buildings at the end of the cul-de-sac. He found a vantage point where he could see Gigi's apartment and the police car parked in front of it. When the police left, he would return.

Inside Gigi's apartment, the questioning continued. The detective showed interest in the ten o'clock appointment. He believed the man who made it was the one who killed Charlotte Novitski. Gigi could not identify him. He asked if Gigi knew of any reason why anyone would attack her secretary. Again, she could not help him.

The detective asked if they could look around the apartment. Gigi had no objection, but wished she had a way to stop the patrolman from looking in the bedroom. She breathed more freely when the patrolman came out of the bedroom with the report: "Nothing in here."

Chapter 22

Den stood in the shadows of a darkened building near the end of the McCord Court cul-de-sac. He was thankful there were no neighborhood dogs to announce his presence. From his vantage point he could watch the squad car and the front door of Gigi's apartment.

As he watched, Den saw another vehicle enter the Court and slowly drive toward the place where he was hidden. He slid behind one of the building's evergreens as the vehicle passed him. It turned around at the end of the street and parked not too far from Gigi's apartment.

At first Den thought it might be some kind of a stake-out. Two men were in the front seat. It was too dark to identify them, but the driver appeared to be watching Gigi's apartment. The other was slumped against the seat, probably trying to rest until it was his turn to watch.

Den didn't think the police would have any special reason to suspect Gigi for the murder of her secretary. *"They may be there to protect her,"* he thought. *"Or maybe it was their policy to keep an eye on people closely associated with violent deaths."*

When the detective and the patrolman left the building, Den was relieved. Gigi was not with them. She was not being taken someplace for further questioning. His relief was short-lived. As soon as they left, the automobile he thought was a stake-out moved forward and stopped in the space the police car had vacated. This was definitely not a stake-out procedure.

Den knew something was up. He watched the men get out of the car and walk to the apartment building and his attention turned into alarm. As they approached the door, he saw both men pull handguns from their shoulder holsters.

Den ran back along the hedge to Gigi's apartment building. He hurried to the window of her bedroom, slid it open and silently re-entered the room.

* * * * *

When she saw the squad car drive away, Gigi went to her bedroom. Den had been thorough. There was nothing to show the police he had been there. She reviewed the questions asked by the police. Nothing indicated the detective suspected Den or anyone other than the man who made the ten o'clock appointment. She was wondering who might have a reason to kill Charlotte when she heard knocking at her front door. *"They're back,"* she thought. *"The detective is back with more questions."*

Gigi went to the door and, without thinking, began to open it. As soon as she disengaged the lock, the door was pushed open. Abdul immediately struck her with his Beretta. She fell to the floor, nearly unconscious and unable to cry out. Abdul ran into the kitchen, signaling Jacobson toward the bedroom. The kitchen was empty. He threw open the door of the utility room. "Ten" was not there. Before returning to the living room, he took a roll of duct tape from the shelf above the clothes washer.

Jacobson, his pistol still in his right hand and the butt of the weapon resting in his left palm, came back through the bedroom door. He had checked the bathroom and the closet, too. "He's not in there," he reported, "She has to know where he is. Make her talk," he said to the Jordanian.

Abdul ran a line of duct tape around Gigi's head, sealing her mouth. By the time she fully recovered her senses, her hands were taped together and she was taped to a chair. She didn't know Abdul. He was a stranger. She immediately recognized Jake Jacobson. He was replacing a pistol into the holster beneath his coat.

He nodded at her and smiled. It was a thin, self-satisfied smile. Jake smiled because he knew Abdul would make her tell where Den Clark was hiding. Then he would kill her. Then he would find Den Clark and Abdul would put a bullet in his head. Finally, he would get the revenge he sought. Both Den and Gigi would be dead.

Abdul did not plan a simple bullet-in-the-head execution. The deaths of the woman called "Gigi'" and the man called "Ten" were tests, set up by the CIA to see if he was capable of killing. Now he would show Jacobson just how capable he was. He would leave no doubt about his ability to kill. He would also leave no doubt about his ability to extract information from people who didn't want to talk.

Abdul grabbed Gigi's hair and pulled her head up. Then, calmly, he began to speak. "I want you to tell me where I can find your friend, Ten, but it would be a waste of my time to question you right now. You wouldn't tell me where he is. I'd ask again and you still wouldn't tell me. Even if you did tell me, it would be a lie. Then I would have to" … he paused to make sure she understood his threat… "convince you to tell me the truth.

"I'm going to skip the first steps," he said and moved his face within inches of hers. "It will save time for both of us. I won't question you and you won't have to lie to me. We'll go directly to the next step. I'll start to convince you to tell me the truth and when I'm finished, you will want to tell me the truth."

Abdul let go of Gigi's hair and took the knife from its scabbard beneath his coat. He ran his thumb across the sharp edge of the knife to test is sharpness and continued to talk to her.

"I'm going to remove your little finger. I'll take the one on your right hand. When that's done, I'll cut off your ear." He ripped open her blouse and tore her brassier apart. "Then I'll ask you where he is. If I don't like your answer, I'll start with your tits. That's what you call them, isn't it?"

* * * * *

By the time Abdul finished taping Gigi to the chair, Den had entered the bedroom. He heard Abdul's threats to mutilate her. He pulled the revolver from his belt. In the living room, Jake didn't have the stomach for Abdul's bloody method of interrogation. He didn't want to see it. He didn't want to be a part of it. He feared the business would make him physically sick.

He quickly walked to Gigi's bedroom to get away from what he knew was going to happen in Gigi's living room. As he opened the door, he saw Den coming toward him with a revolver in his hand. Jake jumped back and dodged away from Den's line of sight. He rushed past a startled Abdul. He ran through the kitchen, out of the building and directly to Abdul's parked car. In seconds, the key was in the ignition.

Den had no interest in chasing him. His concern was the man who stood beside Gigi with a knife in his hand. He entered the living room with his .357 revolver raised and pointed at Abdul. Abdul, confused by Jake's rapid departure, didn't have time to draw his Beretta. His only alternative was to hold his knife to Gigi's throat and bargain for his escape. He again grabbed her by the hair and was moving the knife toward her throat when Den fired.

The bullet hit him in the center of his chest. The knife dropped from his hand and he fell to the floor. His body made a few involuntary jerks. Then it stopped moving and blood from Abdul's shattered chest stained a larger and larger part of his shirt.

Den was removing the tape that bound Gigi to the chair when he heard the screech of tires as Abdul's car careened out of McCord Court and onto Central Boulevard. As soon as she was free, feeling both terror and relief, Gigi threw her arms around him. Den felt her body shaking against him. He held her as she gasped for air. He picked her up and carried her into the kitchen, away from the corpse of her tormentor. "Sit down and drink this," he told her. She sipped from the glass of water and her breathing began to return to normal.

"*It didn't take long for Jacobson and one of his Aegis goons to find me,*" Den thought. "*My God, why did I put Gigi into the middle of this? Now they'll go after her, too. We've got to get out of here and find a safe place.*"

Den retrieved his luggage from the hedge and returned to the bedroom. He grabbed slacks and a couple of Gigi's blouses from the closet, took stockings and underclothing from a dresser drawer and crammed them into her overnight bag.

He went to Abdul's body. He could see his shoulder holster and the butt of his Beretta. He also saw a bulge in his inside coat pocket. A passport, an envelope and a letter carrier type wallet made the bulge. The envelope and the wallet were crammed with hundred dollar bills, some of them being colored with Abdul's blood. Den took the money and, after checking the Jordanian passport, returned it and the empty wallet to the jacket's breast pocket.

When Den returned to the kitchen, the water glass was empty and Gigi, still shaken, was writing a note. She showed it to him. It said "The man in the living room tried to kill me." Den nodded his approval. They left the note on the kitchen table.

Gigi had endured a number of shocks. Her secretary had been shot as she stood in the doorway of her law office. Gigi had been pistol whipped and threatened with terrifying mutilation by an Aegis murderer. She knew Jacobson and the dead man in her living room were Aegis instruments. She knew Jacobson and the man who threatened her were the ones who murdered Charlotte.

Gigi had experienced the reality of an Aegis attempt to kill. She shuddered when she realized they would send someone else to kill her as well as Den. The frightful, naked fact of the danger she and Den faced struck her with full force.

Den led her to the truck and helped her enter it. He threw his suitcase and her overnight bag in the pick-up box and drove from the apartment building. Den had no destination in mind. He knew they had to get out of McCord Court.

He knew most of Gigi's neighbors would be home and waiting for their dinners. They would have seen the squad car. They would have heard the shot that killed Abdul and Jake's tire squealing escape. One or more of them would have called 911. The police were on their way and he and Gigi had to be gone before they arrived.

* * * * *

When they heard the sirens and watched the police cars converging into McCord Court, Gigi's neighbors were of two minds. Some of them couldn't help but go into the street in the hope of satisfying their curiosity and learning the cause of all the excitement. Most of them did not want to get involved. They were content to watch from their windows. They'd get the details from their more inquisitive neighbors or from the television news.

By the time the policeman and the detective who questioned Gigi had returned to her apartment, the scene had been photographed and Abdul's body was ready for removal to the morgue. Later, the detective sat at the kitchen table and reviewed his notes.

One of the policemen in the squad car that answered the 911 call saw a body through the living room window. He cautiously entered the apartment through the kitchen entrance while his partner guarded the front door. The place was empty. The dead man carried a Jordanian passport. It contained a recent Mexican Migración "entrada" stamp showing he entered that country less than a week earlier.

Some of the neighbors said they heard a single shot and then the squeal of tires. One of them said he saw a pick-up truck leave the driveway minutes after the sound of the departure of the first automobile.

The detective didn't criticize the uniformed policeman who drove him to the apartment earlier in the day. What was done was done. He would, however, privately tell him he should have jotted down the license number of the pick-up. At least, he had some information to include in his report. It was a Chev truck - four or five years old.

The detective began to develop a scenario to explain what must have happened. The dead man probably made the ten o'clock appointment with the attorney. The purpose of the appointment was to be assured that Ms Grant would be waiting for him in her office, but he did not appear at ten o'clock.

He waited until noon when the likelihood of the presence of other clients was minimal. He meant to kill the attorney, but murdered her secretary by mistake. Discovering that mistake, he attempted to correct it by killing Grant in her home.

The passport showed the dead man was a Jordanian and nothing to indicate he had entered the United States legally. Did the dead man know the attorney? Probably not. Did Grant know him? Doubtful. If Grant knew him, the detective guessed, the note on the kitchen table would probably have given more information.

The Jordanian was probably a hired gun, imported to kill her. The detective wondered who hired the Jordanian. He wondered about the motive behind the attempt to murder the lawyer. He leaned back in the chair and again read the note Gigi had left. She must have been afraid of another attempt on her life - so afraid that she ran.

The detective shook his head. His scenario was logical but it was incomplete. One question had not been considered. Who killed the Jordanian? The duct tape that bound someone - probably attorney Grant - to a chair had been cut. Bits and pieces of it contained strands of long honey blonde hair. He would be surprised if it wasn't hers. A hired killer wouldn't tape his victim to a chair and then free her and allow her to get access to a gun and shoot him.

There had to be a third person involved. Someone killed the Jordanian and then freed the lawyer and drove away with her. Then the detective again amended his thinking. If the neighbor's recollection was right, there had to be a fourth person present. Someone drove away immediately after the shot was fired, but before the pick-up left the scene. He snapped his small notebook shut and thought this was going to be an interesting case. It would be easier if he could find the attorney and get all of the answers he needed.

Chapter 23

Den drove his truck from McCord Court onto Central Boulevard and headed south. His immediate purpose was to take Gigi to a quiet place where she could regain her composure and they could decide on what they were going to do. By the time he reached the southern outskirts of Tucson he had a plan. It would protect her.

He would expose Jake and Teddy and Aegis. He would contact newspaper and television journalists as well as Senators and members of the House of Representatives. He'd tell them everything he knew about Aegis. The truth would be disclosed. Once that information had been made public, neither his death nor the death of Gigi would hide that truth. There would be no reason for Aegis to pursue him or Gigi and she would be safe.

Den knew his plan would not give him protection. He would run the risk of being returned to Latin America for crimes committed in Guatemala, Bolivia and Chile. The ever-present undercurrent of anti-gringo and anti-CIA sentiments in Latin America would probably fuel demands that he be extradited to one or more of those countries.

He also knew the Belt Line government administrators and politicians would find a way to bring felony charges against him in Washington - conspiracy to commit murder came to mind. He knew he would probably face prison in the United States or, if he was returned to a Latin American venue, death by a firing squad.

When he went public and as soon as it became evident extradition or criminal charges were in the offing, Den would have to run. By going public, he would replace the necessity of hiding from Aegis with the necessity of hiding from felony charges or extradition proceedings.

Where would he go? Chile might be a safe haven. The killer of Humberto del Valle might find a refuge there. Canada's extradition policies might make it an attractive sanctuary. Den would become a fugitive, living somewhere in a self-imposed exile. Gigi could lead a normal life in Arizona. That was the most important thing.

* * * * *

On the far south side of Tucson, a small and tired neon sign fluttered "Vacancy" at irregular intervals. It also tried to proclaim "Sunset Motel" but succeeded only partially. "Suns t Mot l" was as close as it could get. The sign needed attention. So did the motel.

The Sunset Motel needed paint. Weeds grew alongside the edges of the building and in those places where they were able to get a foothold through the cracks in the parking lot black top. It was the kind of motel where the management sometimes changed sheets twice a night and insisted its customers pay for their rooms in cash and in advance.

Den registered at the motel. He signed in as Ernest Adams, the name appearing on his Pennsylvania driver's license. The rooms were reasonably clean and the plumbing worked. While Gigi soaked in the tub, Den paced and once more considered his decision to expose Aegis. He reconfirmed it. It was the best way to assure Gigi's safety.

It was time to tell Gigi what he was going to do. When she had dressed and returned to the room, Den sat on the bed next to her and explained what he had in mind. His last words were: "I'm sorry I got you into this, hon. I damn near got you killed. Now I'm going to get you out of it."

Beneath the stereotypical façade assigned to the female of the species, Gigi Grant concealed an iron structure. Most women have it. Their grasp on reality is more firm than their male counterparts. Their ability to survive is extraordinary. Gigi had left the snug security of a position in a large law firm to step into the unknown terrain of service in the Central Intelligence Agency.

She survived the disappointments that followed and didn't hesitate to leave the Agency and accept the risks of starting a solo law practice in a place where she was friendless and unknown. She had the brains and the ability and the courage to make decisions. When Den first told her of the danger he faced and his plan to disappear to a place where Aegis could not find him, Gigi was willing to hide him in her apartment. Now she made another decision - quickly and firmly.

"What do you mean, 'get me out of it'? Don't you mean: 'get us out of it'?" she said with some emphasis. "Get rid of that 'noble, noble' nonsense, Denver Clark. Do you think you can spend the rest of your life hiding, or in some Guatemalan prison, or worse, just so I can spend every day of my life knowing I was the reason for it?

"No, Den. We're in this together. I know what I'm getting into. My God, Den. I've just seen it. I was there. I heard the threats and I saw the knife. If we live, we'll live together and if we go, we'll go together."

From their first meeting in the cafeteria at the Sherman Kent School, Den knew Gigi was an independent woman. Perhaps, he should have expected her reaction. In truth, he was not unhappy with it. He did not want to vanish from her life.

"You'd have to give up a lot, hon."

"I know. You're giving up a lot, too."

"Being on the run isn't easy. You can't let your guard down. You have to keep looking over your shoulder. You have to be ready to run again."

"I know, Den. I know. It will be fun."

"Fun?"

"We'll be together and that will be fun. Den, listen to me. You know what I've gone through today. I know the danger, but I'd rather live one year with you, fully alive, than ten years away from you, wondering where you were and how you were. Don't worry about me."

Den thought about it. Ten years just being alive? One year with Gigi? He quickly revamped his plan to disappear. This time, Gigi would be with him. Her determination to stick with him trumped his decision to go public.

* * * * *

It was Gigi who found a different way to keep their pursuers at bay. The men in Aegis, she argued, wanted to kill them because they feared exposure. That same fear could protect them. The threat of exposure would be as effective as exposure itself.

"What would happen," she asked, "if someone inside Aegis - Teddy Smith, for example - was told harm to either of us would automatically cause everything you know about them to be broadcast to the world? Do you think Aegis might have a good reason to see to it that nothing ever happened to us?"

Up until that moment, Den had been on the defensive. He couldn't find a way to attack Aegis because, except for Teddy and Jake, he couldn't identify any of them. Gigi's plan didn't depend upon identifying any of them. Den could write his exposé of Aegis and send it to a friend - no, to a number of trustworthy friends - with instructions to make it public if he or Gigi didn't contact them periodically.

When this threat to expose Aegis was explained to Teddy, Den guessed his immediate reaction would be to tell Jake to stop all attempts to kill them. He'd call Jake back to Langley within fifteen minutes of Den's phone call to him. He couldn't afford the risk of letting Jake trigger the mailings of the exposés. Gigi's plan could convince Aegis to terminate all attempts to kill them, but they both knew it might not produce that result. It was not an unqualified insurance policy.

At the very least, Teddy and his Aegis friends would pause to study Den's threat. As far as the danger posed by Jake was concerned, they could only speculate. Jake might not give a damn about what happened to Aegis. On his own, he might look for another assassin.

Den and Gigi also agreed the threat to expose the conspiracy did not guarantee their protection from the Aegis network. Teddy or Jacobson or some other unknown man might find a way for Aegis to survive the publicity that would result if Den's story was made public.

The possibility that their threat might not produce the results they wanted was balanced by the possibility that it would work. The use of the threat might help them. It couldn't hurt them. Den and Gigi made their plans. Den would phone Teddy.

He would tell him he had written his history of Aegis. Den would tell him copies of the report of Aegis activity had sent to a number of trustworthy friends. He might even hint at sealed documents held in trust by attorneys inside and outside of the United States. Den would threaten Teddy and his Aegis friends with automatic and unavoidable exposure if harm came to either of them.

As yet there was no written report exposing Aegis and its clandestine assassination plots. As yet there was no group of trusted friends who would distribute those reports in the event Den or Gigi were killed or disappeared, but Teddy wouldn't know it and he couldn't take the chance of questioning its existence.

Gigi and Den knew their best protection continued to be disappearance. As soon as Den returned from placing the phone call to Teddy, they would leave Arizona and drive into Mexico. There, Den would turn his lies into reality. He would write the Aegis report and he would select ex-SEAL companions to put pre-addressed packages into the mail if regular communication from him ever ceased. Then Den Clark and G. G. Grant would vanish.

* * * * *

While Den and Gigi were developing their plans, in the Sahuaro Inn an uneasy Jake Jacobson watched the 10 o'clock evening news. It reported a man carrying a Jordanian passport had been shot and killed in the home of attorney G. G. Grant. The police were following what they expected would be a number of productive leads. Jake recognized the phrase "what they expected would be a number of productive leads" as a euphemism meaning "They didn't have a clue".

Jake, on the other hand, had more than a clue. He was frightened and he had reason to be frightened. When he decided to enter Gigi's bedroom to avoid watching Abdul torture her, he saw Den coming at him with a revolver. It was a scene he never wanted to see again. He knew Den recognized him. He also knew Den killed Abdul and would have killed him, too, if he hadn't run from the apartment.

Teddy was right. Den Clark knew who was trying to kill him. And now Clark knew he was somewhere in Tucson. Jake expected Clark's reaction would be violent. He might come looking for him. If Clark found him, Jake knew he would be a dead man. Jake needed help. He called Teddy Smith to get it.

* * * * *

In McLean, the phone on the nightstand next to Teddy Smith's bed rang. He roused himself and looked at his wristwatch. The phone rang again. He picked it up. Perhaps there was some crisis at the Agency. Perhaps an emergency meeting was being called. "Yes," he said into the telephone.

It wasn't an emergency call from the Agency. It was Jake Jacobson. *"Why does he have to call me in the middle of the night?"* Teddy wondered, a bit peevishly. "It's damn near one o'clock, Jake," he said. "You've ruined my sleep. This better be important."

"It is, Teddy. Abdul is dead. Den Clark killed him."

"You're sure? How do you know?"

"I was there."

Jake's words abruptly jerked Teddy into full consciousness. His first reaction was one of disbelief. *"It can't be,"* he thought. Teddy couldn't understand how Den could possibly know about Abdul. Even if he had, somehow, learned Jake had hired the Jordanian terrorist, Den wouldn't know where he was or how to find him.

The old questions again visited Teddy. He had been bothered by the possibility of the Jordanian terrorist existed only in Jake Jacobson's devious mind. Maybe a mythical Abdul was part of one of Jake's Byzantine schemes aimed at getting rid of Den. Teddy would keep his suspicion to himself. He would wait and see what Jake had to say. He limited himself to questions about the events surrounding the death of Abdul.

Jake told Teddy of his meeting with Abdul in Monterrey and the terrorist's confirmation of his agreement to work with him. When Jake admitted naming Gigi Grant as Abdul's first target, he expected Teddy to raise particular hell. He was surprised when Teddy took the news calmly. Teddy meant it when he gave Jake complete discretion to select the target. Teddy didn't care who Jake might name as target. His only interest was finding a competent replacement for Den Clark.

"By pure luck," Jake told him, "I found Den Clark. He was hiding out in Grant's apartment in Tucson. He saw me just before he killed Abdul. I managed to get away. I'm sure Clark will stay in Tucson for at least a few days before pulling another of his disappearing acts. It will take him that long to make sure he leaves no tracks for us to follow. If we act fast, I think he can be run to ground. Can you send someone to find him and take him out?"

Jake's question was followed by a long pause. Jake's fears multiplied when Teddy did not immediately agree to his request. The cat was out of the bag. Den Clark would now become the hunter and he, Jake Jacobson, would become the hunted. That was more than merely a disquieting prospect. It was a disquieting immediate prospect. He needed help right now and Teddy was lying in bed in McLean, thinking about it.

"Clark is a loose cannon," Jake said with some animation. "This may be the only chance we get to silence him. We know he's here in Tucson. If you send a couple of good men, they can be here tomorrow. They can find him and finish him off. Then Aegis will be safe. Safe, Teddy. Safe. Nobody will have to worry about a loose cannon, rolling around out there somewhere."

In McLean, with the phone to his ear, Teddy again wondered if Abdul existed. Did Den, in fact, kill him? In the morning, Teddy would contact the Officer-In-Charge of the Phoenix FBI Office. He'd find out if a man had been killed at the Tucson residence of G. G. Grant. If Abdul was not a product of Jake's imagination and if Den had killed him, Teddy would have to deal with an unexpected problem.

Den would surely think Teddy sent Jake and the Jordanian to kill him. Eliminating Den and Gigi would not be easy. Den was hard to kill and time was of the essence. Teddy wasn't sure he could find both or either of them before Den reacted by exposing Aegis. Teddy had to be prepared to face the possibility of disaster.

Already Teddy had sown the seeds for his own personal defense. Deputy Director Brewster believed Clark was a rogue agent - an assassin for hire. If worst came to worst and Teddy's innocence would not be supported by the fact of his disclosures to Cullen Brewster,

Teddy had a second line of defense. He would claim there was no Aegis organization and that Jake Jacobson and Den Clark had acted on their own.

Jake Jacobson was becoming more than just a pain in the ass. His obsession to kill Clark was a threat to both Teddy and to Aegis. Teddy wondered what would happen if Jake were dead? How would that play out? These were the thoughts passing through Teddy's mind as he listened to Jake's call for assistance.

"I can't do much right now, Jake," Teddy told him. "I'll get back to you tomorrow morning. In the meantime, sit tight. Don't stick your nose out of the motel room. Don't do anything until you hear from me. Do you understand me? Don't do anything. Sit tight until you get my call."

Teddy hung up. "*Interesting*," he thought. *"Jake calls Den a loose cannon. I've got two loose cannons on my hands. Den is bad enough. Jake is worse. If Jake's story is true, Den might blow the whistle on Aegis. I'll have to do something soon. Damn Jake."*

Teddy turned out the light and went back to sleep.

* * * * *

Jake Jacobson could never be described as a brave man. When faced with any kind of physical danger, he was unable to overcome an impulse to run. It had been his childhood defense mechanism. He had abandoned Mick McCarthy when the firing began in Damascus. When Den confronted him and Abdul in Gigi Grant's apartment, he ran again. The only time he didn't run from danger was when Den punished him in his Bellavista apartment. He had no option then. He couldn't run.

Now, back in his Tucson motel room, Jake lay on the bed and worried about Den Clark. Teddy wasn't going to immediately send men to kill Clark. He damned Teddy's delaying tactic. Clark was no fool. Jake applauded his own insight in assuming the name of Albert S. Simpson. It would take Den time to find him. Still, it was possible Teddy's delay might give Den enough time to track him down.

Quickly flying back to Langley gave Jake no real protection. Den could follow him. Den could hide in Washington and kill him at any time - some morning when he was driving to Langley, or when he was eating at a restaurant, or standing in front of his apartment window. Jake shuddered at the thought and again asked himself how he could possibly have missed when he shot at Den in Arlington.

Trying to reassure himself, he thought: *"Teddy can't let me down. Teddy can't shut his eyes to my danger. He'll have to send someone tomorrow."* Then another thought occurred to him. *"My God, what if Teddy leaves me here, twisting in the breeze?"* He thought for a moment and then relaxed. *"I know what I'll do. If he doesn't call by noon, I'll call him. If I have to, I'll threaten to phone the newspapers. That'll bring him to heel."*

Now confident that he would soon be out of danger, Jake went to sleep.

Chapter 24

After the third ring, Teddy Smith switched on his bedside light. For the second time that evening he had been awaken in the middle of his sleep. His mood was not pleasant. Teddy looked at his wristwatch. He reached for the telephone and, without waiting for his caller to announce himself, he exclaimed "For God's sake Jake, now it's after one o'clock. Do you have some deep-seated aversion against calling me during daylight hours? What is it now?"

"Hello, Teddy," said a voice from the other end of the line. Teddy's surprise at hearing Den was quickly replaced by wondering whatever possessed him to call. Was Den calling for help? Could it be Den still trusted him? Could Den somehow believe he wasn't involved in the attempts to kill him? He hoped so. He'd try to give credibility to those possibilities.

"Den Clark! It's you! My God, it's so good to hear from you. I thought you had been kidnapped and killed. Do you need help? Do you need money? Tell me where you are. I'll come and pick you up."

Teddy's first words - "For God's sake, Jake" - were proof of his duplicity. It was obvious. Jake called Teddy that same evening. Den knew Jake reported everything that had happened during the day. Teddy's attempted 'innocence' act didn't have a chance and Den wasted no time in disabusing him.

"You know exactly where I am and you know exactly what I'm doing. Jake phoned you this evening. He told you where I am and he told you I killed that Jordanian goon you sent to take care of me. Deny it, Teddy. Deny it. I want to hear just how you'll try to convince me you and your Aegis friends have no plans to eliminate me."

"*Jeesus Christ,*" Teddy thought. "*Now I've screwed it up. Why did I let him know Jake had called? Why, oh why, didn't I keep my mouth shut? Well, what's done is done. No point in denying it.*"

"Yes, Jake called me," Teddy admitted. "Believe me, Den. I had no suspicion of what he was up to. He told me what happened and I told him to stay in his motel room and do nothing. Nothing," he repeated. "I'm glad you called. I hope we can straighten out this whole mess."

"Of course, I believe you." Den answered. Teddy winced at the heavy sarcasm as Den continued speaking. "I believe you didn't send me on a one-way trip to Guatemala. I believe you and your buddies had nothing to do with the shot that nearly got me in my apartment. I believe you didn't send Jake and your paid shooter to kill Gigi Gant and me. I believe in the Easter Bunny, Santa Claus and the tooth fairy, too."

Teddy changed his tactics. "I guess I deserved that," he said. "I know you won't believe me when I tell you I wasn't happy with Ocelot. Jake devised that operation and, I'll admit it, he talked me into approving it. Jake's been after you ever since you beat him up in The Bellavista, but I didn't know he was going to take a shot at you and I didn't know what he was trying to do in Tucson. You won't believe any of this but it's the honest-to-God truth. While I'm at it, I've wanted to tell you some other truths. They are the truths that you should know and now is as good a time as any."

Teddy admitted Jake went to Syria to recruit Den's replacement, how he and the man they called Abdul met in Mexico and how Jake paid him to kill G. G. Grant. "I told him to pick a target and to stick around until Abdul had completed the mission. The target wasn't important. I thought he'd pick some Mexican drug boss. It was only a test. Like the one we gave you in Chile. It was Jake who picked the Grant woman. She knew about some of his shenanigans when he was in Damascus. Jake wanted to silence her. I had nothing to do with it. I didn't know she was the target until Jake called me.

"You won't believe me, but there it is. Jake called about half an hour ago. He told me you were in Tucson and that you killed Abdul. He wants me to send people to …" Teddy paused trying to find the kindest word … "to deal with you. Hell, Den, I wasn't even looking for you. As long as you kept your mouth shut, I was willing to let sleeping dogs lie."

When Teddy paused to take a breath, he heard Den's chuckle, followed by: "Congratulations, Teddy. I'm impressed. That's a great tale. And made up on the spur of the moment, too. You certainly are fast on your feet.

"Do you want to know what I'm doing?" Den continued. "Listen up. I've been writing. The working title of my opus is: The Aegis Conspiracy. You know how difficult it is for unknown writers to get their works into print nowadays. That's why I've called you. I thought you and your Aegis friends might be instrumental in helping me get my little booklet published and distributed.

"If Gigi or I disappear, if Gigi or I get injured, if either or both of us should pass away - by some kind of accident, by suicide, by a heart attack or even by an infected toenail or from a bad case of dandruff - a number of people, here and abroad, will not hear from us. When they don't hear from us, each of them will open the packets they have been guarding. They will all read my unpublished papers and each one of them will send a copy to selected newspapers, radio commentators, television talking heads and politicians.

"As surely as the night follows the day, if anything happens to me or Gigi Grant, the Aegis Conspiracy will be broadcast. If you want to see the Aegis Conspiracy published, all you have to do is take a whack at both or either one of us. Perhaps you will share my comments with the rest of your friends in Langley?" It was a question.

Teddy ran his hand over his forehead and to the back of his neck. *"God damn that Jake,"* he thought. Then he made a decision. "I told you I wasn't looking for you," he said. "You don't believe me. Now I'll tell you something else. I'm sure there are people in the Agency who believe the same things I do, but those people are not a part of Aegis. There is no large Aegis network. Aegis has never consisted of more than three people – you, Jake and me. No one else, Den. No one else.

"I'm not trying to kill you." Teddy paused before adding: "No one is trying to kill you. No one except Jake Jacobson. He wants me to send a team to kill you. He's waiting for my answer. I told him I'd call him before noon today. I'm not going to call him and I'm not going to send anyone. Hell, I don't have anyone to send. If I did, I wouldn't send them." Teddy paused and slowly added: "Jake is staying at the Sahuaro Inn. Room 110."

Teddy waited for Den's reaction. He heard nothing. After a few seconds, he heard a click.

"Den? Den?" No answer.

Teddy smiled and hung up the phone. He leaned back, resting on his bunched-up pillows. He was satisfied. It had been a day of accomplishment. Den would certainly go to the Sahuaro Inn. Jake would be there, waiting for a phone call that would never come. He would have no idea Den was coming for him. Jake would be a sitting duck. Den would kill him.

Teddy hoped he had convinced Den that Aegis now consisted of only two people. If Den believed him, he would know his threat of exposing Teddy would be foolproof - as soon as he killed Jake. With Jake dead, Den would know Aegis consisted of only one man - Teddy Smith.

Den would think Teddy had neither the manpower nor the inclination to pursue him. He would think the threat of exposing Teddy and Aegis would free him and the Grant woman. They could lead their lives without the fear of sudden death. There would be no need for Den to go public.

Jake's death had other important advantages for Teddy. Jake wouldn't be around to blackmail him with threats to talk about unauthorized killings. It would also effectively silence Den. Abdul might be a case of justifiable homicide, but Jake's death would clearly be a case of premeditated murder and Arizona has the death penalty. Denver Clark would keep his mouth tightly closed. Teddy's two loose cannons would be securely fastened to the deck.

"*It's called killing two birds with one stone,*" Teddy thought, "*and I won't have to call Arizona tomorrow.*" He re-arranged his pillows, turned out the light and, for the third time that evening, proceeded to go to sleep.

* * * * *

In Tucson, it was approaching midnight when Den left the phone booth in the mall parking lot. Gigi's blackmailing threat - STAY AWAY FROM US OR ELSE - worked better than either of them had hoped. It must have scared the hell out of Teddy and caused him to volunteer a lot of information.

Den repeated that thought, this time with skepticism. "*It caused Teddy to volunteer a lot of information?*" That didn't sound like Teddy. It was out-of-character. Den's own experience with Teddy was enough to convince him anything and everything the man said was suspect. If Teddy told him the sun was rising in the east, Den would look out the window and check, just to make sure.

While he drove back to the Sunset Motel, Den reviewed Teddy's admissions and tried to make sense out of them. Of course, Teddy would deny trying to kill him. It was very convenient to say it was Jake and only Jake who wanted him dead, but why did Teddy tell him Jake was staying at the Sahuaro Inn? Why did he go out of his way to give him the room number?

The answers to those questions were not hard to find. If Jake was the only one trying to kill him, by removing Jake, Den would be removing the threat to him and Gigi. Teddy wanted him to visit the Sahuaro Inn and kill Jake Jacobson.

Could Teddy be setting a trap? Would some unknown Aegis agent be sitting in Sahuaro Inn - Room 110, waiting there to kill him? It was possible, but Den doubted it. If it was a trap, successful or unsuccessful, the result (as far as Teddy knew) would be the automatic distribution of Den's disclosures about Aegis. It would be followed by a firestorm of media and congressional demands for the identification and punishment of the conspirators. Teddy wouldn't do anything to cause that to happen.

By going to the Sahuaro Inn and removing Jake, Den would remove a threat to himself and to Gigi. Was that why Teddy told him where Jake was staying? Was it because Teddy liked Den and didn't want to see any harm come to him? It was an impossible scenario. Den couldn't believe Teddy was ever motivated by anything except self-interest.

Teddy had been willing to sacrifice Den. He sent him into

Guatemala to be killed. Teddy OK'd Jake's attempt to kill him in Washington. After setting up those two plans to wipe him out, any suggestion that Teddy wanted to protect Den because of some special liking for him was incredible. Teddy had an ulterior motive.

Of course there was another reason for Teddy's disclosures. Teddy was afraid of Jake. If Jake, motivated by some paranoid insistence on revenge, tried to kill him or Gigi, Teddy believed the story of Aegis would become public. The protective cloak of secrecy surrounding Teddy would be dropped.

It made sense. Teddy wanted to get rid of Jake before he could do something stupid and destroy Teddy's career. That, Den concluded, was Teddy's hidden agenda. A dead Jake Jacobson protected Teddy Smith. That it also protected Den and Gigi was only an incidental benefit.

Den's final question was: Why did Teddy tell him Aegis was now composed of only himself and Jake? Den suspected Teddy expressed that second revelation in order to emphasize the unspoken suggestion that he go to room 110 and kill Jake. Teddy was telling him Jake's death did more than eliminate the one man who wanted to kill him and Gigi.

If there were no widespread Aegis organization, the death of Jake Jacobson together with the threat of exposure of the one remaining conspirator, removed all danger Den and Gigi faced. They could move next door to Teddy and he would treat them in the most cordially and friendly manner.

Whatever Teddy's motives might have been, one thing was certain. Jake was like a dog gnawing on a root. He simply wouldn't let go. It was well over a year since Den gave him that beating inThe Bellavista apartment building. Since then, Jake had tried to kill him twice - in Guatemala and in Washington. Now he wanted Teddy to send someone to Arizona to kill him.

"Unless he's stopped, he'll keep trying until he gets lucky," Den thought as he approached the Sunset Motel. *"It would be easy enough to kill him. He doesn't know Teddy wants him out of the way. Teddy has made it easy for me to finish him off."*

At first Den was surprised to find he didn't immediately decide to kill Jake Jacobson. The deaths of Montoya and del Valle might have been justified but there was no excuse for Teddy sending him to kill those kids in Guatemala. That ambush was unjustifiable. It was nothing more or less than plain, simple murder.

Now, Teddy was trying to use him again - this time to kill Jake. Den thought he had joined a group of higher echelon Agency men who were protecting the country. Instead, he had been deceived into becoming Teddy Smith's private executioner.

Den found himself thinking: "*Why should I do that bastard's bidding.*" Of course, there was good reason for Den to do that bastard's bidding.

* * * * *

As he stepped out of the truck, Den found himself thinking: "*What if Teddy was lying to me? What if Teddy has another reason for telling me there were only two people left inside Aegis? What if that son of a bitch is trying to lull me into a false sense of security? What if Aegis is really an active internal CIA network? What if Teddy wants me to let my guard down? What if Aegis still intends to kill us?*" The little voice inside him had given him a nudge.

Chapter 25

Gigi anxiously awaited Den's return from placing the phone call to Teddy Smith. She recognized the pick-up truck when it drove past the motel window and Den found his place in the motel parking lot. Den was not smiling when he entered their room. He seemed preoccupied and it caused Gigi some concern.

Den reported the entire late night conversation with Teddy Smith. Gigi felt somewhat reassured when Den told her Teddy believed the threat of automatic public disclosure. Den told her Teddy knew what would happen to him if his connection to the assassinations became known.

He told her he was equally sure Teddy couldn't control Jake. It explained why Teddy told him Jake was staying at the Sahuaro Inn. Gigi furrowed her brow. Den saw she needed an explanation.

"Don't you see?" he said. "All Teddy has to do is keep away from us and he'll run no risk of being discovered. Teddy can order Jake to back off and leave us alone, but Jake might not back off. He might try to kill us. If he does, the assassinations Teddy planned will become known to everyone. He is convinced our exposure of Aegis will disclose everything. It will give dates and places and, most important to Teddy, names. His complicity will become public knowledge and he will be in serious trouble.

"Jake, on the other hand, may not care about what happens to Aegis or to Teddy. It's very clear. He wants you dead and he wants me dead. If he tries to kill us and the exposé is distributed, Jake will deny anything and everything that might tie him to Aegis. Remember, there is no record of Jake's assassination schemes. They were all verbal amendments to official projects, properly reviewed and approved by the Directorate.

"If that doesn't give Jake adequate cover, he'll claim he was following Teddy's orders. He'll claim he believed those orders were legitimate. If the prosecutors put enough heat on him, Jake will make a deal for immunity and become a government witness. The worst he'll get is a slapped finger. It doesn't take a genius level IQ to figure it out. Going public about Aegis doesn't represent a threat to Jake.

"Teddy knows his own protection consists of getting rid of Jake. Then Jake can't talk and neither can I. I'd have to admit to murdering the little bastard. With Jake dead and me silenced, Teddy is out of the woods as long as my report doesn't become public knowledge. When Jake is dead, two sources of Teddy's potential danger will disappear."

Gigi nodded. She understood. Then her question went to the core of their problems. "Do you think Aegis is more than you and Jake and Teddy?"

"I really don't know, hon," Den answered. "I've thought about it and I really don't know. Teddy may have told me the truth, but I'm not ready to believe anything he says. It's quite possible he was lying to me. You've asked the right question, hon. If Aegis is a wider network of CIA officials, would we still be safe?

"Let's say Teddy lied and Aegis is a much broader organization. If so, unknown Aegis people are another source of danger. Undoubtedly, they know the story of their conspiracy will be distributed when you or I die. And, sooner or later, we will die of natural causes. That means, sooner or later, Aegis will be exposed unless they find a way to insulate themselves from the effects of my report. When they find that way, they'll kill us if they know where we are."

Den looked into Gigi's eyes and became very serious when he added: "I said 'when', hon. Not 'if'."

Now it was Gigi's turn. "So far," she said, "the only evidence we have about Aegis is what Teddy told you. I don't trust him and I don't trust the CIA. If the Aegis conspirators number more than you and Teddy and Jake, the rest of the people in Aegis have to be worried about the effects of a post mortem exposure.

"Until we get some very solid proof to the contrary, I think we have to presume Aegis is alive and well. I think you're right, Den. When someone in Aegis finds a way to avoid the effects of your exposé, we will have to be silenced. I don't think we should take any chances."

Gigi and Den were in agreement. Their ultimate safety lay in the protection offered by continued false identities, by disappearance and by concealment. Den and Gigi had to vanish into a new life. Gigi was a realist. Jake Jacobson was their immediate problem. She knew the course they had to follow. "You're going to kill Jake, aren't you?"

Den expected the question. He had already made up his mind. He knew the death of Jake Jacobson would protect Teddy Smith from blackmail. He also knew the death of Jake Jacobson meant he and Gigi would be free from immediate danger.

Den exhaled softly and answered her. "Yes, hon. I'm going to kill him. I'll do it in the morning. Then we'll have to stay out of sight, at least until I get my story written and sent to some SEAL buddies. As soon as I get back, we'll leave for Mexico."

* * * * *

In the morning, Den checked the chambers of his revolver. They were filled. He pushed the barrel of the weapon under his belt, kissed Gigi and told her he would not be gone long. Then he drove to the Sahuaro Inn Motel.

Jake was shaving when he heard the soft knocking at his motel room door. He wiped the lather from his face and took the .45 automatic from beneath the pillow where it had rested during the night. He stood with his back against the wall adjacent to his motel room door.

"Who is it?"

"Teddy sent me," a muffled voice answered.

Jake was suspicious. If Teddy sent a team to help him, why didn't he call and tell him? Best to play it safe. Careful to avoid standing in front of the door, he pulled back the deadbolt, removed the sliding chain security lock and cautiously reached for the doorknob.

Outside of the motel room, Den watched the doorknob. As soon as it began to turn, he stepped back and threw his weight against the door. He expected his weight and the door would meet the resistance of Jake's body. He expected to knock Jake off balance and drop him to the floor.

Den, unimpeded by the pressure he expected to find, hurtled into the room. He stumbled and fell, the revolver dropping from his hand. He rolled and reached to retrieve his weapon. A shoe stamped down on his right hand, pinning it to the floor. When Den looked up, he saw the round, ominous opening of the barrel of a .45 automatic. It was pointed straight at him. Jake Jacobson was holding it.

Jake picked up the revolver and tossed it onto the bed. He stepped down heavily before removing his foot from Den's hand. His voice exuded cordiality. "Oh please get up, Den. You must be uncomfortable down there. Come. Sit by the table - and be so kind as to keep your hands flat on top of it."

Jake's voice was hard and cold when he added: "If you make a single move, I'll kill you." Den's hand was swelling and throbbing and hurting. He did as he was told. There was no point in fighting unless he had better odds. As long as he was alive, he told himself, he had a chance to disarm Jake.

"It's time you and I had a little talk," Jake said, reverting to his pseudo-friendly tone. "Let's see now. How long has it been since you beat me up inThe Bellavista?" Den didn't react. He was looking for an opening, a chance to get to the gun Jake was holding.

"Answer me you son-of-a bitch," Jake snarled at him and, at the same time, came close enough to hit Den on the side of his head with his automatic. The blow came without warning and Den's body lurched to the side.

"Answer me, goddamn you."

Den straightened up and told him it must have been a year or so. Blood seeped out of the bruise and he put his hand to his head. Jake did not react to the movement and Den put his hand back on the table.

"My, my, Den, you should sign up for a memory course. It will help you recall these important dates. It was one year, seven months and eighteen days ago." He looked at his wristwatch. "In another four hours and sixteen minutes it will be one year, seven months and nineteen days ago. Does that jog your memory?"

Den saw Jake step forward preparing to hit him again as he said:

"Answer me you son of a bitch." Den was able to lean away from the blow, softening some of its effect. Nevertheless it opened a gash on the side of his face.

"Does that jog your memory?" Jake repeated.

"No, Jake, it doesn't jog my memory," Den slurred and spit out some of the blood that came from where his teeth had dug into his cheek.

"More's the pity. I'm going to kill you and you aren't even interested enough to recall the day you beat me up and signed your own death warrant. Tsk, tsk, tsk. Whatever am I going to do with you, Den? Just look at what you've done. You've gotten my .45 all bloody. And, see, you left some hair on it, too." Daintily, with thumb and forefinger, he picked some hair from the barrel of his pistol, held it out for Den to see and then flicked it onto the floor.

Jake feigned concentration. Then he smiled and said: "I know what I'll do. I'll use your gun." Pointing his weapon at Den, Jake carefully backed up until he touched the bed. He reached back and felt around until he found Den's .357 magnum. He picked it up, dropped his automatic on the bed and walked to the front of the table.

"I believe I'll use it to kill you. That would be a nice touch." He raised the revolver until it pointed directly at Den's eye. Den watched Jake's hand, planning a desperation attack as soon as he saw any sign of the finger tightening on the trigger.

Jake enjoyed this kind of torture. He was disappointed when Den showed no indication of fear. Jake brought the weapon down. "Oh yes, Den. I forget to tell you something. Do you remember the man you killed in your whore's apartment? Answer me, asshole." Jake yelled and again pistol-whipped Den, drawing blood from the other side of his face.

"Yeah, I remember him. I killed him. I may kill you, too, but I suppose someone will beat me to the punch."

"Don't get snotty with me," Jake said as he swung the weapon at Den's head. This time Den leaned back and Jake, standing on the far side of the table, missed. He moved closer. He didn't intend to miss next time. "I've got some news for you, Den. The man you killed is the same man who killed that big, dumb Irishman, Mick McCarthy. I saw him do it. Let me tell you all about it."

"Go fuck yourself," Den said in an even voice. "I've got news for you. You're a loser. You're a loser, Jake, and everybody knows it. Even Teddy Smith wants to get rid of you. He told me where to find you." Den's purpose was to enrage Jake. He succeeded. It was too much for Jake to handle.

"You lying son of a bitch," he yelled as he raised Den's revolver and began to swing it in a wide arc, intending to lay Den's head open. It was what Den was waiting for. Jake couldn't shoot him with an uncocked .357 revolver pointed at the ceiling.

Den lunged toward Jake, driving his left fist at Jake's groin and reaching up with his right hand to grab the weapon Jake was trying to bring down on his head. Neither maneuver was completely successful. He missed Jakes balls, but delivered a punishing blow into his solar plexus. Den didn't catch the barrel of the gun. His injured right hand was not strong enough to grasp it, but the blow to Jake's abdomen bent him over and loosened Jake's grip on the revolver. It fell from his hand.

The men wrestled for the weapon. Each touched it at times, but neither could get enough of a grip to be able to use it. Den was able to kick it under the table. He pushed Jake away from him and dove to the bed and Jake's .45. Den had it in his hand when Jake ran for the door. He was in the open doorway when Den fired.

The swollen fingers on Den's right hand would not respond as they had been trained. They jerked the trigger and the slug hit the wall, six inches from its target. By the time Den had the gun in his left hand and ran after him. Jake had turned the corner. He was in Abdul's auto and out of the lot before Den could fire again.

Jake had little on his mind except the need to escape and the fear that he might be followed. He drove north on Highway 19 and finished the hundred plus mile trip to Phoenix and the Sky Harbor Airport in less than an hour and a half. The next flight to Washington required stops in both Dallas and Atlanta. It would board in forty-five minutes.

All of Jake's luggage and personal effects were left in the Sahuaro Inn. He had only a belt buckle, a watch and some change to put in the tray that received x-ray scrutiny. Nevertheless, he was "wanded" and asked to take off his shoes. Jake hurried through Security and stationed himself where he could watch the passengers enter the airline's waiting area. He knew Den wouldn't be able to carry a gun or a knife with him. Nevertheless, he hoped he wouldn't see him coming through the Security checkpoints.

When his plane was in the air, Jake calmed down. He began to wonder if Clark had told the truth. Did Teddy want to kill him? Did Teddy tell Clark he was in the Sahuaro Inn Motel? Clark didn't know he was in Tucson until last night when he saw him in Grant's apartment. Clark crashed through his Sahuaro Inn motel room door at about ten in the morning. That was only half a day later. Could Clark find him in only one nighttime?

Clark had to get Grant out of her apartment and into a place where the police couldn't find her. That would take more time, another hour or so at the very least. There were lots of hotels and motels in and around Tucson. Did Clark have time to call them all? Who would he look for? He didn't know Jake used the name Albert S. Simpson when he registered at the Sahuaro Inn.

How could Clark find him so quickly? Teddy, Abdul and that mouse, Ferdie Robbins, were the only people who knew his Tucson motel address. Robbins was afraid to say 'boo' and Abdul certainly didn't tell Clark. Jake heard the shot that killed him before he started the car and drove away from Grant's apartment building. Abdul didn't have a chance to say much. He was dead.

Did Clark tell the truth? If it wasn't Robbins or Abdul, could Teddy have squealed on him? Jake's apprehension grew and then subsided. When he called Teddy, he told him Clark was in Tucson, but Teddy didn't know where in Tucson. Teddy could have found Grant's address and phone number, but that wouldn't help him.

Was it possible Teddy somehow found Clark after he killed Abdul and talked to him? No. That simply wasn't possible. In his McLean apartment in the middle of the night, Teddy couldn't find Den Clark, hidden somewhere in Tucson a couple of thousand miles away. It simply wasn't possible.

Seated in an airplane high over Arizona, Jake concluded Clark had been lying. He began to feel somewhat more secure. He still wondered how Clark could have found him when another thought occurred to him. Could Clark have called Teddy? The older woman in the seat beside him turned and looked at him in surprise and alarm when Jake suddenly and loudly cried out, "Yes."

Clark must have called Teddy. If Clark threatened to spill the beans about Aegis, Teddy would tell him anything. Jake could almost hear Teddy blaming everything on him and then telling Clark he was at the Sahuaro Inn. That sounded so much like Teddy. It also explained why Teddy hadn't called him. In Washington, it was noon when Den came crashing through his motel door in Tucson. Teddy had plenty of time, but he hadn't called because he expected Den Clark would kill him.

Jake ground his teeth. *"That lying, two faced bastard,"* he thought. *"He wanted Clark to kill me. He'd like to shut my mouth forever. I know too much about him. That stone hearted, calculating son of a bitch. He's trying to get rid of me."*

Chapter 26

Gigi waited in the Sunset Motel, watching the street entrance. When she saw Den drive into the parking area, one of her fears dissolved. Den had not been killed. Her fears returned when he entered the room. His jacket and shirt were covered with blood. Blood oozed from the cuts on his swollen cheek and forehead and from his matted hair. He cradled his right hand in his left. She cried out when she saw him.

Den calmed her. He said he was all right - that he looked much worse than it was. His voice was strong and that reassured her. Den went to the bathroom and winced when he let go of his swollen hand and dislocated finger. He turned on the water and dropped a towel into the filling basin. Gigi was right behind him. She picked up the moistened towel and he winced again as she washed the blood from his face.

"Your hand, Den," she asked. "Have you been shot?"

"No, but it hurts to beat hell. Can you see if they have any tape?" Gigi hurried to the motel office as Den continued cleaning his face and head, wringing the towel in the now almost crimson water in the motel sink. Gigi quickly returned. "This is all they had," she said and handed Den what remained on a roll of masking tape."

"It'll do." Den held his injured hand out to Gigi and told her, "Take a grip on my finger - that crooked one - and give it a good stiff yank. Don't be tentative about it, hon. A good stiff yank." She did and Den gasped when the sharp pain hit him.

The motel room provided its visitors with a machine for heating water, together with packets of instant coffee and the usually accompaniments. Gigi broke one of the wooded stir sticks in half, made a splint around Den's ring finger and, using the masking tape, wrapped it all to his middle finger. Den gritted his teeth and said nothing during the procedure, but he was glad when it was over.

Finally, Gigi asked: "Is he dead?"

Den shook his head. "No, hon. The son of a bitch is still alive." He told her what had happened in the Sahuaro Inn. "I don't believe anyone saw me. Jake left in a hurry and I don't think he stopped long enough to take down a license number."

Together they cleaned up the room, careful to leave nothing that would identify them or draw attention to their stay. Den needed help to get the suitcases into the pick-up. Then he gave Gigi a light kiss and said, "Come on, Mrs. Adams, let's get out of here. You'll have to drive," he said, waving his bandaged fingers in the air."

Gigi, relieved by Den's confidence, managed a small smile and asked: "Where are we going?"

"We're off to see the world. Travel and adventure. We'll start in Mexico. I think you'll like it there."

In an hour and a half they were at the border in Nogales. The bill of Den's cap obscured his bruised face when he looked down and busied himself by studying a map as they drove through the United States Immigration station. Gigi answered a few innocuous questions on the Mexico side and they were safely out of the United States of America and into the United States of Mexico. No one looked in the springs under the truck's front seat. If they had, they would have found a .357 magnum revolver.

Gigi and Den spent the evening in Guaymas. The next morning they drove south to Mazatlán.

* * * * *

On the first leg of his flight back to Washington, Jake damned Den for making him behave in such a cowardly fashion. He damned Abdul for his failure to kill Gigi. He damned Teddy for his duplicity. Jake understood the reason Teddy didn't want to kill Den. Den wasn't a problem. He was running and as long as Teddy left him alone, he'd keep running and he'd keep his mouth shut. Teddy would leave him alone unless he became a threat. That meant Teddy would keep Jake from looking for Clark and getting his revenge.

Jake also realized Teddy may have considered him to be a more serious threat than Den Clark. He knew everything Den knew - and more. Unlike Den, he could talk. He could expose the hidden agenda of Operation Ocelot. He could blame everything on Teddy and claim he knew nothing about unauthorized projects.

Teddy Smith had reason to want to permanently remove him from the scene. What better way than to get Den Clark to do it for him? Well, Teddy wasn't going to get away with it. He'd see to it that Teddy paid for his treachery. Jake promised to settle that score and to settle it quickly.

After layovers in Dallas/Ft. Worth and Atlanta, it was approaching mid-night when Jake's plane landed at Reagan National Airport. He hurried through the terminal and hailed a cab. When it was a block from his Bellavista apartment building, he paid the cabbie and walked to Kensington Park.

Jake entered the Park and followed a lighted jogging trail, stepping from it briefly to pick up a stone larger than his fist. He continued on the path as it slowly ascended and reached the top of a rise overlooking a reservoir. A bench was placed next to the jogging trail. From it, Jake could look down on the water and on the jogging trail he had followed. Jake left the trail and entered a cluster of evergreens growing a few yards behind the bench. There, partially hidden, he found a comfortable place, backed into it and waited.

* * * * *

Teddy's alarm clock buzzed at quarter to six. He awoke and prepared for another day. His day usually began with a before-breakfast jog in Kensington Park. His routine seldom varied. Most of the time, he had the trail to himself at that early hour. That was the way he wanted it.

As he got into his jogging clothes, Teddy experienced an uncomfortable feeling. He knew its cause. More than a day had passed since he gave Jake's motel address to Den Clark. If Jake was dead, he expected Den would have contacted him. If Jake was alive, he would have called to see if someone was on his way to Tucson to kill Den.

Neither one had called. The suspense made him uneasy. Teddy took the elevator to the main floor of the apartment building, nodded at the security guard and didn't bother to acknowledge the greeting: "Good morning. Mr. Smith. It looks like a nice day."

Once in the street, Teddy began his regular run. In a few minutes, as usual, he entered Kensington Park. A few minutes later, as usual, he turned from the main trail adjacent to the reservoir and entered the one leading to the top of the hill. In another few minutes, as usual, he arrived at his destination and rested on the bench placed beside the trail. It was his practice to sit there for another ten minutes, enjoying the scene and organizing his day.

From his place of concealment in the evergreens at the top of the hill, Jake watched as Teddy jogged past the reservoir. He knew Teddy's routine. Often, he had run beside him on that same path. He waited until Teddy reached the bench and sat with his back to him. Without making a noise, Jake crept toward the bench.

He struck Teddy on the head with the rock, knocking him unconscious. To make sure he was dead, Jake hit him several times on the back of his neck where the spinal cord enters the cerebellum. He would make the death look like a mugging. He took Teddy's money and threw the empty wallet to the side. He removed Teddy's Rolex watch. It was not a pirated copy. It was genuine. Jake would keep it.

Jake walked back to The Bellavista. Everything had gone smoothly. He believed he had left no evidence to suggest his presence at the scene of Teddy's murder. No one had seen him enter or leave the Park. He was satisfied. He could direct his attentions to other matters.

Now that Teddy had "met an untimely death at the hands of some unknown petty thief", it occurred to Jake that a Section Head position in the Projects Branch was vacant. The person who filled that position had been an important link in the Aegis organization. The people in Aegis, whoever they might be, would need someone reliable to fill it.

"Why not me" Jake asked himself. *"I've got good credentials. Teddy must have given me glowing recommendations whenever job review reports were written."* Jake wished he knew some of the Aegis people, but, with the exception of Den Clark, Teddy had never

identified anyone in the organization. Jake hoped and expected the Aegis top echelon knew his name.

Jake knew the eastern dilettante, Cullen Brewster, would have a lot to say in the naming of Teddy's successor. He was the Deputy Director of the Clandestine Service, but Jake had only the most casual of relationships with him. Cullen Brewster was hard to get to know. He was born with an aloof nature and he made no attempt to change it. His "stand-offish" manner caused many in the Projects Branch, including Jake, to refer to him as "that patrician son of a bitch."

With Teddy's performance reports, the help of the unknown Aegis people and the support of Cullen Brewster, Jake would be a shoo-in for Teddy's job. He would have to find a way to get Deputy Brewster's help.

Jake had not forgotten his towering need to avenge the humiliation Den Clark had visited upon him in The Bellavista. That humiliation was now compounded. Jake cursed the panic fright he displayed when, like a scared pup about to pee on himself, he had run from Den, first from Grant's apartment and then from the Sahuaro Inn motel. Perhaps he could find a way to get the Deputy Director's support and, at the same time, further another of his major objectives - the killing of Den Clark.

"Could I hang Teddy's murder on Clark?" he asked himself. *"If the ground is properly prepared, I believe it could be done. When I've got Teddy's job I'll have the facilities to hunt down that son of a bitch and finish him off."* Jake smiled and thought: *"The FBI would look for him in the States and the CIA would search for him off-shore. When they found him they would kill him and I'd be rid of him."*

* * * * *

"Thank you for seeing me, sir," Jake said as he entered the Deputy Director's office. Without any preliminaries, he explained his purpose. "Teddy Smith helped me," he began. "He trained me and he gave me opportunities to prepare covert operational plans. He even told me he would be pleased if I were to be his successor. I will always be indebted to him.

"Equally important to me, sir, we were friends outside of the Agency. That friendship and my admiration for Teddy make it impossible for me to keep my suspicions to myself. I believe the newspaper reports of Teddy's death at the hands of a mugger are not accurate."

Cullen Brewster didn't change his expression. Neither did he give Jake permission to sit. Instead, he asked him: "The basis for your suspicion, please."

"I assume you are aware of the disappearance of Agent Den Clark?" Brewster nodded.

"Clark was given the mission of developing information on drug business in Bolivia and, later, in Guatemala. During one of our morning joggings, Teddy told me he believed Clark's assignments in those two countries led him to involvement in a narcotics distribution scheme. Teddy told me he scheduled an appointment with Clark, intending to question him about the matter.

"Before that meeting could take place, there was an attempt on Clark's life. They shot a hole in his apartment window. Teddy told me he thought the Philadelphia mob tried to kill Clark because they feared he would stand between them and their Latin American cocaine suppliers.

I believe Clark thought it was Teddy who tried to kill him. I don't believe a mugger killed Teddy Smith. I believe Clark went under-ground after the mob's unsuccessful attempt to kill him. I believe he returned to Washington and killed Teddy Smith, making it look like the work of a mugger."

The Deputy Director quietly considered Jake's charge before he asked: "Do we know the whereabouts of Agent Clark?"

"I don't know for sure. Teddy sent me to Arizona to follow a lead. We were told Clark had been seen in Tucson driving a pick-up truck with Pennsylvania plates. I looked for him but couldn't find him. I came back to Washington to report to Teddy, but got here too late. Teddy had already been killed."

"Thank you for the information, Mister Jacobson. On behalf of the Agency, let me express our gratitude. We will ask appropriate law enforcement people to investigate." Then Brewster stood. He did not extend his hand. He said: "Please don't let me keep you from your duties" and nothing more. He merely stood and waited for Jake to leave.

Jake made no movement toward the door. "It would be better if Agent Clark were not taken alive," he said. "It would protect the Agency from media accusations of drug trade involvement."

Brewster said nothing. Without moving, changing his expression or making a sound, he stood next to his desk, looking into Jake's eyes. After a few moments of embarrassed silence, Jake mumbled a "Thank you, sir" and left the office.

Cullen Brewster's thoughts were summed up by two words. "Something smells." Jake's story was different from the one Teddy Smith had told him only a few days earlier.

Chapter 27

The Fiesta Hotel was located within the old part of Mazatlán and was favored by a clientele preferring to look at the two-hundred-plus year-old architecture found in "El Centro" rather than gaze at a seldom changing Pacific seascape. Still other tourists preferred to avoid the higher prices charged at the newer, posh, Five Star and Five Diamond hotels that speckled the beaches to the north of the city in the Zona Dorada - the "Golden Zone".

The Fiesta Hotel was not on the beach, but the Bahia de Olas Altas was visible from the rooms that faced the Pacific. The few blocks walk to the Olas Altas beach was no inconvenience to those who preferred a more Mexican and less antiseptic, touristy atmosphere.

The hotels in the Zona Dorada, the more recently developed part of Mazatlán, were built to accommodate the ever-growing number of people who came to enjoy the climate and the beauty of the Mazatlán area. Any one of those hotels could be expected to have hundreds of rooms, fine restaurants, swimming pools and the other amenities that would attract both locals and visitors from the north. An assassin concealed in a large crowd of hotel occupants and visitors would be difficult to single out.

The Fiesta had only thirty-four rooms - tiny when compared with the Zona Dorada palaces. Den and Gigi took a room there because of the Fiesta's size. It was easy to keep track of the hotel's occupants. Even though their stay in Mazatlán would be brief, they wanted to be able to more easily learn if suspicious strangers were present and watching them.

In Guaymas, Den and Gigi spent their first night in Mexico behaving like newlyweds. After they arrived in Mazatlán, Den hardly left the Fiesta Hotel. He stayed in the room and worked on his report.

His swollen hand and bandaged finger hampered him. Nevertheless, he began to document the history of his involvement with Aegis.

It started with the revelation of the existence of a secret organization hidden within the Central Intelligence Agency and described it as a group of men who planned and carried out assassinations. He described, in detail, his first meeting with Teddy Smith and the way Smith recruited him into Aegis. He reported Teddy's explanation of the extent of the Aegis organization and his emphasis on uncompromising insistence on absolute secrecy.

Den named Teddy Smith as the man who involved him in Aegis' plan to kill Humberto del Valle. He set down everything he knew about the deaths of Montoya and the Guatemalan students, identifying both Smith and Jacobson as moving forces behind the planning of those executions. He explained how Aegis wove the assassinations into legitimate CIA operations without the knowledge of the CIA officials who reviewed and authorized clandestine operations.

Though he realized his report would probably be read only after he was dead, Den tried to avoid speculations and personal comments. He accurately reported the part he played in the conspiracies. It was Gigi who insisted he also report his defense of being duped by false representations of Aegis' patriotic purpose.

During the days, Gigi did not stay in the hotel. She thought she would distract Den from the work he had to do. She was probably right. She walked in Old Mazatlán, enjoying its sights and its smells, visiting the Mercado Pino Suarez - Mazatlán's produce market on Avenida Carnaval - and being impressed by the gothic, colonial Catedral de la Inmaculada Concepción de Maria.

She would have enjoyed them more if Den had been with her. She hoped he would quickly finish the writing of his exposé. She wanted to close the CIA chapter of their lives and begin the new one that was so much more promising. When she returned to their room on the third day, Den's look of satisfaction, his smiles and his greeting told her the report had been written.

"Tomorrow," Den told her, "we'll both pretend we're tourists. We'll hire a boat. We'll start at the Marina. We'll go to the rocks and watch for Sea Lions. We'll pack a lunch and picnic on one of the islands - Goat, Wolf, Deer or Bird."

"Goat, Wolf, Deer or Bird? You're making that up."

"You'll see. You'll see. I've already started my new life. I'm a reformed man. I won't tell lies. At least, not to you. At least, not very often."

* * * * *

Early the following morning Den kissed a still sleeping Gigi and left their bed. He dressed and walked from the Fiesta Hotel to a narrow shop operating beneath the one word sign: "Noticias". It identified the business as a newsstand. A bundle of the Mazatlán edition of "El Debate" lay on the counter. The paper carried a few of the major stories from Europe, Latin America and the United States, but most of its articles dealt with Mexican happenings and, in particular, news items of interest to the people of Mazatlán and the State of Sinaloa.

In recognition of the presence of gringo tourists, the news stand also carried a modest supply of North American newspapers. Den went to the shelf marked "Internacional" and picked up a two day old issue of the Los Angeles Times. He stopped at a shoreline restaurant, sat at one of the tables with a view of the beach and ordered coffee.

It was a nice day, warm with very little wind. It would be a good day to visit the islands laying close to the Mazatlán Pacific shore. When the coffee was brought to him, hot and strong and black, the way he liked it, Den had finished reading the front page of the Times. The international news gave him no cause for alarm. The paper blamed a few riots in the Near East on the Administration in Washington and there was another financial mis-management scandal at the United Nations. Nothing new.

Den turned to the Times reports of national news and waved at the waiter. Without direction of any sort, he brought more coffee to the table. Then Den saw the headline of a story that made him draw in his breath. The waiter wondered why the gringo tourist ordered a second cup of coffee, but didn't touch it. He wondered why he sat at the table for such a long time, staring out at the ocean. He wondered why he didn't finish reading his newspaper. The reason for Den's behavior was the story appearing as a small item in the middle pages of the Times. Teddy Smith had been murdered.

Den hadn't expected Jake would kill Teddy. Perhaps, he should not have been surprised. During their confrontation in the Sahuaro Inn, in order to distract Jake, he taunted him with the claim of Teddy trying to get rid of him. Den was well aware of Jake's nearly pathological need to punish anyone who injured or threatened him. Two plus two equals four. Jake killed Teddy.

That morning, as Den sat at the restaurant, with coffee cooling on the table before him, he again considered a re-emerging question. With Teddy dead, did it make any difference if Aegis was really a web of people inside the CIA or merely a hoax Teddy had used to turn him into an assassin?

Den's answer was: "No." The death of Teddy changed nothing. As long as Aegis existed, he and Gigi ran the risk of sudden death. If Teddy told the truth, though there may be no continuing threat from Aegis, the threat from Jake remained.

Nothing had changed. Their safety still lay in flight and concealment.

* * * * *

Gigi, half awake, rolled on her side and reached out, expecting to feel Den's warm body next to her. She awakened abruptly when her hand couldn't find him. Then she smiled and remembered how he would sometimes quietly leave their morning bed without disturbing her. He'd go out for coffee. Then he'd come back and they'd go to a restaurant for breakfast. Gigi was dressed when he returned to their room.

The pleasant prospect of a day on a boat with Den had brightened her spirits. Her mood changed as soon as Den entered their room. Perhaps it was Den's just a bit subdued greeting or Gigi's recognition of a subtle hint of distraction. Something had happened. Then she saw the newspaper Den carried in his hand.

"What is it Den?" she asked. "What's happened? Is there something in the newspaper?" Den nodded. He found the report of

Teddy's murder tucked away in the center of the paper. He spread the Times on the table where Gigi could read it.

"Theodore James Smith, an officer in the Central Intelligence Agency, was murdered yesterday morning while jogging in Kensington Park in McLean, a suburb of Washington, D.C. He was killed by repeated blows to the head. His empty wallet was found at the scene. Police suspect robbery as the motive for the killing."

The story reported Teddy's position in the CIA as that of a senior analyst and briefly described a bland version of his history in the Agency. The story concluded with reference to the growing number of assaults and muggings in the DC park system.

Gigi hoped the death of Teddy Smith might mean she and Den would no longer need to hide. That hope quickly disappeared. Jake was still alive and, as before, there was no evidence to show Aegis was no longer active. Gigi believed as did Den - the death of Teddy Smith didn't change anything. Jake Jacobson and, possibly, the rest of the men in Aegis continued to imperil them.

Gigi looked up at Den. "Jake killed him, didn't he?"

Den nodded.

Her next question was, "Is he going to get away with it?"

Den was unable to answer her question. He hoped Jake would have to face justice, but he believed it was a forlorn hope at best. He told Gigi there was little they could do, but he had something in mind. He would send a letter to Langley accusing Jake of murdering Teddy. Would it do any good? Den doubted it.

His letter might be received by an Aegis conspirator who would destroy it. It might be received by someone outside the conspiracy, but Den knew his reputation in the Agency had been blackened. After his disappearance from Washington, Teddy, Jake and their unknown Aegis friends would immediately build their defense against exposure by damning and slandering him. They would completely destroy his credibility. His letter would probably be disregarded. Nevertheless, he would send it.

The letter wouldn't mention Gigi. The letter wouldn't mention Aegis. Den had a reason for those omissions. The way the Central Intelligence Agency treated the letter could provide evidence to show Aegis was still alive and consisted of more than just Teddy and Jake.

The letter would detail Jake Jacobson's involvement in the killing of Agent Mick McCarthy in Damascus. It would recount Den's friendship with McCarthy and his decision to make Jacobson pay for his Damascus deceit. Den would admit administering the beating at The Bellavista Apartments and report Jake's subsequent attempt to kill him, first in Guatemala, and, later, in Arlington.

The letter would report his late night telephone call to Teddy Smith and tell of the struggle in the Sahuaro Inn. It would emphasize Jake's anger at discovering it was Teddy who gave him Jake's Tucson address. Having established a motive, the letter would accuse Jake of murdering Teddy Smith.

If the CIA decided to thoroughly investigate the charge and if Jake was subsequently accused of murder, Jake might offer to tell everything he knew about Aegis in exchange for a favorable sentence. If that happened, the newspapers would have a field day reporting it and Aegis, if it existed, would have been exposed by Jake, not by Den and Gigi. After being exposed, there would be no reason to kill either of them.

On the other hand, there might be no investigation or accusation. Den's letter might never come to light. It might actually "go up in smoke." His letter might not cause a ripple. For Jake and the Project Branch, it might be business as usual. If nothing happened to Jake, to be on the safe side, Den would have to presume Aegis protected him just as it protected him in Damascus.

If Jake was not prosecuted, nothing would be proven. The letter could have been disregarded because Den had lost all credibility. The letter could have been disregarded because of a cover-up engineered by Aegis - or by the CIA itself.

Den explained his reasoning to Gigi. She listened to his analysis and boiled in down to a simple sentence. "Your letter can't hurt us," she said, "and it might help us."

Den didn't tell Gigi everything he was thinking. If the CIA shoved his letter under the rug and Jake was not accused of Teddy's murder. Den would have to return to Washington and kill him.

Den drafted his letter and decided to send it to Deputy Director Cullen Brewster. The only thing Den knew about Brewster was his reputation as a "cold, smart, independent, patrician son of a bitch." Den would mail the letter from Guadalajara. It was over two hundred and fifty from Mazatlán. It was far enough away to mislead anyone attempting to find them.

Any pursuer would spend days searching for them in Guadalajara. Before they found any trace of him, he and Gigi would leave Ernest and Maggie Adams in Mexico and vanish into other identities at another place.

Den and Gigi drove to Guadalajara. There was no need to hurry. They spent the night there. In the morning, Den Fed-ex'd the letter to Cullen Brewster and mailed his other statements to a few trustworthy SEAL friends.

Chapter 28

In Langley, Deputy Director Cullen Brewster studied a letter received in the overnight mail. He closed his eyes and leaned back in his chair. It helped him focus on problems and clear his mind of inconsequential matters. Den Clark's letter gave him cause for concern. The letter from Clark, the information received from Jake Jacobson and the report of Teddy Smith all pointed in different directions.

Any one of them, or all of them, could be false. People were always lying to him. He expected it, but this matter involved the additional element of urgency. Unless the truth was uncovered and protective measures taken, the Agency could be faced with major problems.

Teddy Smith said Den Clark had become a rogue agent, a killer for hire. Jake Jacobson said Clark was trafficking in drugs and killed Teddy Smith. Clark said Jacobson had murdered Teddy Smith was trying to murder him.

The Agency couldn't stand the heat occasioned by the publicity that would develop if it became known that one of their men had become a hired assassin. It couldn't stand the publicity that would develop if it became known that a cocaine trafficker was operating within the Agency's Clandestine Service. It couldn't stand the publicity that would develop if it became known that Teddy Smith was murdered by a CIA officer and not by some unknown mugger.

Cullen Brewster had to put out three fires and he had to do it quickly. He wondered which one of the stories contained truth. More accurately, he wondered what parts of each story may have contained an element of truth. He relaxed and considered the character of each of the three informants, hoping his sub-conscious mind and his intuition would come to his assistance.

Clark had appropriate credentials. His SEAL record was impeccable and there was no hint of drug trafficking or use in his file, He had produced an excellent report on narcotics activities in Bolivia, but he was a new man. As far as the Agency was concerned, he was still an unknown quantity. There was a lot of money in the assassination business as well as in the drug business. Love of money is the root of evil.

Jacobson's story was the least credible. Cullen Brewster was aware of the Damascus cover-up. Jacobson's history in Syria was not one calculated to establish a reputation for honesty. The opinions of Jacobson's associates in the Agency did nothing to support the profile of a trustworthy man. Still, even pimps and prostitutes and drug addicts and crooks often produced valid information.

Teddy, on the other hand, had a good track record. Brewster had known him for years and was inclined to believe him. He also knew Teddy was capable of disregarding the rules. He smiled when he recalled how Teddy had saved him when, so many years ago, he sat in that old Barranquilla prison. After an ill-thought out plan to blow a hole in the prison wall failed, Teddy paid no attention to his superiors or to the rules. He used Agency funds to bribe prison guards. Teddy set Brewster free.

Still, Cullen Brewster was not satisfied with Teddy's version of the Clark matter. One single fact put Teddy's story into question. Police Incident Reports showed someone shot a hole through Clark's apartment window on the night before he disappeared.

When Teddy told him Clark was a rogue agent, he also said he'd done a thorough search for Clark and had visited his Bellavista apartment. Surely he knew about the window and the attempt on Clark's life. Why had he withheld that information? Was it possible Clark ran because someone shot at him? Was Clark a target and neither a paid assassin nor a drug trafficker?

Jacobson's story disclosed the bullet hole in Clark's window and claimed his disappearance was drug related. His story of Clark's involvement in the drug trade would be a good reason for running. Jake's report contradicted Teddy, but it did not automatically make his version true.

The story Clark told in his letter from Mexico could have been the truth, but, clearly, his version was meant to save his own posterior. Still, Jacobson's reputation bothered him and Teddy Smith's failure to disclose the attempt on Clark's life was strange. Deputy Director Cullen Brewster stared out the window for another half hour. His old friend Teddy Smith, he reluctantly concluded, had tried to mislead him. He returned to his desk. He had made a decision.

* * * * *

Den and Gigi knew the Agency would know he was in Mexico as soon as Cullen Brewster received the letter. They expected the CIA to arrive in Guadalajara and begin a search for him within 24 hours of its receipt. Den planned to leave no trail for Aegis to follow. He would leave as few footprints as possible. If he could help it, there would be no clue that might help Jake or anyone else follow him from Guadalajara to Mazatlán.

The pick-up truck was a problem. If it were found, its license plates would lead to the Pennsylvania Department of Motor Vehicles. There, the truck's registration records would identify the owner as Ernest Adams. That name could be found in the Guadalajara hotel guest registration book. If the truck were found, it would be better if it were found in Guadalajara. It would let their pursuers falsely narrow the area of their search.

Automobiles stolen in the United States find good markets in Mexico. Securing a bogus local registration may not be legal, but it is not a difficult operation. The Mexican government officials who issued Certificates of Registration welcomed any source of extra income.

Den sold his truck at a used car lot in Guadalajara. When Den admitted he had no Registration Certificate, the lot operator merely shrugged and reduced the amount of his offer - "because of special additional expenses" was the way he put it.

Den carried his Pennsylvania license plates with him when he and Gigi embarked on what might be described as the ordeal of a two hundred and fifty mile trip in a Mexican bus. Den planned to throw the license plates into the Pacific Ocean when they got back to the Fiesta Hotel. Then he and Gigi would begin their new life.

* * * * *

In his McLean apartment, Jake used his forefinger to move the ice cubes around in his highball. He was pleased by the way his life was moving. He could hardly believe Teddy Smith had turned on him. If he hadn't been cautious when he opened the door of his Sahuaro Inn motel room, Den would have killed him. But he was alive and it was Teddy Smith, the treacherous son of a bitch, who was dead.

Jake was particularly pleased with the way he directed suspicion to Clark. It was hard to read Cullen Brewster. He never gave an indication of what he was thinking. Still, Jake believed he had given him good reason to believe Den killed Teddy.

Jake was ready to plan his next step. Jake knew Brewster had a problem. An agent in the Clandestine Services was thought to be a drug trafficker as well as the murderer of Teddy Smith. Jake knew the Deputy Director couldn't allow the CIA to be exposed to the publicity that would surely occur if it became know that an ex-CIA Agent and drug trafficker murdered Teddy Smith.

To add to the Deputy's concerns, the presence of an international drug trafficker within the structure of the Agency's Clandestine Services could destroy the stuffy Boston reputation of Cullen Brewster.

If it were up to Jake, he'd solve the problem in a hurry. He'd order the quiet and quick elimination of Den Clark. Cullen Brewster, that wimpy, eastern, patrician, son of a bitch, would never do it because Executive Order 12333 wouldn't allow it. Brewster's only alternative was to do nothing - let the whole thing slide.

"*Well,*" he thought, "*I'm in no hurry. I can wait.*"

* * * * *

A small group of intellectuals living within the Belt Line, together with the much larger group of Washingtonians who want to be considered as intellectuals, view Hollywood productions as a kind of opiate of the masses. Foreign films, on the other hand, draw their attendance and, on very rare occasions, their very mild criticism.

McLean's Cine Clasique specialized in showing foreign films. Jake Jacobson often spent Saturday afternoons there. Watching the sub-titles of some strangely plotted foreign movie was, somehow, pleasing to his ego. He told himself he understood the subtle nuances of the story which, he was sure, must have dealt with some profound problem of the human psyche. And there was always the chance that someone in a position of authority might see him there and be impressed.

Jake left the Cine Clasique and started to walk across the street to the lot where his Audi was conspicuously parked. He made his way between the cars lining the street in front of the theatre. When he got to the traffic lane, another car was double-parked to his left, its driver apparently waiting to pick up a movie patron.

Suddenly the vehicle surged forward, as if someone had stepped on the gas pedal by mistake. The middle of the vehicle's bumper smashed into Jake's legs and knocked him backwards onto the pavement. The car's tires rolled over him as it sped away. The driver made no attempt to stop.

* * * * *

Thomas Rosenow, the Special-Agent-in Charge of the FBI's Phoenix office was unhappy. Washington had advised him of the pending arrival of a visitor. Rosenow was asked to fully cooperate with him. It was all "hush-hush". It was a matter of national security.

Alone in his office and awaiting the arrival of the visitor, Rosenow snorted: "A matter of national security! Fully cooperate!" He knew what that meant. It was the cloak and dagger boys, the goddamned CIA. They were going to stick their noses into his operations. They were going to come in, take charge and tell him what to do. He couldn't do a thing about it.

When Washington spoke to him, Tom Rosenow knew he had to be a good soldier and fully cooperate. He even had to appear to be happy to cooperate. There might be a half dozen of them taking up office space, propositioning his secretaries and screwing up office routines, but he had to put up with them. The only satisfaction he had came from his knowledge that no one in Washington or in the entire world could keep him from hoping his visitors would get the hell out of Phoenix in a hurry.

Tom Rosenow's foul mood changed soon after Llewellyn Keating entered his office. Keating didn't fit Rosenow's preconceived notion of what a CIA man should look like. He didn't wear a dark suit or dark glasses and he didn't have a lean and mean look about him.

Llewellyn Keating wore a sport coat. It covered a decidedly unflat stomach that would have been better covered if the sport jacket had been an inch or so wider. The man was not yet middle-aged, but he was balding. He had a pleasant expression and showed no signs of being an aggressive or hostile sort. Best of all, he wasn't accompanied by a crew of associates. He was alone.

Llewellyn Keating endeared himself to Rosenow by apologizing for the inconvenience and promising to get out of his hair as soon as he could. Then he explained his mission. A man traveling under a Jordanian passport had been killed in the apartment of a Tucson attorney. The dead man was a terrorist and the attorney was G. G. Grant, a woman who once was a CIA operative in Syria.

After swearing Rosenow to secrecy, Keating told him Grant was a part of a covert scheme to uncover terrorist cells within the United States.

In Syria, a story had been planted. G. G. Grant, it claimed, had been fired and her reputation ruined when she was used as a scapegoat to cover up Langley incompetence. According to the rumor, Grant hated the CIA, wanted revenge and was willing to get it by working with terrorist organizations. Of course, none of it was true. The woman, Keating explained, had been set up by the CIA as an attorney.

In time, Keating confided, Grant was contacted by the enemy and she agreed to provide terrorists with a safe house after they were smuggled into Arizona from Mexico. There the terrorists waited to form new cells or move to cells already established in other parts of the country. When they left the Tucson safe house, the terrorists didn't know they were being followed. They didn't know they and the cells they visited were being identified and watched.

Keating suggested close cooperation between the FBI and the CIA was essential. Rosenow told him he didn't have to put too fine a point on it. He would be happy to "fully cooperate". Keating smiled and went on with his narrative. He told Rosenow something was wrong when the recently killed Jordanian terrorist arrived in Arizona. He meant to kill G. G. Grant. He must have been tipped off.

After a failed attempt at her office, the Jordanian entered Grant's apartment and tried to murder her. Luckily, two CIA agents had been assigned as Grant's back up. They were in her bedroom where they usually operated the hidden television and recording instruments. They were the ones who killed the terrorist.

One of the men took the terrorist's car from the scene. The other drove the attorney to California. Grant was no longer an Agency asset. It wouldn't take long for Al Queda and its various terrorist associates to find out Grant was a CIA plant. They would kill her if they could find her. She would soon have another identity and enter into the CIA's version of the FBI Witness Program. She probably would never return to Tucson.

Keating again emphasized the absolute necessity of keeping the entire story concealed. Two imported terrorists had already been taken into custody. The men in the cells they visited may not know they have been compromised. Keating told Rosenow it was particularly important that they didn't learn it from "a newspaper, a TV news program, a radio talk show, a blogger, or from any other conceivable source." Rosenow smiled as Keating ran down the list. He told him he got the idea and promised he would keep his mouth shut.

Then Keating asked Rosenow to perform a function for him. The Tucson police were investigating the murder of the Jordanian. They had to be called off, but they couldn't be told the real reason for terminating their investigation. Rosenow was asked to use his good offices to provide cover for Grant and the sting operation.

He was asked to contact the Tucson police and convince them to drop the matter. Keating proposed a method of reaching that objective and Rosenow suggested a few amendments to the plan. The CIA picked up the tab for their cordial early lunch and Tom drove his new friend, Lew, to the Sky Harbor airport where he boarded an Air West flight to Mazatlán.

The next day, Rosenow drove to Tucson. He visited the Chief of Police and convinced him the death of the Jordanian was drug related. He told him the dead man was an important element in an ongoing federal investigation of an international drug ring. It transported Afghanistan's heroin through the Near East to Europe and America. Any publicity or local investigation might unwittingly damage the work of the FBI and the DEA.

That same day, the Chief called one of his detectives into his office. He removed him from the investigation of the murder of the Jordanian. He told him the case was closed and reassigned him to a shooting that took place in a cantina in a heavily Mexican section of the city.

The Chief also told him the case was in federal hands and suggested the detective might keep his mouth shut about anything he ever knew about the killing of the Jordanian - unless he wanted to be thrown off the force and lose his pension.

Chapter 29

It is not uncommon for North Americans to retire in Costa Rica. Many of them are businessmen who have spent their lives living abroad while representing the international interests of United States corporations. During their offshore careers, these people lose their connections with their homeland. Their families have grown up and scattered. They have neither homes nor close friends in the country of their birth.

For many of them, Costa Rica is an appealing place for retirement. It's a quiet county. The crime rate is insignificant. The health facilities are acceptable. The climate is wonderful and the cost of living is attractive. The expatriates comfortably fit in with other Americans who already share their experience of, in effect, having become displaced from their United States homeland.

When Gigi and Den returned to Mazatlán, they decided to begin their exile in San José, Costa Rica. They would destroy their Adams identities and adopt the one Ferdie Robbins created in his second set of bogus documents. In San José, they would become a part of the North American colony.

* * * * *

The Libertad was a ship of Panamanian registry. It was launched after the end of the Second World War and had been built to carry military supplies and personnel to the South Pacific Theater of Operations. After a decade of virtual inactivity, it began more active use as a tramp steamer.

The Libertad sailed from California to Panama on an irregular schedule. It moved up and down the coasts of Mexico and Central

America with cargoes of industrial goods and returned to California carrying Panamanian, Costa Rican and Mexican products. As was the custom with tramp steamers, a few compartments were set aside for passenger usage. The shipping company optimistically called them staterooms.

The tramp steamer business became less attractive when air, railway and trucking carriers took more and more business from them. The Libertad became no more than a marginally profitable operation. It was sold at a bargain price to a group of men whose business experience consisted of inheriting large amounts of money.

They planned to refurbish the Libertad and enter the tourist cruise business. Their business plan proved to be ill-advised when the investors began to understand the costs of refurbishing and fitting the Libertad for cruise work. The ship again changed hands at an even lower price.

If the Libertad's chain of ownership were traced through complicated offshore corporate and partnership records, some of its major present day owners would be recognized as figures involved in organized crime. The Libertad still sails between California and Panama but, in addition to legitimate cargoes of industrial products and bananas, the Libertad now often carries stolen automobiles and products used in the drug trade.

Den did not identify himself when he talked to the Mazatlán Freight Agent who was suspected on importing shipments of stolen automobiles from California and exporting shipments of Mexican marijuana back to that State. Den saw an advantage in working with people involved with organized crime. They were conditioned to keeping their mouths shut.

In the world of organized crime, if a man had any plans for longevity, there was more than ample reason for him to remain silent. You could ask one of them: "What time is it?" You might very well receive the answer: "I don't know. I'm not from around here."

Den's interview with the Freight Agent was satisfactory. The Agent and the Captain of the Libertad didn't require identification from Den or Gigi. They not only agreed to provide them with a passage, they promised there would be no record of their departure from Mazatlán. Neither would there be a record of their arrival in Panama City.

In Mazatlán, the Libertad was unloading its cargo. It would embark for Panama at midnight. Den made the final arrangements with the Freight Agent who insisted on payment in American dollars. He wasn't asked to give a receipt. He and the Captain split the fare. They would be doubly interested in keeping everyone, including their New Jersey bosses, from knowing two unidentified gringos boarded the Libertad while it was in Mazatlán.

Understandably, the passenger accommodations aboard the Libertad were somewhat primitive. Gigi suspected the cuisine might not reach up to the standards of the Royal Caribbean Line. She went to a Mazatlán abaceria and laid in a substantial supply of crackers, cheese, bottled water, canned sardines (Den liked them), chocolates (she liked them) and snacks. The foodstuffs requiring refrigeration were limited to two rings of baloney sausage. She was well prepared for the voyage.

It would take about a week for the freighter to arrive in Panama. From Panama City, Gigi and Den planned to use bus transportation to travel north following the Pan American Highway, first to the city of David and then on to San José. They would travel separately in order to insure their tracks would be well covered.

Den and Gigi spent the rest of the early afternoon on the beach, perfecting their tans and watching the shorebirds and the Pacific waves. When Gigi had enough sun, she and Den shook the sand from their towels, left the Olas Altas beach and walked toward the Fiesta Hotel. Along the way, Den stopped twice to study store window displays. He was uneasy. Gigi recognized his uncharacteristic behavior.

"What's up, Den? Are we being followed?"

"I think so, but I can't find him. He may be back there somewhere. It might be my imagination." Den's concern emphasized the possibility, perhaps the probability, of having to abruptly leave a place in order to avoid the real or an imagined danger of being identified.

They detoured into a narrow alleyed grid of streets crammed, cheek to jowl, with shops that sold caps, T-shirts, post cards, sea shells, coffee beans and whatever else an enterprising Mexican thought might attract the gringo dollar. A Coral Princess cruise ship had docked that morning and the souvenir business was brisk.

Gigi and Den lost themselves in the crowds of tourists. They unexpectedly turned corners, they entered shops from one door and left from another and, finally, they hurried down a winding street and returned to the Fiesta Hotel.

By this time, Den knew someone had been following them. He could catch a split second glimpse of him and sometimes see only a disappearing shadow, but he was sure he and Gigi were under surveillance. He believed he had shaken the man in the tourist traps. "*Damn it all,*" he said to himself. He wondered how someone could find them. How could they find them only a few days after his letter was delivered to Cullen Brewster in Langley?

Den took some comfort from the fortuitous timing. The Libertad would leave Mazatlán before midnight. He and Gigi would leave the Fiesta as soon as possible. They would find a way to board the Libertad without being seen and remain below decks until the Libertad was at sea.

They had to move quickly. They started packing as soon as they returned to the hotel. Den kept the .357 with him. He suspected the man who followed them might have discovered their presence in the Fiesta Hotel. If he was waiting for them, Den was prepared to kill him.

They were packed and ready to leave the room when they heard a knock on the door. Den pulled his revolver from his belt. He shifted his weapon into his left hand and put his still bandaged middle fingers to his lips. He motioned Gigi toward the door and signaled her to jerk it open.

When the door flew open, the man in the hallway, a stranger to them both, had his hand in the air, ready to again knock. Using only the uninjured fingers of his right hand, Den grabbed him by the necktie and roughly hauled him into the room. At the same time, he tripped him and the man fell to the floor.

Gigi locked the door and closed the drapes, shutting out most of the afternoon Pacific sunshine. Den's knee was on the man's chest. He still held the necktie, now uncomfortably tight around the man's neck.

The barrel of the .357 magnum was inches away from the man's unnaturally wide-opened eyes.

"Talk," Den ordered.

Without moving, the man squeaked out: "I'm Llewellyn Keating. I'm from the Agency. I'd like to talk to you and Gigi. Could you, please, let go of my necktie?"

Den released his grip and stood up. He kept the revolver pointed at the space between the man's eyes and careful took a position where legs could not kick him. Keating loosened his necktie and took a deep breath. He moved his head in a circle to get the circulation and the neck muscles back in working order.

Keating took a few more deep breaths and got to his feet. He promised Den he would keep his hands stretched out straight above his head. Then he turned around and asked Den to search him. "I'm not carrying a weapon," he said. "I was told it might be safer if I was unarmed."

After being searched, Keating made his way to the table. He sat, looked at them both for a second and said: "I had an awful time finding you. The manager of the Fiesta told me you were at the beach. I tried to catch up with you, but I don't run too fast." He looked down at his stomach and smiled.

Den disregarded Keating's attempt to put him at ease. "Talk," he repeated. Keating showed a small, cautious and almost embarrassed smile. There was a tentative quality about him. He acted more like a clerk who didn't quite know what he was going to say rather than a man the CIA would send on a mission into Mexico.

"You don't have to live this way," Keating said. The statement got no reaction from Den or Gigi. "Please, sit down, Mr. Clark. Let me bring you up to date."

Den moved a chair away from the table. He did not want Keating to be able to push it into him. He sat, keeping his left hand on his lap. It still held the revolver. Keating reached toward his breast pocket and when he saw the barrel of Den's weapon immediate rise and point at his head, he slowly, very slowly, withdrew a package of cigarettes. He shook one out and dropped the pack on the table. "Have one," he said.

"I don't smoke," Den answered. "It's a dangerous habit."

Keating carefully took a lighter from his shirt pocket, lit the cigarette and said he had been trying to quit. He again smiled his little boy's smile and said he was told Den had a number of bad habits. Keating folksy attempt to put Den at ease didn't work at all. Den showed no reaction to his chatter. His expression didn't change. He sat without movement, holding the .357 in his lap and looking into Keating's eyes. He said nothing.

Keating spoke openly and carried no weapon, but Den had no reason to trust him. He could be a part of one of Jake's intricate schemes that would end in an attempt on his life. Den had no real idea of just who this man was. In spite of his manner and appearance, Den was cautious. He asked Keating how he found them. Keating chuckled and said it would have been difficult if Jacobson had not stumbled upon them in Tucson.

"When Deputy Brewster showed me your letter, I was ready to get to Guadalajara as quickly as possible, but he had a different idea. He said Guadalajara was a red herring. If we wasted time there, you'd move out of Mexico and we'd have a terrible problem trying to find you.

"Jacobson told Deputy Director Brewster you were driving an older pick-up truck with Pennsylvania license plates. That was the thread that allowed us to trace your movements. I looked at the Immigration Service's video tapes of the cars crossing through their station at Nogales. Those that came close to fitting Jacobson's description were checked out.

"The home address of the owner of a Chevrolet pick-up with Pennsylvania license plates was found to be in the center of a public park in Germantown. The name of that owner was Ernest Adams.

"From then on, it was just a matter of time," Keating said. "I put a team of Spanish speaking agents on the phones. They began to call hotels and motels, starting at Nogales and then moving down the highway to Hermosillo and then following it south along the Pacific highway. It didn't take long for them to learn a Mr. and Mrs. Ernest Adams spent a night in Guaymas and the following night in Mazatlán at the Fiesta Hotel.

"You lost me in those shops today," Keating admitted. "Please don't tell anyone about it," he added, rather sheepishly. "I stopped to buy a T shirt for my wife. She's a cat person. The T-shirt shows the head of an independent looking animal and the legend: 'Just what don't you understand about MEOW'. I just couldn't resist it."

"*He's a disarming son of a bitch,*" a dubious Den thought.

Keating read Den's suspicious attitude and divined its reason. "I think I understand why you're so cautious," he said. "I don't believe you know Jake Jacobson is dead." Involuntarily, Den's eyes opened a bit widen and he straightened in his chair.

"Yes," Keating confirmed, "the day after the Deputy Director received your letter, Jacobson was involved in a hit-and-run accident. He was killed. Deputy Brewster identified his body. Incidentally, Jacobson was still wearing Teddy Smith's Rolex. That was proof positive that Jacobson was not telling the truth when he said you killed Smith. It proved the accuracy of your letter.

"You don't have to keep running. The Deputy wants you to know you and Miss Grant are safe now. Aegis consisted of only Teddy Smith and Jake Jacobson, and they're both dead. The Deputy," Keating explained, "is a very smart man. He thinks you found out about the extent and true purposes of their assassination operations.

"Of course, Smith and Jacobson knew you'd blow the whistle. They decided to kill you before you could tell us about Aegis. Incidentally, the Deputy Director has already decided the Agency will take no further investigations or disciplinary actions against you for anything you may have done. It's best to allow sleeping dogs to lie, don't you think?"

Keating went on to tell them they had no problems in Arizona either. Obviously, he was proud of the way he arranged the Tucson police department's decision to terminate their investigation into the murder of the Jordanian. He grinned as he told how he convinced the FBI that it was a terrorist sting operation that went bad and how he got the FBI to convince the Tucson Chief of Police it was a drug sting operation that went bad. Both the FBI and the Tucson Chief of Police would keep quiet, Keating said, "as a matter of national security".

"You're a lucky man, Mister Clark," Keating said. "Deputy Director Brewster understands what has happened to you. He has gone far out of his way to completely clean your record. He has pulled a lot of strings to protect you. He told me he couldn't blame you if you decided to leave your CIA career far behind you, but he wants you back in Clandestine Services."

Keating was sincere when he referred to what he called Den's most unfortunate experience. "I know you've had a bad ride," he said, "but please think about coming back. You've got a good future in the Agency."

Den stood up, and tossed his .357 onto the bed. He apologized for treating Keating in such a violent manner. Keating waved off the apology and admitted he would have acted in the same way if he were in Den's shoes.

"Well, Keating, I guess I'll have to recall those letters."

"Letters?"

"Yes. A protective measure. Friends have a report to mail out if anything happens to Gigi or me. They're not necessary now."

Gigi, standing at the window, had been silent during Keating's discourse. She didn't believe him.

Keating cautiously smiled when he admitted the CIA had given him a liberal expense account. That evening he asked them to be his guests at a posh restaurant in one of the Five Diamond hotels in the Zona Dorada. He suggested they all plan to meet at the airport in the morning and begin the trip back to Washington.

When Den agreed, Gigi, from her position behind Llewellyn Keating, signaled her disapproval by slowly, but emphatically, shaking her head. Den disregarded her. After the friendliest of good-byes, Llewellyn Keating returned to his hotel in the Zona Dorada.

Chapter 30

From their hotel window, Gigi watched Llewellyn Keating enter his taxi. She turned to Den intending to tell him she distrusted Keating and doubted his story. She was surprised when Den stopped her in mid-sentence and agreed with her. Den's disclosure of his exposé letters was meant to convince Keating he believed his story. Neither of them believed the death of Jacobson offered them the protection they needed. Keating's assurance of their safety wasn't close to being convincing.

Gigi's suspicions were aroused by the announcement of Jake Jacobson's death. Jacobson's accident occurred less than 24 hours after Cullen Brewster received Den's letter. Gigi did not think it was an accident.

Den's letter alerted the Deputy Director to the danger represented by a murderer in their midst. Den's letter sounded an alarm. To protect the Agency, Gigi argued, the Deputy Director could not run the risk of allowing Jake to be tried or even accused of Teddy's murder.

Gigi questioned the Deputy Director's motivations in extending so much effort to protect them. She was skeptical. The hit-and-run accident, so soon after the Deputy's receipt of Den's letter, was suspiciously fortuitous.

Deputy Brewster, she decided, would quickly recognize the problems that would be created by public knowledge of Jacobson's murder of Teddy Smith. The avalanche of adverse media publicity, the political fall-out, the demands for firings and for reorganizations, as well as the demands for even more stringent congressional oversight could do great injury to the Agency's ability to function.

Deputy Brewster would certainly recognize those threats. Gigi believed he arranged the accidental death of Jake Jacobson. If

Brewster would kill Jake to protect the Agency, why wouldn't he kill Den Clark and Gigi Grant, the only other people who knew Jake killed Teddy?

Gigi thought Llewellyn Keating was sent by Cullen Brewster to dispose of them. She was unwilling to go to dinner with him, let alone run the risk of returning to the United States with him. She much preferred saltine crackers and baloney sausage with Den on a rusted tramp steamer over caviar and champagne with Llewellyn Keating at a Five Diamond hotel.

Den needed no convincing. His little voice had not been whispering to him. It had been shouting at him. Everything was just too neat. The end of the threat from Aegis, the elimination of the problem presented by the unsolved murder of Abdul in Tucson, the Agency's decision to cover up Den's involvement in assassinations, even the offer to come back to the CIA - it was too much like a Disney movie. "And they all lived happily ever after."

When Keating began to talk, Den saw the warning flags begin to fly. The inconsistencies in his story drew Den to a conclusion. Keating could not be trusted.

Den's letter to Deputy Director Brewster didn't mention Gigi. Her name didn't appear in the Guaymas, the Mazatlán or the Guadalajara hotel registries. In each case, they signed in as Ernest and Maggie Adams.

How did Brewster know her name and how did he know she was traveling with him?

Keating told him Brewster wanted to assure him the investigation into the killing of the Palestinian had been quashed. It no longer endangered him.

How did Brewster learn he killed Abdul and needed to be shielded from the Tucson police investigation?

Keating told him Brewster wanted to assure them they were no longer threatened by Aegis because the conspiracy consisted of only Teddy Smith and Jake Jacobson. Den never heard the word "Aegis" spoken by anyone other than Teddy. The secrecy surrounding the conspiracy was unconditional and absolute. None of the conspirators would acknowledge its existence.

How did Brewster learn of the Aegis organization?

The Palestinian was dead and unable to tell anyone what he knew. Only Jake and Teddy knew Den and Gigi were together. Only they knew Abdul threatened Gigi. Only they knew Den killed Abdul. Only Jake or Teddy could have been the source of Cullen Brewster's information.

Teddy and Jake were Aegis conspirators, Neither would disclose the existence of Aegis to any stranger to the conspiracy. They would pass Aegis related information to Deputy Director Brewster only if he was a member of Aegis. Brewster would share information with Keating because he, too, was a part of the conspiracy.

Den knew what would happen if he and Gigi joined Keating for dinner. They would be killed and their bodies buried somewhere in the Mexican desert. Den accepted Keating's dinner invitation and let him know about his exposé letters for a single reason. He wanted to delay any plans Keating had to assassinate them.

The presence of exposé letters might cause Keating to report back to Brewster for confirmation of instructions to kill him. The acceptance of the dinner invitation was intended to assure Keating he had no suspicion of the danger that might await them after the evening dinner as well as sending Keating back to the Zona Dorada and giving him and Gigi the opportunity to disappear into the interior of the Libertad.

By the time Keating realized his dinner guests were "no shows", he and Gigi would be safely hidden and, soon, on their way to Panama.

Something else was obvious. Den and Gigi lost the protection they hoped would be afforded by their threat to expose Aegis. The deaths of Smith and Jacobson would be used to insulate Aegis from the damaging revelations of Den's exposés. He could foresee what could happen.

Brewster would tell the world he became suspicious when he learned of the killing of the four Guatemalan students and ordered a quiet internal investigation. The result of that investigation, he would say, was the discovery of the del Valle, Montoya and Guatemala assassinations. Brewster would use Den and Teddy and Jake as his scapegoats. They would be accused of planning and carrying out the murders.

The Deputy Director would claim the three CIA officers had a falling out. Smith or Jacobson tried to kill Clark in his Arlington apartment. Clark ran and was probably living somewhere under an alias and with a new identity. Jacobson killed Smith and then died as a result of a hit-and-run accident. If Clark were ever found, Brewster would promise to extradite him back to the United States and the appropriate law enforcement facilities would bring criminal charges.

All loose ends would disappear. Den and Gigi would be silenced. So were Jake and Teddy. No investigation would uncover their planning of Aegis killings. No investigation would uncover Abdul's ties to the Aegis conspirators. The FBI had been finessed into believing Gigi's disappearance was a result of a CIA terrorist sting. The Tucson police would never look for her. They had bought Keating's CIA witness program story.

No one would bother to look for Den. He, presumably, would be well hidden in Latin America. No one could ever find him.

Later, when the politicians and the media received the reports from Den's SEAL friends, Brewster's explanation of the assassinations by the three rogue agents would have already been accepted as fact. Den's warning of a larger Aegis network would be dismissed as poppycock. They would be passed off as the self-serving declaration of a murderer. With Den and Gigi in some unmarked desert grave, the potential of the exposure of Aegis would die with them.

* * * * *

Before Llewellyn Keating's taxi arrived at his Zona Dorada Hotel, Gigi and Den, unseen by anyone, went to the docks and quietly boarded the Libertad.

CODA

The guard at the gatehouse saw a black Lincoln approaching. It stopped and the darkened window on the driver's side rolled down. The guard recognized its occupant and the gates swung open. Deputy Director Cullen Brewster's automobile moved forward and started down the quarter mile drive that ended at a large, white pillared home. Its architecture, its appointments and its surroundings proclaimed its owner to be a man of considerable wealth.

Minutes later, Cullen Brewster sat in a comfortable wicker chair on the veranda of the Virginia country estate. His host, a tall, silver-haired man in his early seventies, sat next to him. A bottle of Chardonnay in an iced bucket and two long stemmed glasses rested on the small table separating their chairs. They were alone.

The older man looked out at the Virginia countryside. He sipped from his glass. He liked white wines. As he enjoyed the view, he thought about Aegis and the events Teddy Smith had set in motion. Teddy's decision to turn his back on Aegis, the organization which the older man had so carefully constructed, was a disappointment to him. Teddy had violated the core principles that justified the creation of Aegis. His Guatemalan venture could have destroyed the organization.

Neither Brewster nor the old man had been aware of the mission Teddy had hidden within Operation Ocelot. They had been unaware of the unauthorized assignment Teddy gave to Den Clark. In spite of Aegis' rejection of Colonel Rodriguez' proposition, Teddy Smith took it upon himself to honor his request. He and Jake Jacobson planned the assassinations and hid them inside Operation Ocelot.

"In one way, I'm sorry to lose Teddy," the older man said, "but his judgment went bad, very bad." He paused and sipped from his glass. "We had agreed on Clark before Teddy recruited him. Teddy followed the rules in recruiting him. I wonder whatever possessed him to insinuate that man Jacobson into the organization without seeking our stamp of approval. I wouldn't have approved him and, I'm sure, you wouldn't have done so either."

Cullen Brewster was in agreement. "You're right, sir. Deception is an important tool in our business, but within our group there is no room for it. Being completely open and honest among ourselves is an absolute condition precedent to our continued existence. Jacobson's history in Damascus proved he was both uncontrollable and untrustworthy.

"Of course, Teddy should have let us know he wanted to recruit him. Obviously, Teddy didn't want us to know what he was planning. He knew we'd never approve Jacobson." Brewster took his first drink of the Chardonnay. As soon as he tasted it, he smiled. Impressed, and looked at the bottle's label.

"Clark," Brewster observed, "performed well in Chile and in Bolivia. I had hopes for him." Brewster's host made no comment. The old man raised his chin slightly, looked at the Deputy Director for a second and, rather pointedly, changed the subject.

"I simply cannot understand why Teddy would agree to undertake the Rodriquez project," he said. "I can't believe he thought we'd have anything to do with the killing of student dissidents. My God, didn't he understand what happened in Chile when they started killing youngsters? Teddy's Guatemalan venture could have exploded in our faces. He could have sunk us and there is so much more appropriate work to be done. What do you think caused Teddy to go wrong?" the old man asked.

Brewster had already given that question considerable thought. "Teddy didn't like our philosophy behind target selection. He didn't tell us about Jacobson because he wanted to set up his own organization. Of course, he knew we wouldn't support the Guatemalan Junta or have anything to do with that fascist Colonel. That's why he didn't tell us about the scheme he concealed inside Ocelot. I hate to think of what might have happened if Teddy's plan to cover his tracks had succeeded."

"We would have thought Clark was killed by some Guatemalan

drug lord," the old man said. "Teddy and his man Jacobson would have continued their private schemes without letting either of us know about them and, sooner or later, Aegis would have been uncovered.

"Then, at some time in the future, this country would have to face dictators and madmen rather than enjoy the peace resulting from our preemptive early removals." He slowly shook his head as he asked: "Whatever caused Teddy to put us at risk?"

The Deputy Director answered. "That is a question I've asked myself many times. I don't believe it was ego and I don't believe it was a messiah complex. I think Teddy believed only dictatorships and military juntas could protect our Latin America flank. I believe Teddy was unduly frightened whenever Latino politicians made speeches condemning the so-called Colossus of the North. Of course, we have to carefully watch them when international alliances are potentials, but Teddy went overboard."

The old man nodded briefly. He again looked out over the countryside and slowly turned his wine glass. When he looked back from that peaceful scene, his pensive mood had changed.

"Well, Cully, you acted quickly and you acted effectively. Smith and Jacobson are gone and our problem has diminished substantially. We may be in for another bit of heavy weather when Clark's report is distributed. Let's hope it won't come too soon."

A cautious smile appeared and quickly disappeared on the old man's face. "With Jacobson and Teddy to shoulder the blame, I'm sure we'll survive the storm."

Cullen Brewster nodded, but made no comment. Then he gently brought up a delicate subject. "It is too bad Teddy mishandled Denver Clark. He could have been one of our most important assets."

The old man smiled. "You are a subtle one, Cully. I know what you're up to. Please stop. I said our problem was diminished substantially. I didn't say it had disappeared." He leaned back in his chair, cleared his throat and again changed the subject.

"We'll have to find a replacement for Teddy. Llewellyn Keating is a possible candidate. I can find only one blemish in his record. It's too bad he failed his Mazatlán assignment - although he did uncover Clark's exposé letters. With Jacobson, Smith, Clark and the woman all out of the way, all testimony would be gone and Clark's report could be deflected"

The old man sipped from his Chardonnay, looked up at Cullen Brewster and said, "The Mazatlán matter is the only mark I can find in Keating's record. Comment, please."

"Llewellyn Keating," the Deputy Director answered, "leaves the impression of being a nice guy, but not particularly imaginative. That disarming impression is one he has carefully cultivated. It had misled many. In addition to being a very competent field agent, Keating had been very effective in carrying out missions. I don't believe he should be faulted for failing to kill Clark and Grant."

Cullen Brewster got his host's attention when he added the word "but".

"But, I don't think Llewellyn is the man for the job. Carrying out assignments is one thing. Creating them is quite another. I don't think Llewellyn has that special kind of intuition - that ability to foresee the unforeseen and make provision to handle it. Teddy had it. His plans usually covered all the bases."

"Very well, Cully. You sound like you have someone in mind." Privately, the older man hoped he wouldn't hear what he was sure he was about to hear. Now it was Brewster who took a sip from his wine glass. He had to screw his courage up a notch before saying, "Denver Clark comes to mind."

This was the third time Brewster brought Clark's name into the conversation. The old man knew Brewster was opposed to killing Denver Clark.

"You are a persistent lad, Cully," he said. "We've been through this before. I know you appreciate Clark's various abilities, but, as long as that man and that woman are alive, Aegis is endangered. He can sit off-shore and give interviews and send letters to editors and Senators and the like. Dead men cannot testify before Grand Juries, Cully. It will be much easier to point the finger of blame at people who are no longer among the living."

"May I comment, sir?"

"Go ahead Cully. I'll listen to you one more time. I hope we will never discuss the matter again."

"Agreed, sir," was Brewster's immediate response. "Clark's Guadalajara letter is quite revealing." he began. "It told us Jacobson killed Teddy and it told us why he did it."

"If I were a cynic," Brewster's host interrupted, "I might conclude the Guadalajara document was meant to get you to…" he paused and selected the right word, "to get you to neutralize Jacobson." It was apparent to Brewster that his "debt of gratitude" argument had not impressed his older companion.

Brewster agreed with his host. "Of course, sir, you are correct." The Deputy paused and used the older man's word. "I did neutralize Jacobson, and, yes, Clark's report was meant to protect him and the woman." Then he continued his argument.

"Clark's letter also allowed us to protect ourselves. It alerted us to something about the Guatemalan Operation that just didn't pass the smell test. Clark told us Jacobson tried to kill him in Guatemala. Clark was wounded in Guatemala. At the same time, students were killed in Guatemala. Clark's letter alerted us and gave us the opportunity to clean up Teddy's mess in a timely fashion

"I believe it is significant that Clark's letter didn't mention Aegis. I don't think Clark wanted to cause problems for the Agency. Remember, he could have publicly exposed Smith and Jacobson's operations. If he did, the fat would have been in the fire. Clark elected to advise me privately rather than send a report, say, to the Washington Post."

The old man scowled when he heard the words: Washington Post. He countered Brewster's argument. "He wouldn't send a report to the Post or to anyone else because it would lay him open to a prison term at the very least." He looked at Brewster and said a single word. "Continue."

Clearly, Brewster had not convinced the old man to change his mind about the need to eliminate Clark and Grant. "It has been two weeks since Clark left Mazatlán and fell off the face of the earth," Brewster emphasized. "He's hiding and we can't find him. Of course, we'll keep looking for him, but suppose it takes us two years to find him, or five years?"

"Whenever Clark dies, his exposé will become public. Then we will have to defend ourselves by blaming Smith and Jacobson. Do you think the media or anyone in the House or Senate might question why our investigation was conducted so late after Teddy and Jacobson's deaths and so soon after Clark's demise?"

The older man removed his glasses, crossed his arms and looked down at the table while he assessed Brewster's question. Brewster saw he was beginning to make headway. When the old man raised his head, Brewster was quick to resume his argument.

"When I was a child, much to the consternation of my mother, my grandfather, would put me on his knee and talk to me about the world of business and his rules for success. I use the word 'consternation' because grandfather was not always careful with his language. I specifically recall him telling me, 'It is better to have someone inside your tent pissing out than outside your tent pissing in.' I believe I could convince Denver Clark to come back inside our tent."

The old man stifled a laugh and limited himself to a smile. "All right, Cully, you silver tongued devil. I'll go this far with you. We'll continue to look for Clark and Grant. You can send out the word they are not to be eliminated without your specific direction. The decision of what to do with them will be postponed."

He stopped and, with emphasis, repeated "Postponed, Cully, not overruled. Postponed. When we've found them, I will want you to personally visit them. If you have any doubts about their sincere commitment to return to the fold, any doubts at all, Cully, I will want them killed, instantly.

"The decision will be yours and yours alone. I'm sure you understand how important that decision will be." His tone was serious when he added: "I trust you will not allow your personal feelings to guide your judgment."

Cullen Brewster nodded.

There was nothing else that needed their attention. The older man confirmed it by lifting his glass. "To the shield of the Republic," he said.

Cullen Brewster nodded in agreement. "Yes," he responded. "To Aegis."

Other Books by Galen Winter

LEGENDARY NORTHWOOD ANIMALS

Quasi-Scientific Studies of the Invisible Moose, the Shovel Nosed Beaver, the Blunt Billed Rockpecker and Other Fabled Creatures. Charles Darwin, Roll Over in Your Grave.

THE BEST OF THE MAJOR

A Compilation of Stories of the Shotgunning Pursuits of Major Nathaniel Peabody (USA, ret.), a Bird Hunter, a Rascal and a User of Cigars and Aged Single Malt Scotch Whisky.

THE CHRONICLES OF MAJOR PEABODY

The Questionable Adventures of a Wily Spendthrift, a Politically Incorrect Curmudgeon, an Unprincipled Wagerer and an Obsessive Bird Hunter.

BACKLASH

A Compendium of Lore and Lies (Mostly Lies) Concerning Hunting, Fishing and the Out-of-Doors.

BACKLASH II

Tales Told by Hunters, Fishermen, and Other Damned Liars.